Richard Dacre and The Murder Room

>>> This title is part of The Murder Room, our series dedicated to making available out-of-print or hard-to-find titles by classic crime writers.

Crime fiction has always held up a mirror to society. The Victorians were fascinated by sensational murder and the emerging science of detection; now we are obsessed with the forensic detail of violent death. And no other genre has so captivated and enthralled readers.

Vast troves of classic crime writing have for a long time been unavailable to all but the most dedicated frequenters of second-hand bookshops. The advent of digital publishing means that we are now able to bring you the backlists of a huge range of titles by classic and contemporary crime writers, some of which have been out of print for decades.

From the genteel amateur private eyes of the Golden Age and the femmes fatales of pulp fiction, to the morally ambiguous hard-boiled detectives of mid twentieth-century America and their descendants who walk our twenty-first century streets, The Murder Room has it all. >>>

The Murder Room
Where Criminal Minds Meet

themurderroom.com

T0352160

Richard Dacre (pen name of Donald Thomas) (1926–)

Donald Thomas was born in Somerset and educated at Queen's College, Taunton, and Balliol College, Oxford. He holds a personal chair in Cardiff University. His numerous crime novels include two collections of Sherlock Holmes stories and the hugely popular historical detective series featuring Sergeant Verity of Scotland Yard, written under the pen name Francis Selwyn, as well as gritty police procedurals written under the name of Richard Dacre. He is also the author of seven biographies and a number of other non-fiction works, and won the Gregory Prize for his poems, *Points of Contact*. He lives in Bath with his wife.

By Donald Thomas

Mad Hatter Summer: A Novel of Lewis Carroll, Nightmare
The Ripper's Apprentice
Jekyll, Alias Hyde
The Arrest of Scotland Yard
Dancing in the Dark
Dead Flowers for Lady Blue
The Blindfold Game
The Day the Sun Rose Twice

As Francis Selwyn:
Sergeant Verity and the Cracksman
Sergeant Verity and the Hangman's Child
Sergeant Verity Presents His Compliments
Sergeant Verity and the Blood Royal
Sergeant Verity and the Imperial Diamond
Sergeant Verity and the Swell Mob

As Richard Dacre:
The Blood Runs Hot
Scoop: Blue Murder
Money with Menaces

The Blood Runs Hot

Richard Dacre

An Orion book

Copyright © Richard Dacre 1988

The right of Richard Dacre to be identified as the author of this work has been asserted in accordance with the Copyright, Designs and Patents Act 1988.

This edition published by
The Orion Publishing Group Ltd
Carmelite House
50 Victoria Embankment
London EC4Y 0DZ

An Hachette UK company
A CIP catalogue record for this book is available from the British Library

ISBN 978 1 4719 0447 9

www.orionbooks.co.uk

For Christopher and Catherine

For Christopher and Catherine

For Christopher and Catherine

CHAPTER ONE

The sound reverberated on the verge of earshot. It rose from the far shore of the bay, where vulcanised rubber tore and shrilled on hardtop. For three or four seconds the high-pitched skid jammed and skated in a mad dance. It broke at last in a scream of tyre-tread, forced out like pain unendurably prolonged.

Hoskins heard it through the air of the May evening. On that Bank Holiday Monday the first warm weekend of the year was drawing to a close.

'It's the photographs,' Harold Moyle was saying across the marble table of the Cakewalk terrace. 'The other girls in the fifth form swear he keeps following her. They think he holds the camera under his coat. And not only that. She has to walk past his house on her way to school. Two of them saw him edging the curtain back and taking pictures of her from his front room as she goes by. For God's sake, Sam, this is not a joke!'

Hoskins' mild blue eyes looked past Moyle's shoulder at the rippling calm of the full tide. He stretched his attention to catch the far-off sound again. To look at the two men together, it would have been easy to mistake Chief Inspector Hoskins for the one who was a teacher.

'And what does young Elaine have to say about it?' he asked quietly. 'Better still, what does she know?'

He heard an engine wail, more distinctly across the shimmer of tide. The throttle was open now as if the beast had turned against its tormentors.

'Look,' Moyle said indulgently, 'I wouldn't give you earache for nothing. We're not talking about a girl of fifteen and a bit of nooky with her boyfriend. It's a man probably two or three times her age. And all I want is someone to warn him off. That's the lot. Nothing heavy.' The kindly face with its abundant greying moustache chided Hoskins for his own good.

It could have been a car, open-topped and supercharged.

1

Somewhere on Highlands Avenue, the overcliff drive among tall rhododendron hedges. Houses built like toy Balmorals or green-tiled Spanish villas. More probably it was a bike, a powerful German brute or a Jap with shining flanks of pearl grey or firebox red and the bounding energy of a thoroughbred stallion. Hoskins smiled understandingly at Moyle and listened for it. The engine roar faded behind a rise in the wooded cliffs. It broke cover again with a snarl. The riders of the Chain-Gang might be out for speed, rending the peace of the suburban avenues for the fun of it. But the bike sounded out of their class. Possibly someone was being killed across the bay. More likely it was fun.

'And it's not just that,' Moyle persisted. 'The others in her group reckon he walks after her from school. Right to her gate sometimes. And across those back yards, his upstairs window can practically see into her bedroom. She told Joanne Taylor that she thinks he tries to watch her undressing at night.'

'She could always close the curtains,' Hoskins said sceptically. His carefully cut and flattened hair was almost grey, but the smooth tan of his cheeks had not yet given way to jowls. In his grandfather's day he would have been looked on as a man in the prime of life. To a less tolerant generation he was a grandfather himself, a figure of indeterminate middle age. The tint of blue in his rimless spectacles magnified and darkened his eyes. It gave him the owlish look of a hopeful and lecherous clerk. He spoke quietly and patiently as a matter of habit. It was sometimes hard to catch his words.

He had never hit a suspect during interrogation and never raised his voice in favour of the noose or the birch. Such reserve made him an oddity in 'A' Division. But in twenty years the quiet manner had produced results, precisely because every fledgling criminal in the grimy streets of Canton or in the Bank Holiday bother-gangs of Ocean Beach saw him as easy meat. Hoskins had never been easy. In the end, his height and bulk betrayed him as a policeman.

'Look . . . ' said Moyle.

'Shut up a minute, Harold, and listen to that engine.'

The roar faded again behind the trees and cliff walks. Moyle spread his palms helplessly and listened.

'Sam! What's an engine on a Bank Holiday night? The warriors on the warpath. We've got Hot-Rodders and Chains in the fourth form now. A shootout at Ocean Beach. That's Bank Holiday to them. What I'm talking about is Elaine Harris. She's fifteen. A man of two or three times that age is following her from school in Salisbury Road and taking pictures on the sly. Ask yourself why, Sam.'

'Just listen a minute,' said Hoskins patiently.

But now there was nothing to be heard above the slow homeward drone of cars in procession below them on the wide sweep of Bay Drive. Across the water towards Sandbar the sun was going down with the promise of a storm to come. A rippling tide stretched violet and shot-silk to the bronze rim of the horizon, under a sky of gunpowder grey. On the terrace of the Petshop, known more grandly in Hoskins' youth as the Winter Garden, the stored warmth of the day struck upwards from parterre. At the lower level, the pink paving of the 'Cakewalk', once the promenade of youth and fashion in the 1930s, edged the sands of Ocean Beach. At its mid-point a green neon arrow on the deck of the New Pier stabbed outwards through the thickening light to the engineering din of the funfair pavilion by the landing-stage. A girl in black leather with hair like a mauve thistle-top stopped and looked up by the shrubs of the promenade, as if she recognised the two men.

'Before the war,' Moyle said, 'you'd be turned back from the Walk on a Sunday night if you weren't dressed for it. Even the colliers and their girls from the valley towns used to come down in coloured suits and shoes that shone like knives. Like Monte Carlo it was then. Look at it now! You could at least have a word with this bloke, Sam. Turn him up in your records and see if he answers. At least that.'

'I'll have a look, Harold. See if he's been booked. He doesn't start bells ringing, though.'

Beyond the bulky timbers of the landing-stage a red-funnelled steamer churned backwards in its paddle-wash and swung towards its berth in the Canton Railway Dock. The pier amplifiers carried a woman's voice, wailing indolently across the slack water.

> I dreamed of an island in paradise,
> And you were there . . .
> I stood by the ocean in starlight
> And you were there . . .
> You alone . . .

Ocean Beach was the city's resort, screened by its headland from dockyard cranes and the chimneys of the smelting works. It had no history, only nostalgia. Everything that had happened to it was within living memory. Fifty years before, the fashionable restaurants and rendezvous had been smart as advertisements for Imperial Airways or Pullman trains. What survived the war had since become the kingdom of club-owners and speculators. Men like Carmel Cooney, owner of the Petshop, Peninsular Trucking, Coastal Ground Rents and the Royal Peninsular Emporium. They dreamed of a cut-price waterside Las Vegas on the coastal strip of industrial Canton.

There were more 'special hours' drinking certificates in the mile and a half of Ocean Beach than in the whole of Canton city centre. In the cocktail clubs and palais de danse, where the young bourgeoisie of the 1930s had tango'd and samba'd, girls from the back streets of the dockland Peninsula and the high-rises of Barrier now danced or stripped or waited table for the punters. Their young faces wore contempt like a badge of office.

'Has he ever tried to touch her? Ever flashed it at her? Ever spoken to her?'

'No,' said Moyle defensively. 'Not that I know of. Why?'

'Because I'd rather not begin, Harold, by stepping into the largest cow-pat in the field. If that's all right with you.'

Hoskins listened again, staring at the empty glasses on which the last condensation of the chilled drink lay wan as windows in a February dawn. But he heard only the distorted and amplified yearning of the woman's voice from the pier. Half a mile away, she might have been crooning at him from the basket chair at the next table.

> I heard music by Gershwin
> And dreamed of you . . .

'A quiet word, Sam. That's all. Just enough to do the trick.'

Hoskins grunted, without gratitude for the concession.

'If he walks down the same road without soliciting her or touching her or even speaking to her, I can hardly do him for that. If he hangs about, I could have him for obstructing the footpath without reasonable cause. But even that'd be dodgy. There's insulting behaviour, of course, but I wouldn't like to chance that in court if he never makes an approach. And you can hardly get him for taking a picture out of the window of his house.'

'He's got the camera when he's walking down the same road as her, Sam! He had it in his hands when she walked past his place once and he was outside, pretending to do something with the car. He'd timed when she'd walk by and he must have been waiting for her. She told the others she saw him use the camera, from the corner of her eye.'

Hoskins sighed.

'There again, Harold, if he's that gone on her, he'd try something. That's the form as a rule. Not photographs. In any case, it's no good saying that taking a photograph of someone against their will is a form of assault. It's been suggested before. There was a test case about it. They decided it didn't amount to a crime. Photographing a road isn't illegal. Anyone who's in the frame gets photographed and there's nothing they can do – legally.'

Moyle turned a face that had the beginnings of a fifty-year-old tragic mask.

'Suppose he's making some evil little collection of photographs of her. . . . Suppose . . . you know, wishing things. Like witchcraft, only sex.'

'I'd need a search warrant to find it, Harold. You imagine the grief there'd be if nothing turned up! I could ask the Super. But Ripley wouldn't go to the stipendiary for a warrant. Not on what you've given me.'

The two friends since boyhood were sitting where the terrace was sheltered by the length of the ballroom. Concealed lights flushed the tall windows that overlooked the pier and the Cakewalk. What had once been the Winter Garden ballroom was spacious and elegant as a lounge on an ocean liner. Individual tables were ranged round a floor of polished parquet. The square pillars with their mirrored surfaces supported a stucco ceiling, an art deco design of elongated nymphs and fauns. Hoskins noticed that the first of the dinner parties had sat down at two tables near the bandstand, recessed into the rear wall with a dais that curved into the main area. Few dance bands played there nowadays. No dinner guests came to tango or samba. Mel Cooney's entertainments offered skin and din.

'So there's nothing to be done?' Moyle asked. His tone suggested that the meal was to be a glum and reproachful occasion.

Before Hoskins could reply, a young woman appeared on the terrace. She was wearing so little that she might have come from the beach in her bikini. But high heels and fishnet stockings accompanied the breast-halter and briefs in black silk. Her uniform was completed by a black bandana headpiece on which was a brooch with her name: Heather. Her blonde hair had been bobbed and curled to give her a fluffy appearance, but the sharp-featured young face, Hoskins noticed, had a look of hardened enamel. It would be like kissing a car door or a refrigerator. She was tall and slim, with an air of pursing her lips during a moment of surprise.

'Mr Moyle? Table ready in five minutes, if you'd like to come then.'

She turned and walked away, the legs taut and agile, the hips performing a controlled squirm.

'Cooney likes them tall,' Hoskins said. 'Must be something to do with getting older. Prefers them in the driving-seat. That's one of his shopgirls, like most of the rest out here. Let the boss hump you and you shall be a showgirl at the Petshop. First you wait table, then you show your all on the bandstand where the talent scouts can see. Talent scouts! Still, if you come from Barrier or Peninsula, that's a promise of heaven on earth. Cooney's heaven and someone else's earth.'

Moyle nodded and reminded him of the previous conversation.

'We've got to wait until he attacks her, have we?'

'I never said that, Harold. There's things I can do and things

6

you can do. I can have a quiet word with Superintendent Ripley . . .'

'If you wait for the Ripper, Sam, you'll wait for ever.'

'All right, Harold. I'll see if I can get a uniformed man to walk that road when school comes out. Or have one of the "Afternoons" parked where everyone can see it.'

Moyle looked doubtful.

'What can they do if he starts using his camera?'

Hoskins smiled. 'You know how it is, Harold. Quiet approach. Friendly chat. "Should be careful with that camera, Sir. Unless we want the folks round here to think that Sir is taking pictures of their little girls. Wouldn't want Sir to get a thumping while the police aren't here to protect him, would we, Sir?" Works wonders, as a rule. And then escorting him at a distance until he gets home. Glimpse of policeman outside noting down number of house and so forth.'

'Harassment, they'll call it,' Moyle said gloomily. 'I thought perhaps if you had a quiet word. You know.'

'Let's see,' said Hoskins evasively. 'I'll try to take a peep myself in the next few days.'

As they stood up to go inside, the roar and the slithering shriek of rubber on tarmac came across the water, shrill and hard as fingernails drawn sharply down a slate. They stood there a moment longer, listening.

'Wait!' Hoskins said.

A chill played on the bones of his back. The duel on the overcliff road no longer had the sound of fun to him. A renewed skid rose through soprano frenzy to an uncontrolled screech that went almost off the end of the auditory scale. The sleek-flanked beast was being done to death.

'Wait!' he said again, daring Moyle to move or speak. There was a moment's silence across the stillness of the violet tide and then, unmistakably, the massive collision of metal like an avalanche of loose rocks. Its echoes died away. Hoskins walked slowly along the Cakewalk terrace and looked out across the rippling flood. He could see nothing on the shore beyond the resort. But just at the headland, where the beach was hidden from him, the gunpowder grey of the storm-sky was lit intermittently by a pale reflection of fire.

7

CHAPTER TWO

A pang of guilt at cheating his friend nagged Hoskins as he slid behind the wheel of the Vauxhall in the Winter Garden car park. An hour ago he had looked forward to Harold Moyle's dinner. Now his gratitude went out to the riders who had rescued him from a lugubrious conversation. It was only to be half an hour's reprieve. One of the Evening Patrols out of Ocean Beach would be there long before that. Perhaps, when he got back, the dinner could be resumed without Elaine Harris as an invisible guest.

He went for the overcliff avenue, up the tight curves that climbed through spruce and pine from the western end of Ocean Beach. For two miles, along the overcliff, the wooded slope dropped away to the lower promenade of Bay Walk. The upper road edged the cliff-top suburb of Highlands. Where coal barons and shipowners had once built a weekend settlement, the young executives with their look-alike families and corporate prosperity were now firmly in possession.

A few ornamental paths led down to the shore, between banks that flourished with pink-feathered tamarisk and the yellow flower of broom. Through the dark interstices of the pine branches, sweet and resinous in the warm aftermath of the day, lay a glimpse of quiescent sea. On the other side of the gently curving road, the barbered rhododendron hedges rose like a fortress wall. Through the bars of electronically controlled gates there were filmland visions of scaled-down mansions in Gothic baronial and the whitewashed Spanish arches of the newly rich.

What made it worse was that Elaine Harris was far from a stranger to him. A year or two older and she might have been done for soliciting by now. The sturdy adolescent with the broad oval of her face, the lank fair hair loose upon her shoulders, the narrowed eyes and thin lips, had been booked in Hoskins' memory. Her slum-child face was matched by a school uniform and a pleated skirt that would have looked scanty on a ten-year-old. From the ankle almost to the groin the pallid legs were bare. He had no intention of discussing this with a civilian – not even

8

Harold Moyle. But, more than likely, the enthusiast with the camera might by now be one of her clientele.

Putting the girl from his mind, Hoskins turned on to the beginning of Highlands Avenue. He had driven only a few hundred yards when the traffic burst upon him. The Vauxhall Cavalier was engulfed, like a dowdy crab in a shoal of exotic fish swarming the other way. He counted twenty of them. They blasted and swerved and swooped one after the other upon Ocean Beach, like a dive-bomber squadron. The shrilling of the horns blotted out even the engine din and the shouts of the drivers.

The cars were recognisable at once as the customised creations of the Hot-Rodders. Their drivers were the disaffiliated children of Canton accountants or solicitors, the fashion-conscious rebels and a sprinkling of criminals who were young but extremely professional. Elongated fins and cantilevered roofs smashed past him, with twin exhausts and pastel designs that were sleek as a tight swimsuit. Some of the battle-wagons had been rebuilt in the style of a pre-war Lagonda or a Chrysler Airflow saloon from a Bogart–Cagney movie. One or two might have been an artist's impression of a 1950 spaceship. The warriors showed style, even in their choice of weapons.

The Hot-Rodders and their younger brothers in Harold Moyle's fourth form took a pride in their cars to equal that of any rider to hounds with the Pytchley or the Quorn. Several of the windscreens were inscribed with the names of the sharply dressed boys and their girls. *Suzy—Hooper*. . . . *Jacqui—Gash*. . . . *Louise—Neville*. . . . *Chopper—Monnella*. . . . Others bore their painted titles in ice-cream colours at the prow: *Two-Pipe Poppa*. . . *Was That a Red Light?* . . . . *Stepaside*. . . . *Pass Me the Blood, Bub*. . . . As if by agreement, the family parties began to shamble away to the car parks and the single-track metro-rail to Canton. The Cakewalk with its boiled-sweet colours of neon and its rippling tide became the property of the gangs.

Hoskins emerged from the swarm where the road curved round the headland. A panorama of Ocean Beach fell away behind him. The pier and its pavilion on fretted arches had the look of a crusader palace adrift on the sparkling tide. Above the fish-scale silver of its towers and pinnacles, the little flags stood out bravely

9

in the freshening breeze. The white holiday houses and the black scar of the railway track mapped the town at twilight. He steered the car round the corner. Ocean Beach was gone and the cloud ahead of him was dark with smoke.

A black plume of it had risen from the beach and now hung in a dark wind-pattern of slow dispersal. Smoke but no sign of flame. Hoskins pulled in and switched off the engine.

He was too late for glory. Parked just ahead of him were two of the Evening Patrols out of Ocean Beach Division. The registration numbers identified them. Whoever had been in the cars was down on the shore by now. Without enthusiasm, he locked his door and walked towards the smoke. A stench of hot tyres hung in the air, but there was not a mark on the asphalt. It was the one point on the overcliff road where the slopes and pine trees gave way to a steeper drop, just at the headland. Whoever missed the turning had probably gone over at full tilt. A thick odour of smoking rubber and scorched paint filled his nostrils.

He went to the nearest path and began to negotiate the tiled steps. The tropical pines with their bare trunks and branches black against the sky gave an air of the Mediterranean or the Pacific to the summer cliffs. The last of a dappled sunlight filtered through their fronds on to the grass, where the land dropped away in green chasms to the sea.

Until he reached the lower promenade of Bay Walk, raised just above the sands, the banks to either side hid the scene from him. Presently he saw it all.

Four uniformed men from the patrol cars were staring at the scattered remains of a bike, spread across fifty or sixty feet of firm sand. One of them had a car fire-extinguisher in his hands. With a feeling of relief, Hoskins saw that there was no rider. No corpse then, only the dismembered bike. Someone had probably pushed it over in an access of spite. The answer to a seduced wife or a stolen girl-friend was frequently to take it out on the guilty party's car with a sledge-hammer or a shotgun. Cheaper than divorce or marriage, it had become a tribal custom of the Canton proletariat. If a car, why not a bike? Virile self-respect would rather destroy than steal. Theft was anonymous. Destruction was personal as a monogram.

Hoskins consoled himself with the belief that this one could be tidied up in minutes. At least, so far as his part was concerned. After all, he was strictly off-watch. Half an hour and he would be back with Harold Moyle, taking dinner off him at Cooney's Petshop. Watching Heather on the stage with the technique that teased, so long as the enamelled and varnished face was out of view. Despite his distaste for Carmel Cooney, he had nothing against Heather and her sisters in the skin-trade. He was in the mood to be led on this evening. And there would be enough story in the crashed bike to keep Elaine Harris out of the talk.

'Oi! Chief!'

As Hoskins jumped down to the firm sand, it was the young patrolman with the extinguisher who turned and bellowed across at him.

'Back on the walk! The beach is closed off!'

Hoskins kept going, savouring the moment to come. He had never understood why the moment Traffic Division issued a flat cap, the owner slashed the peak, hooding his eyes and assuming the air of the Waffen SS. The hooded eyes and the macho moustache came closer.

'You deaf? The beach is closed!'

Hoskins scarcely did it justice. He drew out the little oblong of plastic, his face and identity on the warrant card apparently photographed through a light green fog.

'Family,' he said, quiet and even-tempered still. 'You ought to have known me from a distance, Scottie. Who's in charge here?'

There was satisfaction in seeing the colour mount in Scott's half-hidden bandit face.

'Sorry, Mr Hoskins. No one's exactly in charge. We just got here and put the fire out. Haven't even had a chance to call in yet.'

'No one with the bike?'

'Not that we saw, Mr Hoskins. Bloody shame to see one of those end up in pieces. Fuck's sake, Mr Hoskins, he could have given it to me if he didn't want it. BMW K100. Top of their range, that is. Bloody crime, I call it. The tank must've broken off and exploded when it hit the beach. Big tank, too. Almost five gallons when it's full. No wonder it burnt. Caught one of the tyres alight. That's where the stink's from.'

11

The young patrolman was less abashed than Hoskins considered proper.

'No rider?' They were walking back to the scattered pieces and twisted frame.

'No sign, boss.'

'Someone pushed five thousand quid's worth of bike off a clifftop. Why would that be?'

'We only got here five minutes before you, Mr Hoskins. No one's had time to work that out. Probably someone squaring a rumpus by dumping the other boy's bike over the edge. Mean, though, I call it. Don't you?'

One of the patrolmen was measuring with a tape, the traffic policeman's kneejerk at disasters great and small.

'Camera,' said Hoskins softly.

'In the car, sir.'

'Someone go and get it. You'll need to have all this packed away before the tide comes in and covers it. Call up forensic and lifting tackle. No sense getting a hernia.'

'You go, Lewis,' said Scott.

The young probationer, a schoolboy in complexion, doubled away. Hoskins considered the wreckage.

The BMW tourer had been a beauty, certainly top of its class. Not a yobber-bike, though. Not a mount for the Chains with their flying hair and scuffed black leatherwear. It had a finish of silver satin, its frame shaped like a flying fin. The front wheel had been wrenched from its telescopic forks by the impact, the rear one thrown far off. It was the front tyre that had caught the furnace roar of the petrol going up. The steel of the frame had been convoluted like a propellor blade. Which of the warriors, Hoskins wondered, would push it over the cliff as a ritual sacrifice? Even the Hot-Rodders had a taste for smashing up the riders rather than the bikes.

'That's where the main fire was, sir.' Scott pointed to the scorched and twisted shape of the fuel tank on a patch of blackened sand, the container torn away by the impact or by its own explosion. 'It must have gone with a hell of a bang.'

Hoskins nodded.

Alone with Scott, he said casually, 'There's a regulation about cap-peaks, even for traffic patrols. They're not to be slashed. Makes you look like the bloody Gestapo.'

Under his moustache, Scott grinned and did not care.

'You don't live up the estates behind Boot Hill, Mr Hoskins. There's three of us there on the cars and about two hundred neighbours not working. Fiddling the old king cole into the bargain. I'd as soon not be recognised when I'm on the job. Civil servant, that's my story round the neighbourhood. Processing forms. I'm not in a hurry to have the windows put in or the kids spat on in the playground. Lucky if it's only spit, the way things are. All right?'

'Of course it's not all right,' said Hoskins helplessly. 'What happens when you have to arrest someone you know? They'd recognise your voice for a start.'

'We'll see,' said Scott cheerfully, 'if it happens. Amazing what you can get away with, though. I was in the bridewell once. Just going off duty in civvies, like, when they brings in this face I know. Even then he never twigged it. "Bloody hell, Mr Scott," he says, "have they got you too?" Told him I'd come to identify a push-bike I'd had impounded.'

There was no sign of the young patrolman who had gone up to the car. Impatient to get back to Moyle, Hoskins turned and began to walk up the beach towards the lower promenade, a tall and weighty figure in the long shadows. Where the tiled steps of the path led up to Highlands Avenue through the wooded slope, he stopped and listened. There were movements among the trees.

A little valley divided the cliffs, its stream running between paved banks. Clumps of rhododendron grew wild, among beech and white cherry in blossom. To either side lay shrubberies of holly, magnolia and camellia. The parks department had once turned the ravine into a fake glen with grassy glades and rustic fences. Now the fences were down and the paths tangled.

He straddled the smooth metal rail and dropped down on to the mossed earth. There was a groan of revulsion and a sound of retching. Moving forward, looking for someone who might be the rider of the BMW or the agent of its destruction, he saw through the twilight a man crouching. A figure in dark trousers and jacket. The man was vomiting beyond a bush, one arm round the trunk of a tree to support himself. His gurglings and heavings stopped and then, after a moment's pause, began again. The dark clothes might have been a rider's but, as he lifted his head, he was the young policeman whom Scott had sent back to the car. His cap had gone and without it the ginger hair and fresh face seemed more childish than ever.

Hoskins turned, shouting for Scott and the others. Then he took another step forward, hauling himself up the slope between the trees with one hand gripping the slim grey trunk of a sapling. There was nothing amiss that he could see, as he moved towards the crouching figure of the young policeman.

It was when he took hold of another sapling and pulled that a monstrous shape sprang through the dusk at him from the branches. Hoskins was not a man easily frightened, but his heart beat in his throat at the shock as he recoiled from the obscene apparition. A pair of elephantine leather-clad arms swung down and thumped into his chest. A man did a half-somersault from the tree and hung by his feet, his face looking upside down into Hoskins' own. The mouth was open in a derisive gape. The eyes bulged through heavy goggles, as if through pebble-lens spectacles. The scalp was covered by a tight leather balaclava to fit under a crash-helmet. Hoskins, who had raised his arms to defend himself, let them drop and stood back. Reason dispersed the nightmare vision.

He had found the rider of the BMW. That was all.

The man hung head downwards. The young patrolman with the tender stomach had looked up and found him first. By pulling on the sapling trunk, Hoskins had dislodged the torso but the legs were still caught in the branches of a stouter tree. The arms swung lightly as if in a stirring of the breeze. Then, as Hoskins stepped back, the corpse slipped clear under its own downward weight and tumbled with extraordinary softness on the bare earth. How long he stood, staring at the grotesque form of death, he could not have said. It was Scott's voice that he heard first behind him, reproaching his idleness.

'He mightn't be dead, sir.'

Putting aside the childish horror with an effort, Hoskins

guessed that Scott was about to undo the rider's balaclava to release the pressure on his neck.

'Leave that, Scottie!' he said softly. 'It's probably the only thing that's holding the poor bugger's brains in. I'd say he must have copped it outright. He fell on the ground just now as if he hadn't got a bone in his body. He could be pulp inside those clothes.'

Now that the drama was past, he went through the ritual as he always did in the occasional ghastliness which punctuated the boredom of police routine. He explained it to himself as being on 'automatic pilot'.

'Ambulance,' he said to the young constable who had finished being sick, 'and warn the duty commissioner. It might be an accident. But there's a good chance that it's deliberate.'

He watched the young man scramble up the slope towards the cars and then returned his attention to the body. It was like that of a drowned man, bloated and swollen by the black protective gear of the biker. Scott found the crash-helmet twenty feet away. Hoskins imagined the scene that was to come. The call at one of the mean prefabricated concrete houses on the Boot Hill estates, officially known as Parklands, behind the municipal cemetery of Ocean Beach. Enquiries as to whether some teenage Kevin or Gary was the son of the family. The breaking of the news. Finding a neighbour to sit with the tear-swollen mother. Coaxing the father – if there was one – to identify the Hot-Rodders' latest victory. That, thank God, was not for him. Nor to enquire how a resident of the estates came to be riding five thousand pounds' worth of bike. Ocean Beach was not his territory. He was just a passing friend doing it a good turn.

'He went over at full throttle, Mr Hoskins,' Scott said. 'For the bike to have shot from under him and gone down on the beach, and him thrown into the trees, he must have done.'

Hoskins shook his head.

'He was probably pushed, Scottie. Chased and then pushed by some sharp young dresser in a fancy car. The warriors are out in Ocean Beach tonight.'

Turning his face aside to avoid the pop-eyed gaze of the corpse, he checked for a last flicker of vitality. There was no pulse at the throat. He touched the cool plucked-turkey skin, as if it were a duty to look for hope that he knew had gone. Gingerly he drew down a zip. He slid his fingers through the opening of the leather tunic and felt a jacket inside. There was a breast pocket with a hard oblong shape. He drew out the driving licence and unfolded it.

Presently he looked up at Scott as the two men stood in the twilight under the trees. Hoskins' expression betrayed incredulity and despair at human vindictiveness.

'They've killed a civilian.'

Scott looked at him, not understanding.

'The warriors hunt one another,' Hoskins said, 'not civilians. That's the rule. If the name on the licence means what it says, they've killed Robin Redlitch-Smith. Robbo Smith.'

The surprise on Scott's face suggested excitement rather than dismay.

'Robbo Smith? Sports reporter on City Radio?'

'Sports writer on the *Western World* since he lost the CR contract.' Hoskins went patiently through the wallet. 'If it's him, the warriors seem to have declared general war. Wait here a minute.'

He went up to the cars and laid a hand on the shoulder of the red-haired patrolman. The lad, who was talking into his radio, looked round.

'Have you asked for the name that owned the registration number of the BMW?'

'Not yet, sir. I got the ambulance, the lifting gear in case we need it, the duty superintendent CID and the assistant commissioner operations.'

'Good man. Now, before you do anything else, ask for that number. The ops room can get it from computer records in a minute.'

Hoskins walked back to his car, unlocked the door and tuned the radio to police frequency. The last fire of the sun and the rippling sea through the pine branches gave Highlands Avenue a look of Honolulu or Tahiti. To the coal-owners and shipping bosses of the age of steam, Ocean Beach in summer had been the South Seas on their own doorstep. A voice, which might have been trying to make itself heard in a rolling-mill, spoke from the radio.

'Redlitch-Smith. With a hyphen. Robin Royston Redlitch-Smith. Registration dated last March. O.K.?'

'Delta patrol, message received. Thanks.'

Hoskins sat back in the driving-seat and tried to make sense of it. He watched in the growing darkness as the lights of the vehicles gathered. There was the ambulance and the truck from the police motor-pool. The surgeon's car came and went. The body was carried up from the trees and the ambulance left. Another party with white tape closed off the wooded slope. A generator was unloaded and an arc-lamp on its cable was carried down to the spot where the body had been found. There was nothing to be done about searching the beach. The tide was covering that already.

The war between the warriors was strictly a private affair. The Hot-Rodders with their slick hair and pressed clothes were a debased version of the 'Beautiful People' their grandparents might have been. The Great Gatsbys of the violent young. The children of the bourgeoisie striking back against the 'monkeys' and the 'yobber-bikes' of the lower orders. To catch a monkey and his girl on a bike and hunt them down was a sport and a purging of the social stock at the same time. The Chains riding in packs of a dozen took such revenge as they could. Speed and mobility were their advantage, overtaking and hemming in, blinding a driver by a shattered windscreen or forcing a collision, bringing the Hot-Rod to a halt and devising a one-way journey for its occupants.

So far the serious casualties had been surprisingly few. Seven bikes had been ridden down by the cars in the past year with considerable injuries but only one death. Several cars had been forced to a halt. In one case the boy and girl had been badly beaten. In another, his body was found by the car and hers near the municipal tip. The precise details were kept from the public as a matter of policy. Mechanised class war was not to be an item of Canton news.

But Redlitch-Smith was a civilian. The Chain-Gangs did not ride BMW K100s. Their machines had a more plebeian appearance and sound. Their gear was embroidered with signs and names of allegiance and defiance. The Hot-Rodders knew their enemies. It made no sense.

Ken Martin, the duty chief inspector from Ocean Beach, took Hoskins' statement as they sat together in the car.

'I should think he was hunted, Sam,' he said at last. 'He didn't even brake on this corner. They were too close behind him, I suppose. You can't see it here, but the hardtop further back has his rubber all over it. He did everything but pirouette on one wheel. By the time he got here, he was going so fast that he went straight over – with a bit of help. We're closing the road until forensic does a check with the tyres. But it was his mark all right.'

'Then you won't want me any more just now, will you, Ken?' Hoskins looked innocently at the chief inspector. 'Harold Moyle was about to buy me dinner on the old Cakewalk terrace when all this happened.'

'Your appetite still as good as ever, is it, Sam?'

'You know how it is, Ken. I do all right.'

Martin eased himself out of the car. He closed the door and put his face to the open window.

'You don't want to be seen round places like Carmel Cooney's more than you need, Sam. It gives a man a reputation.'

'It's the food, Ken; I can't keep away from it. He may be the biggest villain in Canton, but he can't half cook. Best four-courser in town. I'll be sincerely sorry the day he gets banged up. And there's a new girl on the rostrum with the old now-you-see-it-now-you-don't: Heather. And the tall one, that works in his window. I think I'm in the mood to see a bit this evening.'

'You're a hard man, Sam,' Martin said.

'Not yet, Ken. But I hope to be.'

With an assumed look of fatuous innocence masking his plump face, Hoskins did a three-point turn and drove slowly back to Ocean Beach.

CHAPTER THREE

By the time that he parked the Cavalier below the Cakewalk terrace, it was fully dark. Clouds obscured the starlight, but the heavy drops of the storm had not yet begun to fall. Glancing up at the ballroom windows he saw, like a Victorian mantelpiece silhouette, Harold Moyle's profile in reproachful contemplation, staring at the girl on the bandstand. Hoskins put his conscience to sleep. He walked down towards the blaring and shouting of the Cakewalk at 10 p.m..

They were gathered on the promenade as usual, on either side of the pier gates. On the far side were the Chains in their ribboned leather and helmets, beer-bellied at twenty and shabbily whiskered. Their girls, slouching by the parked bikes, joined in the "ere we go! 'ere we go! 'ere we go!' football supporters' chant as they faced the Hot-Rodders across the no-man's-land of the pier approach. Four uniformed men of the Evening Patrol were positioned near the turnstiles. A panda car had drawn up outside the Atlantic Royal Hotel on the opposite pavement of Bay Drive.

On the nearer side of the pier, the confectionery creations of the Hot-Rodders' battle-wagons filled the parking spaces. About thirty of the drivers, trousers creased knife-sharp and hair brilliantined, were sauntering with their girls beside the railings. At first glance they might have been fashion-plates from an old copy of *Esquire*. Seen closer, they had the same slack-mouthed malevolence and stupidity as their rivals with the bikes.

In the darkness there was a beat of music from the pier pavilion and a cascade of lamps reflected over and over in the dark ripples of the night tide, now flooding against the sea-wall of the Cakewalk. Green and orange, like ornamental candy or the lights of Aladdin, the reflections danced and shimmered and melted together in a mesmeric display. The warm air carried a clean smell of washed sand and the hot-nougat scent of candy-floss drifting from the stall on the jetty.

By now almost all the middle-aged and middle-class Bank Holiday trippers had gathered up their children and left. A few

19

still ran the verbal gauntlet of the warriors at the pier entrance. They made for the town end of the Cakewalk, beyond the white-tiled modernism of the sea-front Odeon – opened by Anna Neagle during the Abdication crisis. Their sanctuary lay among the sub-tropical gardens and big stores of the Parade. Neither the Chains nor the Hot-Rodders impeded them, except by an occasional shout of abuse. Civilians had no interest for them, Hoskins clung to the truth of that.

Ignoring the four uniformed men who stood guard on the pier turnstiles, he walked slowly by the parked cars. *Two-Pipe Poppa. . . Was That a Red Light? . . . Louise—Neville. . . Chopper—Monnella. . .* Like a nondescript prat-trousered punter, he admired the style and flair of the customised creations. A car that had hit a bike with sufficient impact to send it over the cliff would have a dent the size of a dustbin-lid. One by one, he studied the ice-cream-coloured roadsters.

'Want a ride, dad? Oi, you! Want a ride?'

The derision came from a group of scruffy eight-year-olds, admirers of the Hot-Rodders, perched on the blue promenade rails. Childish innocence was not a feature of Canton or Ocean Beach. The middle-class motorist whose car went missing was apt to blame an adult thief or adolescent lout. Last month's figures, Hoskins recalled, showed that a third of all vehicle theft in the districts of Barrier and Orient was the work of those under the age of fourteen. One midget, too short to reach the pedals from the seat, was caught in Canton city centre driving a Jetta standing up.

'Hello, Mr Hoskins. Seen anything you fancy, like?'

It was not what Hoskins had intended, but as soon as he saw the name *Neville* on the car, he had braced himself for recognition.

'Not yet, Mouse,' he said equably, 'but I'll keep looking.'

Neville, 'The Mouse', was the product of a Welsh sailor and a Caribbean girl from Peninsula. Blunt-faced and humorous, also an artist with a knife or a car ignition, he kept his head almost shaved to disguise the premature greyness that afflicted him at twenty. He had been done once for pimping, in a house off Martello Square, and twice for taking away and driving uninsured. His nickname was a tribute to virility. In dockland brothel-slang, a circumcised penis was traditionally called a bald mouse.

'You only got to say, Mr Hoskins. If there's anything catched the eye. Anything. You know. I can tell you a few jacks down "A" Division wouldn't say goodbye to that.'

Hoskins looked past Neville's sardonic grin at the girl who stood back a few paces. The Mouse had her on a leash, the tail of it in his hand and the collar round her neck. She looked neither subdued nor excited, but indifferent. It was no more to her than a pearl necklace. Hoskins, small-talking Neville, made a note of Louise for future reference. A check on the occurrence book of the dirty squad, perhaps. Not tall, he thought, and her pale shape just a little plump. She had the air of an impudent soubrette, eighteen or nineteen years old, with a boldly rounded young face, a firm nose and chin. Her dark hair was pulled back straight and slick, her blue eyes seeming saucily rounded by virtue of the darkened lashes. She looked at Hoskins.

'Anything for you, Mr Hoskins,' the Mouse said. Louise gave a preposterous little snort of laughter.

'I'll be in touch, Mouse,' Hoskins said amiably. 'You can count on that.'

Neville chuckled and turned away. The girl in tow was dressed almost like a Petshop waitress in the punk chic of long boots and black bikini pants. The Mouse gave Louise a sharp flick behind with the leash, as if to display his mastery for Chief Inspector Hoskins' benefit. Louise made no response, one way or the other. It was all part of the game to her.

There were days when Neville almost showed willing. An informant. Hoskins wondered about this as he walked on. The Mouse as a plant, in exchange for a little easing up by the Vice Squad. Worth consideration. As things were at present, pimping was the least of the city's troubles. On the whole, the ponces kept order in the trade. They sometimes did the squad's job for them. So, at least, it seemed to Hoskins in a realistic mood.

Not a mark on any of the cars, which in itself wasn't surprising. A Hot-Rodder, after a bash like that, would have made for home and some judicious panel-beating. But Hoskins knew most of the cars in the pack. So far as he could see, there was no one obviously missing.

The lights on the pier went out and the gates closed. From somewhere on the Chains' side of the Cakewalk a bottle rose in the air and came down a few feet from the Hot-Rodders. It did not so much smash as burst into a pool of fire about the size of a large dining-table, trickles of flame running in every direction. The Hot-Rodders drew back and the blue light on the panda began to flash. A fight broke out in the unlit entrance to the pier jetty, metal shutters now locked over the turnstiles.

A uniformed inspector appeared from a newly arrived car. The men of the foot patrol, caught between the two factions, were targets for both. In the unlit pier arch, Hoskins just made out a police cap falling and a young face going down with distorted tension, as if the lad were trying to concentrate on his pain.

'Get hold of her! Get her!' shouted the uniformed inspector, indicating one of the girls with the Chains. A second bottle, fortuitously inaccurate, hit the rail of the promenade and spilt its fire down the sea-wall stonework towards the tide.

'Get her!'

Hoskins found himself among Hot-Rodders who were content to be spectators of the main event. They stood jostling and nudging for a view, forming a human arena round the fight. He edged his way between the packed bodies, across the promenade, and found the second car of the Evening Patrol. The uniformed inspector was talking angrily into his personal radio.

'Zed Alpha Fox to all mobiles. Disturbance at the pier approach. Require immediate assistance. Two gangs, estimate one hundred persons in all. Two petrol bombs thrown. One officer assaulted. No information on extent of injuries. Ambulance and fire service to stand by.'

On the flank of the crowd, unnoticed by those watching the pier approach fight and the beating of the young policeman, two uniformed men were dragging one of the girls from among the motor-bikes. She looked to Hoskins no more than fifteen or sixteen, dishevelled red hair loose on her shoulders, fair skin, hazel eyes and a hint of freckles. By comparison with the girls of the Hot-Rodders, she appeared dowdy and poor in her boots and jeans. The regulation black leather jacket with its frills was embroidered on the back with the partnership of Angie and Digger.

'Let go!' she screamed, frightened for the first time by the consequences of her act. 'Take your hands off me! Get your fucking hands off!'

Hysterically shrill, she bowed against their grip and lunged her hips against the two policemen, trying to brace her legs in resistance as her arms were held in a firm lock.

'Hoskins,' said Hoskins to the uniformed inspector. 'Canton "A" Division, CID, off-duty.'

Amongst the girl's screaming and the shouts of the crowd at the fight, the inspector ignored him.

'Get that girl into the car! Don't let her wipe her hands! I want her tested for petrol!'

He turned to Hoskins without any sign of recognition or of having heard what was said to him.

'Now! What do you want?'

'Nothing,' said Hoskins humbly. He had recognised that this was much worse than an earful of Elaine Harris. 'Sorry. It doesn't matter.'

His reluctance was reinforced by the sight of two more cars, lights flashing and sirens whooping, hammering down Bay Drive towards the pier. Where, he thought, was the use of enlisting in the cavalry now that the battle was over? The Hot-Rodders' war chariots were what interested him. Nothing more. By now the spectators had drawn back from the improvised arena near the turnstiles. The injured policeman and two of the warriors were being attended to.

Neville the Mouse saluted Hoskins with a beer-scented belch, Louise still on her leash with an air of patient contempt. With his lager can, the Mouse indicated the patrol car and the red-haired prisoner, Angie, inside it.

'You should've let us have her, Mr Hoskins. Our bother, wasn't it? Trouble with you jacks, you always have to go and spoil people's fun. Still, I 'spect we can always find her again when we want her.'

By the time Hoskins reached the Petshop, Harold Moyle had gone. Only a message remained, gentle and uncomprehending. An hour later, from the phone in the sitting-room of his flat, he spoke to Ken Martin at Ocean Beach Division and ate baked beans one-handed with a fork.

'I'll bet you it's not what you think, Ken,' he said indistinctly.

'You don't know what I think, Sam. How much are you putting on?'

'I'll do a fiver, if you like. I checked their cars along the Cakewalk afterwards. Not a mark anywhere. I made a list. I'll put it in the divisional mail for you tomorrow.'

'And then we see which little piss-artist isn't on your list and take his car apart? He'd gone home to hide the dent? Life's not that simple, Sam.'

'Mine is. Yours may not be,' Hoskins said morosely and put the phone down.

Next morning, driving down the pink-tarmac Mall between the almond blossom, towards the white cliff-face of the City Police Headquarters, Hoskins listened to the early bulletin of Coastal Radio. The death of Robbo Redlitch-Smith, 'the thinking man's guide to the drama of the game', was reported as a hit-and-run accident. Other events of the Bank Holiday weekend received a collective obituary.

'Apart from the tragedy on Highlands Avenue,' said the toothy tough-chinned voice reassuringly, 'police report a quiet weekend at Ocean Beach, with none of the widespread violence on the Cakewalk that marred the Easter opening of the holiday season. One arrest was reported and one policeman was slightly injured. That was the news. This is Coastal Radio at sixteen minutes past seven on Tuesday the fifth of May . . .'

In the Memorial Gardens, behind low hedges on one side of the Mall, rose the pale arches of a monument to unremembered wars and regiments long disbanded. As Hoskins drove past, the cherry trees along the paths formed clouds and arches of blossom. But there was something acid in the earth of Canton. It produced a blossom of deep chemical pink, the colour of bubble-gum spat out upon the stained and sticky summer pavements of Atlantic Wharf or Martello Square. Not that it would last long, Hoskins thought. The first stiff breeze from the deep-water anchorages was already bringing down the petals to mingle along the gutters and paths. They lay indistinguishably with wedding confetti from the harsh brick of the Register Office yard.

CHAPTER FOUR

In deference to his rank, Hoskins had a small corner room to himself on the fifth floor of the headquarters building, opposite the main row of CID inspectors' offices. Next door to him on one side was the sergeants' room, eight desks wedged in tight and stacked with paperwork. The court files, the crime report books and the Form 52 booklets overflowed desks, filing cabinets and window-ledges. Hoskins' immediate assistant, Jack Chance, known amiably as 'Fat Chance', had a desk in there.

Hero of the CID just now was Wallace Dudden. Superintendent Maxwell Ripley, Hoskins' neighbour on the other side, had ordered the removal of 'sexually offensive' posters from the wall of the sergeants' room. The Police Committee had recently debated the social attitudes and prejudices of the headquarters building. Dudden's offence had been a lady in black stockings and white skin leaning on a mantelpiece.

'It's only a keepsake of me mum, boss,' Dudden had said, failing to raise a smile from the 'Ripper', as Superintendent Ripley was inevitably and universally known.

With ingenuity beyond his usual range, Dudden replaced the photograph with an unobjectionable print of a lady in evening dress around whom four bald-headed men were performing a bow. When the figures of the men, apart from their bald heads, were covered up, it became a lewd and fetishistic masterpiece at front and rear.

Dudden's stock went up. Opinion in the sergeants' room was in any case scornful of the Ripper. It held unanimously that he was running scared of the Police Committee. Particularly of Councillor Eve Ricard whose interests, as her introductions on the local networks put it, were women's issues and media bias.

In disputes such as this, Hoskins was apt to feel like a stooge for both sides, the confidant of Ripley and the sergeants simultaneously. It was not a role he enjoyed.

With the time of arrival noted in his duty diary, he folded his arms on the high window-sill and stared out across the city, thinking about Robbo Smith and Ocean Beach. The corner room allocated to him had two windows. The present one looked inland towards the affluent ridge of Hawks Hill, where the gardens had mature trees in them and the roads were quiet between high walls and gabled roofs. At the city's verge, the terrain opened out into a long valley edged by the first slopes of a mountain landscape. A toy castle with conical turrets, a Pre-Raphaelite design of the 1870s from a mediaeval tapestry, rose distantly among the trees. To the nearer side of Hawks Hill was the beginning of Mount Pleasant, the fortress tower blocks of council tenants, where the single-storey pubs with their thick roofs of concrete slab and slit windows to reduce breakage had the appearance of air-raid shelters left over from the last war.

The other window was the one Hoskins preferred. It showed the real Canton, built on a wide alluvial plain that was almost below sea-level. Ahead of him stretched the civic centre and the pink tarmac of the Mall with its Memorial Gardens and cherry trees. City Hall and the Museum in their slabs of pale Edwardian stone were topped by domes and flying chariots in bronze like Parisian pavilions for a long-forgotten world fair. Beyond them, the buses and department stores of Great Western Street led down to Atlantic Wharf and the protective bank against the sea, the route upon which the railway had been raised.

A hundred years before, east of the Wharf, Dutch engineers had constructed a barrier against the tides. It had given its name to the thousand shabby rows of back-to-back houses sheltered by it. The Barrier district once provided a work-force for the ships and the coal trade. To the western side of Atlantic Wharf lay Peninsula and the docks, the flat compacted silt jutting out to form a bay or natural harbour. Between Hoskins and Peninsula was the final district of Canton proper, the narrow streets and little houses, the clubs, pubs and restaurants of Orient. Its name had come from the first overseas trade of the city docks, long before the coal or the development of the city's 'Chinatown'.

Hoskins turned and sat down at the pile of crime reports, the booklets of Form 52 left for him over the weekend by diligent uniformed colleagues. It was an hour and two purse-snatches later when the door opened and the Ripper appeared. Superintendent

Maxwell Ripley was a tall grey man in his middle fifties, blunted and worn by experience. He had a drooping and breathless air like a beagle at the end of a long hunt. It was common knowledge that his retirement was now two years away and that he was nursing his blood pressure. All the Ripper wanted was a quiet spell to coast home.

'Got a minute, Sam?' he said hopefully, as if half-expecting Hoskins to order him from the room.

'Yes.' Hoskins' voice had the strained affability of a man interrupted in more important matters. 'Yes, sure, Max.' He followed Ripley to the superintendent's room and closed the door.

'How's it going, Sam?'

He had rarely known Ripley to begin a private conversation on any topic with a remark other than this. And he had never known him to take the least notice of the reply.

'It's busy, Max.' Hoskins said. 'There's been a well-organised team of purse-snatchers working Balance Street and Riverside the past weeks. Catch people coming out of the banks.'

The superintendent nodded and dismissed the subject.

'Bit of excitement at Ocean Beach, then?' he said enquiringly. 'Robbo Smith. Not one of our friends exactly, but the wash is likely to catch us. There's some tidying up that'll need to be done at this end.'

'Is there, Max?'

'Yes, there is, Sam.' It was almost a snap. Behind his own desk with the framed photograph and the personal ruler, Ripley was in command once more, back in the driving-seat. 'Take Sergeant Chance this evening. We need a statement from Robbo Smith's woman. Nothing known about her, but we want a word or two. She's on our patch. If there's a connection there, I'll have to know.'

'I'm short-handed just now, Max.'

'And we're one down in the sergeants' room. You know about Stoodley?'

'No.'

'Yesterday. Four tearaways apparently laid a trap for a homo. Public conveniences in King Edward Square. The man got out and they grabbed him again on the corner of Jones and Gower.

27

Stoodley saw him run and get caught by them. Thumping him as Stoodley drove past, going home off watch. Stoodley gets out. Three of the yobboes leave the man and grab Stoodley. Throw him straight through Jones and Gower's plate-glass display window. Shard of glass goes down under his ribs and pierces the gut. He's in the Royal Infirmary. They've got to do a second op today. He'll be all right eventually. We've lost him, though. Pity. He was a good man.'

'Bloody hell,' said Hoskins glumly. 'What time last night was this?'

'Yesterday afternoon, Sam. Broad daylight. No one noticed anything; not a witness anywhere. Only Stoodley saw him run from the toilets with the others after him. The yobs and the man they attacked scarpered opposite ways. We've only got Stoodley's word that he didn't throw himself through the window. No one went to him even after the gang had done a bunk. The pain was bad. He was screaming with it. That could've been the second murder of the Bank Holiday. People thought he was another paralytic drunk, I suppose.'

Hoskins nodded.

'You heard about Ocean Beach last night, Max? On the Cakewalk?'

'There was something in the paper.' Ripley sounded suddenly disapproving.

'Not on the radio news there wasn't!' Hoskins said. 'Cosy rubbish about a quiet weekend on the Cakewalk! None of the violence that marred the Easter holiday! I saw two petrol bombs thrown on the promenade and two gangs of warriors mixing it. There's a uniformed probationer in hospital and a female petrol bomber under arrest. She could've burnt someone to death – and not for want of trying!'

Ripley sat back and sighed, as if about to pass on bad news.

'There's a feeling among our political masters, Sam. There's a policy even on the Police Committee and elsewhere in the committees – about negative reporting. The media hasn't always been responsive. Report news, OK. But playing up violence only leads to worse. And it's bad enough as things are. The argument is that you won't get better community relations if every broadcast is full of items about crimes committed by the young, or the blacks, or the warriors, or people who live in Barrier or Peninsula. Their civil war thrives on that kind of publicity. Locally, there's real pressure building up on the networks to cool it. Negative reporting makes people think they're living in south-side Chicago or somewhere. And the better-off won't vote money to be spent on the poorer areas if they think they're full of thugs and vandals. I'm not saying it's right, Sam, but that's definitely the policy that prevails in the council committees. Coastal Radio and the TV people are playing ball at last. Not the *Western World*, though; they're part of the Rockwell chain and they've got shareholders. Bad news sells copies for them.'

Hoskins sat down uninvited.

'It's that bloody woman Ricard and her crap about media bias,' he said savagely. 'With the May elections coming up, the only way she can hang on is by making people believe that it's all sweet-ness and light. Hide the bad news. Bloody hell, Max! You can't walk through the city centre in broad daylight without a fair chance of being thrown through a plate-glass window! And if you take an evening stroll along the Cakewalk, watch out for the petrol bombs!'

The outburst left him feeling foolish and helpless. Ripley sniffed and nodded.

'I know, Sam. I'm not trying to force a view on anyone. I've no right to and I don't want to. I don't necessarily agree myself. But I can't go into discussions with these people and argue for the money and facilities we need, and then tell them by the way that their policies are crap as far as the Division is concerned. In three weeks' time, you get your chance at the election. Vote Ms Ricard and the Comrades out of office, if you want. Pity you don't live on Hawks Hill. You could vote Conservative there.'

Hoskins stared narrow-eyed through his tinted glasses. 'Why there?'

Ripley smirked under his moustache.

'You really haven't read your *Western World*, have you, Sam? Carmel Cooney is standing as Conservative candidate in a ward that even he could hardly lose.'

'Cooney?' Hoskins' face contorted with incredulity. 'But he's been done for corruption in the Crown Court!'

'Acquitted, Sam, not done. In fact, you could say that he's the only one of our councillors that's ever proved himself not to be corrupt. See how you like having him on the Police Committee.'

And the Ripper relaxed, as if for the first time he had begun to enjoy the sunlit and windy May morning.

'This evening then, Sam,' he said encouragingly. 'I'll have the WPC out there first. It's one of the little streets on Lantern Hill, across from the docks. No need to stage a grand opera about it. We just have to be sure that Robbo Smith's woman didn't pay someone to shove him and his bike off the cliff.'

CHAPTER FIVE

'Cooney?' Sergeant Chance smiled with delight over the steering wheel. He turned past the Florentine tower of the Keep, a Victorian shipowner's folly whose grounds stretched west of the civic centre. 'Cooney? Bloody hell, Sam! They wouldn't let him, would they?'

Hoskins stared out of the window as the shops of Longwall sped past and they crossed the river bridge into Orient. The sodium lights splashed orange and gold on the sleek flanks of the mud-banks at slack water.

'He's a member,' he said philosophically. 'There's not much of a rush to be a Tory on a council that's rarely been anything but Labour. Cooney was tried for corruption when he was a councillor last time – fifteen years ago. Building contracts on the Mount Pleasant estates. Him and three others. They all got off. No convictions then, not a stain on his character. Look far enough back and you'll find he was copped several times for violence and theft when he was in the Army, National Service. A right little villain. But you won't prove anything now.'

'Still,' said Jack Chance reasonably, 'you wouldn't think they'd actually choose him.'

Hoskins turned from the view of terraced shops.

'Listen, my son. Being on a council like this is a game. No one cares. They have to put them up for election but, short of Hawks Hill and a couple of others, there's not a snowball's chance in hell. When Cooney had his spot of bother at the Crown Court, he was the only Tory. The other three were Labour councillors. They all got off. One of 'em lives in Bermuda now.'

'Straight through Osborne Road and Orient, Sam?'

'Back way to Lantern Hill. Up the hill and then left. Arran Street. It's one of that mass of streets across from the docks. Number eight.'

'Right-o,' said Sergeant Chance equably. He was a plump, well-muscled young man with a round fresh-cheeked face and a flop of black hair that gave him a look of natural amiability. Even when he was carrying out an arrest, it seemed a good-natured and cheerful occasion. From his expression, Jack Chance might have been about to forget his instructions and fall into company with the suspect. Miscalculation was so easy that, two weeks previously, Chance had inadvertently broken the elbow of a fugitive who tried to shake off his armlock.

Despite the Ripper's orders, a necessary interrogation in the purse-snatching case had delayed Hoskins' visit to Robbo Smith's woman. After dark, the low-roofed terraced houses of Orient recalled the shabby Victorian market area they had once been. Shopfronts had been built out from their ground floors: second-hand furniture and bookmakers, fish-bars and video rentals, costume jewellery and off-licences. A watchful light shone in the upper window of the 24-hour funeral parlour. By the traffic lights Hoskins heard a rattle of female clogs on dry pavements. At intervals, the steel umbrellas of filling stations sprouted like white double mushrooms among the radiant yellow and blue of the petrol signs.

'If I had to,' Hoskins said presently, 'I think I'd vote for Cooney rather than the Ricard woman. At least he's a straight-forward villain. You know he'll screw you, more or less. When, where and how.'

'I bet you would, Sam. Straight up the hill here?'

Hoskins made a confirmatory gesture at the windscreen.

'And Cooney's lived his life here. So have I. That young

woman's never been anywhere but a snotty college and a well-paid job in a political office. That horrible whining so-called classless accent! The accent of the new masters, Jack Chance. The new rich. Stupid bitch never set foot in Canton until she saw a juicy public career waiting for her!'

'Sam!'

'Grizzling on about media bias! Or telling me that unless I'm a bloody pouve I'm guilty of a male-dominated perversion called heterosexuality! The networks put out crap like that! Not a word about people being petrol-bombed on the promenade! Give me the *Western World*, Jack. "Rear of the Year" swimwear competitions and all.'

'Sam! You want to turn off this road or keep on going into the sea?'

'Turn here,' said Hoskins sourly. 'Top of the side street and pull in beyond the house.'

Chance drove slowly up the uneven road whose terraced houses had the unmistakable air of workmen's cottages gentrified by a young professional class buying for the first time. Some, though they did not know it, were also buying for the last time, Hoskins reflected. From the top of the street, there was a view across the constantly dredged waterway and mudbanks of the outer harbour towards the dock wall and pierhead of the Peninsula. Hoskins paused after Chance had stopped the car. He let out a long breath and smiled, reflecting on his outburst.

'Good!' he said with an accession of energy. 'I feel a lot better for that!'

They walked back together along the terraced street, salesmen's Volvos and Mercedes parked outside the homes of the Victorian labouring class. Hoskins paused by the narrow-fronted house, the light showing behind the curtain of the front room. He nodded at Chance and rang the bell. As he expected, the door was answered by the young policewoman from the uniformed branch. He held up his warrant card, then guided her on to the pavement, out of earshot of the front room.

'All right, love? What's the state of play?'

'Taking it all very calmly,' the young woman said. 'Not delayed shock either. Easy come, easy go, where men are concerned. She walked out on the last one to live with Robbo Smith. The house is rented in joint names but they were planning to buy. So she says. I don't think she's seriously attached to anyone but herself. I shouldn't think this was her first affair. Probably screwing around and proud of it. What they used to call emancipated.'

'Right, thanks,' said Hoskins gently. 'You go and sit with the nice sergeant in the car. You'll be all right with him. He's not the least emancipated. I'll go in and have a word with her alone first.'

'Scream if you need help,' the young policewoman said and turned away with Sergeant Chance.

Hoskins glanced at his watch and saw that it was even later than he had supposed. He went through the doorway, closed the door behind him and stood in the hall. There was a man's rucksack with a black and white arrow motif upon it. A pile of posters proclaiming a variety of Robbo Smith's radical causes lay on a chair. It all fitted the known politics of Robin Royston Redlitch-Smith and, presumably, his current partner. Hoskins turned to the half-open sitting-room door, tapped it lightly and went in without waiting.

The young woman who stood before the sofa was plain rather than beautiful. Hoskins judged that she was twenty-seven or twenty-eight years old. She was quite tall and her figure suggested a firm erotic maturity in the jeans and cream sweater, which she wore like the uniform of her class and type. Her face had the firm and fair-skinned look of a spoilt daughter of the middle class. She would be a teacher or a professional government employee of some kind, he thought, college educated. There was a cool, indifferent stare from her blue eyes, a certain sulky weight to the jaw and a petulance in the line of the mouth. Definitely not Hoskins' idea of fun. Her straight fair hair was cut in an almost perversely plain pudding-basin crop, trimmed short at the nape and worn in a long parted fringe. Quite why it was that he found a sensual stimulus about her, he could not say. Perhaps it was the challenge of her manner, the dismissive blue eyes and the almost resentful sullenness of her mouth and chin.

He stood for only a few seconds, about to speak. Then, to his dismay, he realised that he was about to call her Mrs Redlitch-Smith. The meeting of their eyes or the confrontation of their faces had let slip the other name from his memory. Lesley someone. He could not very well call her Lesley. Hoskins swore silently in the depths of his mind.

'Sit down,' she said, in that modern classless voice about which he had complained so savagely to Jack Chance. Why was it so grating in Eve Ricard and so unobjectionable now?

'Thanks.' Hoskins accepted but waited until she had sat down first. 'I'm sorry to bother you this late. I'll be as brief as I can. I'm sorry that this should have happened at all. A lot of people respected Robbo Smith, personally and professionally.'

But not 'A' Division, he thought. Better to have let the compliment alone.

She shook her parted fringe into place with an impatient gesture.

'I'm not sure what you want from me. What I can do.'

The manner of a sulky little girl, he decided, even though she was old enough to have kids of her own. That was the key to her.

'In the first place,' Hoskins said, 'I want to make sure you're all right. There's no reason that you shouldn't be, of course. It looks as if this was a hit-and-run accident of some sort. But I shall need your help as well for the moment.'

It was the high crown and the plain hairstyle that suggested to him a little girl on her way to her first ballet class. Prim and yet sensual. But WPC Frith had been right. Robbo Smith's death was not a tragedy to this young woman. More of a bloody nuisance.

'Why should I help you?'

Hoskins had been half-prepared for something of the kind. To her he was the police. The enemy. Friend of South Africa. Truncheon and rhino whip. The cordon or the gas grenade. It was time for a little shock of reality.

'You should help me,' he said, 'because there is at least a possibility that someone could have a grudge against both of you. Unlikely but possible. Sexual jealousy or political animosity.'

She still looked at him in childish disdain. With a nagging frustration and a spur of excitement, like a descant over a melody, the thought of going to bed with her overlaid his interrogation. To escape Eve Ricard on the island of Eros, he would have swum through a shark-infested sea without a second thought. But there was something about this rather plain and arrogant young woman, promiscuous yet self-possessed, that plagued him like a physical discomfort.

'A lot of people had it in for Robbo,' she said coolly, 'not for me. His enemies were people who were scared of what a journalist of his sort could do when he turned from sport to investigation.'

'Anyone in particular in mind?'

'Everyone,' she said. 'Tories on the local council. Brothel-keepers down the Peninsula. National Front. It's not hard to have people hating you in a city like this.'

'But not a specific name?'

She brushed her fringe back with the edge of her hand, sweeping away a troublesome hair.

'Not that I know of.'

Hoskins tried a different tack.

'Were you here yesterday evening?'

'No,' she said, 'I was at a meeting.'

'You never rode the BMW? It's important, because in that clothing it would be hard to identify the rider.'

'Never.'

Hoskins realised that he had allowed his eyes to drop to the smooth tightness of the jeans over her firm mature young thighs. He raised them at once.

'Do you have a licence of any kind?'

She paused before her answer, as if to show her indifference to the accusation.

'No. I have an ordinary bicycle. That's all.'

'Is there any reason you know of why anyone would have done this deliberately?'

'Is there any reason . . .' Lesley's voice had a peevish tone which he guessed, in her case, might be the prelude to tears. 'Is there any reason why any human being would do it to another? I don't know of any. Not to him. Not to anyone.'

'Of course.' Hoskins headed off the outburst of grief. 'There's no reason to think it was anything but an accident. The other party drove on in a panic. That's all. It happens quite a lot in that way. I'm sorry that I have to bother you about it. I know how you must feel.'

She bowed her face and shook her head without speaking. Hoskins could see her teeth worrying her lower lip.

'You?' she said indistinctly. 'How can you know? You've seen it all before. But only from the outside. I'm just a duty visit – the sort that you'd rather not make.'

Hoskins leant forward and spoke as if to reassure her. It was a quiet and competent voice, a hushed confidence that might describe the ball leaving the bowler's hand in a cricket commentary.

'Fifteen years ago, I sat where you do now. A wife and a baby daughter. A message about a motorway collision. A car into the back of a lorry. That was all. You know the oddest thing? I thought afterwards how easy it was to get the news like that. Everything over. No slow disillusionment and no long-drawn-out partings. It was over for me as suddenly as for you.'

She looked up at him with doubt in her eyes, still not speaking, and shook her head as if she did not understand. It was the first time that Hoskins had told this truth about himself in the course of his duty.

'The main thing,' he said gently, 'is to make arrangements for you now. I can leave the policewoman here for the time being. Is there anyone you'd like to come and stay with you for a while? A girl-friend, perhaps?'

She shook her head again without raising her face to him this time. Hoskins took out a card and wrote on it.

'If there's anything you need or anything you think I ought to know, phone me on these numbers, day or night. If I'm not at one, I shall usually be at the other. Or someone will take a message on the first one. The second one has an answering machine.'

She was almost twenty years younger than he, and not in her first youth. She did not even look as he imagined an object of desire must appear in his fantasies. Perhaps it was the challenge she presented, the feminine sexuality heightened rather than diminished by the urchin crop and the perversely cultivated lack of glamour. The notion that a boyish haircut and a pair of jeans made a woman unfeminine was something Hoskins had never understood. There was a sexual warmth and a coded desire which made it immaterial whether a girl wore an evening gown or a siren suit. Put this one in football boots and a school cap, it would make no difference. Perhaps it was the defiantly hidden and guarded femininity that drew him on.

'I won't bother you any more than I have to,' he said, putting the card down on a small occasional table by the chair. 'There's no need for you to do anything further. The identification and everything else has been arranged. I'll come back later on and make sure you're all right.'

'I'll be all right,' she said. But the face she turned to him at last was that of a self-pitying child.

'Of course,' said Hoskins gently, 'but I'll come back somewhen and see if there's anything else we can do.'

He got up and went out to the door, the policewoman coming back down the street at his appearance. Even if he never again saw Lesley Wiles, as he now recalled her name, he had broken the first and last rule of his profession. Never get involved. He *was* involved. It was bad news, according to the book, and he cared nothing for the book. In any case, it would turn out to be fantasy and nothing more.

The young policewoman went into the house to resume her benevolent surveillance. Hoskins walked slowly up the uneven Victorian paving towards the car.

Initial liking that turned to something more was an experience he had known on a good many occasions with a woman. His present response to a challenge that was almost hostile was something beyond his experience. It was like an arrow of the gods that struck in the myths of antiquity. But so far as Hoskins could remember, there had never been a mythical occasion when the passion was engendered through antipathy.

He sat down in the passenger-seat of the car.

'Well?' asked Sergeant Chance.

'Just drive back,' Hoskins said.

'Nothing to say?'

'Just drive back.'

Chance did as he was told. On the hill running from Harbour Bar to the first houses of Orient, there was a police station in Victorian stone with a blue lamp. Hoskins smiled.

'Just for a moment in there, Jack, I really fancied Ms Wiles. I really did. I thought you might have to pull up at the Harbour Bar nick for me to turn myself in.'

To mention it to Chance would exorcise the ghost. But Chance was grinning with something more than amusement at the revelation.

'Good thing you was able to keep yourself under control, Sam. You might have had a nasty shock.'

'Why's that?'

Sergeant Chance giggled and turned into the neon-lit slum of Osborne Road.

'I was talking to WPC Gillian Frith about Robbo Smith's lady-friend. Seems she got a lot of advanced ideas from him or from somewhere. Good thing you kept yourself on the leash.'

'Mousetrap in the pants?'

'Worse than that, Sam. For about a year, she was volunteer secretary to a friend of yours.'

'Who's that, then?'

'Eve Ricard,' said Sergeant Chance, accelerating towards the river bridge and the lights of the civic centre with a snort of delight.

CHAPTER SIX

On the following morning, Jack Chance edged the motor-pool's last Ford Fiesta patiently through the summer traffic-jam of the Parade at Ocean Beach. In the warmth of the coffee hour a caravan of day-trippers wound through the sub-tropical shrubs of the central gardens towards the Cakewalk and the sands. The sky was already hot and overcast, the colour of dull pearl. House banners hung in an airless heat on the flagpoles of the modern-tiled department stores that looked across the trees to the promenade. A mineral odour of hot engine-oil seeped into the car's interior through the air ducts.

'You were lucky, Sam,' said Chance confidently, reproving Hoskins' complaint about the engine smell. 'This was the last mobile in working order. The Division's got five non-operational and only Jock or Dave to patch them up. All emergency calls will in future be answered on foot as a measure of economy.'

Hoskins stared bleakly out of the window at the pavement crowds. A hot sky yielded grey and gleaming sunlight.

'What a sodding fiasco,' he said helplessly.

Chance did a quick change of lane, making for Clifton Hill with its franchise garages and the little hotels that smelt perpetually of fried breakfast and ancient carpeting.

'You could have had Tango Three,' he said consolingly, 'except that the state of the seats looks like it was used by three or four Paddies that went on the blanket the minute they was nicked.'

Hoskins grunted. Below him, he watched a gull burst upwards from the water in a feathering of spray, beyond the New Pier landing-stage where the emerald sea darkened to a black horizon band. Sergeant Chance began to sing softly to himself, 'Yoo doo something to mee, something that reely gets inside meee. . . .' Girls in the brief elastic skins of white or black or blue bikinis lay like battlefield casualties the length of the sands. Below the bandstand in the central gardens of the Parade their parents or grandparents in wide-brimmed sun-hats filled the green regiment of deckchairs. White flowers perfumed the hot shade and Hoskins thought that for some people the summer had come. Even for Jack Chance. But not for him.

'Turn here,' he said, indicating the corner at the top of Clifton Hill, marked by the orange awning of an ice-cream parlour whose interior was all mirrors and cool marbling. They followed the side road, a lane on to which commercial back gates and lock-up garages opened.

'You doo . . .' Chance began again.

'Park there,' Hoskins said. 'Stay with it. There's a mob of young monkeys operating in Ocean Beach with a push-button starter and a couple of crocodile clips. I'd as soon not come back and find we've mislaid the last working mobile in the Divison.'

He slammed the door and walked through the warm May air to the front of a new three-storey building in red brick. It might have been the inconspicuous premises of an architectural partnership or a computer programmer. In the jargon of the trade, it was

Area Forensic One, otherwise the rear of Ocean Beach Division.

'Been to the main desk, sir?' asked the duty sergeant when Hoskins presented himself at the ticket-window.

'Just ask for Dr Blades,' said Hoskins patiently.

The uniformed sergeant turned and spoke to someone else not immediately in view. A few words came from behind a partition.

' . . . something for Chief Inspector Hoskins.'

A face appeared, and then the rest of a thin man of about forty with an intent and worried expression. This had nothing to do with being worried at all. Dr Blades' malignant stomach had been removed in order to preserve the rest of him. His face seemed to have been caught for ever at that moment in his present expression of concern, as if the wind had changed and taken him by surprise.

'Hello, Charlie,' said Hoskins amiably. 'What've you got for me, then?'

'Not much cause for rejoicing, Sam. Better come round the factory and have a look.'

He whistled a nondescript little tune as he led the way.

'How's life in Ocean Beach, then, Charlie?'

'Keeping busy, Sam. Just busy.'

'Had your leave yet?'

'Noaw!' said Blades disparagingly. 'August. Sharon and the two little bleeders from her first marriage. Not so bad when I'm at work – but a couple of weeks of sun and fun! Pisses me off, Sam. I'd sooner be in here. Each time some belly-acher on the television tells me something's a threat to family life, I know whatever it is can't be all bad.'

'They'll grow up and leave home, Charlie.'

'They could go now, eight and nine respectively, Sam. I'd buy their tickets. I wish their old man would do a tug-of-love snatch on them. I'd give a hand on his side of the rope.'

Whistling again, Blades pushed open a door into what appeared to be a saleroom of secondhand car spares. On a long bench lay the grey satin fin of the BMW bike sheathed in clear polythene.

'What's all this rubbish, Charlie?'

Blades in his white coat picked up a clip-board and pulled a face.

'Did what we could for you. There's a hell of a lot of damage, but most of it from the impact with the beach. You wouldn't think sand could do it, but there's some rock about an inch or two down. He must've ridden right up through the sky on that bike. Horseman of the apocalypse, you might say. It was only when the bike looped the loop that he came off. Hit a tree-trunk head-first, still doing about sixty miles an hour without his bike. Helmet gone, brains knocked out. No pain felt he, Sam; I am quite sure he felt no pain.'

Hoskins looked at the wrapped fin of grey metal.

'And that's all?'

'Not quite, Sam. He *was* pushed. Unless you believe that someone had dented the bike before with a hell of a bang. It's mostly on the luggage pannier at the back.'

Blades walked away and came back with three envelopes of clear plastic.

'We got these off the metal, Sam. Primer. Undercoat. Top coat. Not off a car bumper, obviously. Someone probably caught him with the car's off-side wing. Nudged him sideways, I'd say.'

'Could you testify that the dent must have happened when he was elbowed off the cliff, Charlie? We'd have to know before it went to the prosecution service. Or could we have some prick in a wig and gown telling us that it might have been done before Robbo Smith went on his last ride?'

Blades massaged his chin a little and pulled a sour mouth.

'It's not fireproof, Sam. You can have an opinion, but it's not proof. What I could say, for instance, is that with an impact of the force that seems likely, the bodywork would have been smashed so hard against the rear tyre that the wheel wouldn't turn. And I could say that if the damage had been done some while, there'd have been signs of corrosion or rust where the paint had gone and the air got underneath. There wasn't anything like that.'

'That'll do to be going on with,' Hoskins said.

Blades shook his head.

'It's no guarantee, Sam. You and I know it must've happened on the cliff, but I wouldn't put it past a smart brief and a pet witness to leave a jury wondering.'

'Robbo Smith wouldn't go riding round on a smashed-up bike. Not his style.'

'Juries don't convict on what a man's style may or may not have been, Sam. They need blokes like me doing the scientific expert bit. It might not work with this one. Probably would, but might not.'

Hoskins resigned himself to that.

'All right, Charlie. What've we got exactly?'

'Three paints, Sam. They've been tweezered and puffed off with loving care. Dark grey primer. Off-white undercoat. Top coat that almost matches metallic gold. But none of them quite tallies with a British Standard paint. Foreign stuff. A bit flash. The sort of finishing touch the Hot-Rodders might like for their scrolls and filigree work. Not the sort they'd use on an entire body.'

Hoskins grunted.

'One thing we have not got time to do, Charlie, is round up all the Hot-Rod cars and start stripping the paint off to see what might be underneath. As of yesterday, the motor-pool is down to two men, Jock and Dave, on part-time contracts. There's three mobiles in the Division still in working order. Once they've gone, anyone who dials three nines is going to be a bit unlucky. The CID will arrive by bus, or taxi, or horse and cart. If it arrives at all. All right?'

Blades chuckled and put the samples in his overall pocket.

'Stop bleating, Sam, and come in here a minute.'

The office that opened off the laboratory contained the visual display units, a row of small electronic screens on a bench, each flickering with sea-green luminescence. Blades waved Hoskins to a seat, whistling and talking alternately as he prepared a sample.

'What's your interest in Robbo Smith exactly, Sam? Why can't Ken Martin handle the whole thing from Ocean Beach?'

It was one of the few occasions in his professional career when Hoskins felt his face getting hot with self-consciousness.

'The Ripper wants our end tied up as well. Robbo Smith's woman's on our patch. If there's marks on the bike, I'll have to ask her whether she can remember seeing them before that night. She could even have given him the elbow off the cliff for all I know. It's official, Charlie. Ask Ripley, if you like.'

Blades nodded and thought about it. He laid a hand on Hoskins' shoulder.

'Never thought it wasn't, Sam. Now, keep your eye on that screen.'

Blades sat down and tapped the keyboard. At once there appeared on the green background a series of angular peaks. The little skyscraper shapes resembled a panorama of New York or Chicago.

'High-energy electron-beam microscope,' said Blades proudly. 'Analysis of the primer in the paint sample. Each strip is one of the chemical constituents and a measurement of the quantity. Tin, zinc and so forth. Now watch this.'

He tapped the keyboard again. The little green skyscrapers were overlaid by a new landscape that failed to fit them.

'Nearest British Standard primer,' said Blades. 'No use. Now watch again.'

The pattern flicked off the screen, to be replaced by one that corresponded precisely with the sample. Blades went through the routine twice more.

'Shouldn't waste your time stripping down cars, Sam. What's on that screen was never sold to the general public. Manufacturer's exclusive. You can get a touch-up paint that looks like it, but the chemical constituents would be different.'

'You know what it is, Charlie?'

Blades winced. The twinge of the phantom stomach.

'I had the Home Office research people on this morning,' he said. 'This combination of primer, undercoat and top-coat is a Cadillac exclusive. Cadillac UK used it on imported models of the Fleetwood Brougham. Two years ago, from January to May. Not a common colour, Sam. Not a common car, either. Has that square expensive look of a Rolls or a high-price Merc.'

'They're sure of this at Aldermaston?'

'Never wrong yet, Sam. They've got specifications for everything down to the latest one-yak-power Volga saloon. But you're lucky, my friend. Suppose it had been an Austin Princess in beige with half a million owners? Imagine the footwork and the grief. Only a handful of cars like this one, I should think. This time you are in luck.'

'That's more like it, Charlie!' Hoskins said. 'I'll come back at twelve for lunch. I owe you a nod and a smile down the drinker.'

Blades gave another little wince.

'Best not,' he said quietly. 'Thanks all the same. You go and have a drive round. Look for a motorist with £15,000 or more to spend and a respray on his off-side wing. All in all, Sam, I'd say you were looking for a very nice class of lunatic indeed.'

Hoskins went out to the car and slid into the passenger-seat, reporting his progress to Sergeant Chance. The last of the pearl-grey sky had dissolved into a pale intense blue. A sudden access of heat was reflected back at them from the brick walls. In the stillness, the grasshopper chatter of a film projector from an open window at the shabby back of the tall buildings signalled the progress of the morning matinée at the Ocean Beach Gaumont.

He relaxed and pondered.

'You know,' he said contentedly, 'when I was first sent to CID, there was this old bull of an inspector, Mike O'Hara. Just on his last lap. Done thirty years of arresting and thumping down the Peninsula. Built like a brick shit-house, but straight as a ruler. He'd always say there were two sorts of crime. Most, if you can solve them at all, get sorted fast. Average detection time for a murder, about thirty minutes. The rest you have to work at for yourself. It's not like a crossword puzzle, he used to say. It's not like the body in the library or logic or common sense. It's like hanging on with your finger-tips to a New Pier roller-coaster that's out of control and the passengers screaming their heads off. You can only reach the brake-lever by taking one hand off the edge you're hanging from. And down below your feet there's a drop of forty or fifty feet straight into the machinery. So you could choose between smashing through the buffers and into the sea, or falling into the mincer. But in the end, all you do is hang on and follow the ride, and end up in one piece if you're lucky.'

'Sam Hoskins as a sprog DC?' asked Chance sceptically.

Hoskins shook his head and grinned, as if despairing at his own lack of direction.

'I'd matriculated at school,' he said ruefully. 'Even thought of being a teacher like old Harold Moyle. Bloody glad I didn't. Lip from the kids and aggro from their parents. I had two years National Service in Malaya. In the jungle. Saving the Empire from Chinese bandits. Half my platoon copped it. Not the Chinese. We never heard from them. Colour-blind pilot in an

RAF Hawker Hunter couldn't tell black from white in the forest below him, nor his arse from his elbow in the cockpit. Let fly with four rockets, just in case. All we found of Corporal Suitor was a finger with his ring on it. After that, my son, I came back and joined the Force. And glad to do it. A punch on the nose down the Peninsula on a Saturday night isn't half what the RAF can do to you.'

CHAPTER SEVEN

The same afternoon, Hoskins left Jack Chance to check vehicle registration and ownership on the licensing office computer. He parked the Fiesta in the motor-pool and took his own Cavalier to the little streets of Lantern Hill above Harbour Bar. The two communities made a small town of their own. A century ago, shipowners would go down to Lantern Point, on the shabby esplanade at the foot of the headland, to hail the masters of their vessels leaving or entering the dredged channel. The wharves and dry docks of the Peninsula lay half a mile from the muddy foreshore, across the tidal estuary. Lantern Hill had been a suburb of senior clerks and junior managers in semi-detached houses, as well as the little terraced streets overlooking the docks. There were tennis courts and Tudor bars. Cafés with stained lace curtains and shops with gabled turrets tried to look as if Lake Lucerne rather than the fouled water of the tidal channel lay at the foot of the hill.

With its children still at school, the uneven slope of Arran Street was quiet in the sunlit afternoon. Hoskins, turning to pull in and park, saw the door of the house open and a man of about thirty coming out. Casually dressed and scraggily bearded, the stranger paused to take his leave. Hoskins felt a policeman's suspicion giving way to a throb of personal jealousy. It was absurd. To judge by his first meeting with the young woman, she would be unlikely to regard him with anything but hostility. All the same, unwilling to encounter a possible rival for her attention, he drove on.

For five minutes he parked round a corner at the top of the road. The old iron railings edged a steep grass slope that fell away to the sparkle of sun on sluggish dock-water. A dredger was moored in the main channel, the rattle of its bucket-chain carrying clearly through the still air. Across the silt-banks at low tide lay the flat expanse of the Peninsula and the high-rise blocks of Canton behind it. In the warm afternoon haze, it might have been a distant vision of the New Jerusalem.

When five minutes had passed, he turned the car and drove slowly back. She was in view now, standing in the little garden that divided the front door from the pavement by about six feet. It looked as if she had dressed for labour of some kind in the cream sweater and a trouser suit of thin black cotton. Hoskins pulled up on the opposite side of the road. He watched her draw off the black jacket and lay it on the low wall of the garden plot. She took a small fork and began to chivvy the weeds along the path. Self-absorbed, the young woman paid not the least attention to the car.

Once she straightened up and brushed the fringe across her forehead. Then she braced her legs apart a little and stooped to use the fork. It crossed Hoskins' mind that there might be a sexual deviation which had to do with watching the almost sensual feminine exertion of physical toil. If so, he was fast beginning to appreciate it. He found something provokingly suggestive in the way she stooped with her bent knees forward a little and her feet apart. There was exertion, if not passion, in the muscular tension of her thighs, no doubt kept trim by the use of the bicycle. The experience of childbirth had in no way fattened or coarsened her. There was an erotic appeal in the appearance of Lesley's figure at that moment which made her far more exciting to him than a sylph of eighteen. What stirred in Hoskins' heart and loins was not love nor even desire. He recognised it as that compelling lust warned about in adolescence and preached against in adult life. Why should he feel it for this young woman, who was not stunningly beautiful nor in any way glamorous? She was not even attractive in her manner. He accepted it as an instinctive and perverse chemistry of sexual collusion.

Uneasy at the thought that she might turn while he was watching her, he opened the car door and got out. It was the sound of his footsteps that caused her to straighten up and look round. There was neither hostility nor welcome in the blue eyes under the long fringe. Lesley showed only the incuriosity that betrayed her self-possession. What lay behind such self-assurance was something that he could not yet imagine.

'You have more luck with your garden than I do with my window-boxes,' he said cheerfully. 'I grow mustard. The birds bring it.'

But her face scarcely relaxed with recognition and the rehearsed informality of the window-boxes fell flat.

'Your sergeant phoned to say you were coming. I don't always hear the bell when I'm indoors. Have you found something out?'

'A little,' he said truthfully. 'I've made a start. That's what I came for.'

It crossed his mind as he spoke that she was explaining herself when she had no need to. And if she had known he was on his way, then the display to which he had been treated while sitting in the car had been put on in the expectation that he might see it. The thought appealed to him and he nourished it. Lesley picked up the little gardening fork and led the way. Hoskins made a ritual of scuffing his shoes on the door-mat.

'It's a small matter,' he said encouragingly. 'We've found some marks on the bike. They were probably made at the time of the accident. On the other hand, it's possible they were there before that. You might remember them.'

She looked up at him with cool reserve.

'I shouldn't think it's the sort of thing I'd remember.'

Hoskins lowered himself into a chair. It was feebly sprung and he felt it give ominously under his bulk. Two unwashed coffee cups remained on the table from the previous visitor. As she sat opposite him, the nerves in his hands could almost sense the firmness of her hips and thighs. He wondered how much of this his face might betray.

'Just in case,' he said reassuringly. 'Can you remember a dent on the near side of the luggage pannier at the back?'

She shook her head with the characteristic little gesture of slight impatience.

'It's not the sort of thing I'd notice.'

'You might have seen this, if it had been there before that evening. It was a dent the size and shape of a large dinner-plate on the pannier nearest to the pavement.'

'Then I didn't.'

He took out a note-pad and glanced at it.

'Was Robbo Smith in the process of making a claim against his insurance policy on the bike? We know there hadn't been a claim form received by the company. That gets checked as a matter of routine. But he might have had it in mind. Said something about it, perhaps?'

Lesley stroked the short length of her fair hair thoughtfully, just like a little girl again. Posing. Self-admiring, as if there might be a concealed mirror. Hoskins guessed that she did it in self-contemplation, rather than for the admiration of others.

'Not that I know of,' she said. 'He didn't mention anything to me.'

He nodded, flipped the pad shut and put it away in his pocket. He had asked the only question that mattered. Now he was obliged to fabricate those that did not, in order to explain his visit.

'You don't know if Robbo ever thought of making an insurance claim on the bike at an earlier time, but never submitted it?'

She shook her head dumbly and indifferently.

'Do you know anyone who drives a gold-coloured Cadillac, a Fleetwood Brougham?'

'I don't even know what it looks like. I don't know about cars.'

Her voice became more peevish and almost resentful as he pressed the questions about an alien world of machinery and money. The two used cups stood like stained monuments on the table. It was clear to him that he was not to be offered coffee. He got up, feeling tall and bulky in the little room. Perhaps she had exchanged married life in a suburban semi-detached for forbidden passion in this workman's terrace.

'Thanks anyway for your patience,' he said genially. 'From the point of view of all that's happened to you, I don't suppose the police force is your favourite organisation.'

For the first time, she looked surprised.

'I don't hate policemen,' she said coolly. 'I sometimes feel sorry for them and what they're made to do. That's all.'

Hoskins smiled, as if he understood.

The smile was not returned and the understanding irony lay soured between them with the coffee dregs. He held out his hand in an unnecessary courtesy. She took it. If he wished to indulge in such formality of physical contact, she appeared indifferent either way.

'I'll leave you to your garden,' he said.

Only when they were outside did she put her question. There was curiosity now but not hostility.

'That wasn't really necessary, was it? Coming here this afternoon for those two or three questions.'

Hoskins felt his smile hardening into a smirk.

'I was in Harbour Bar this afternoon anyway. Apart from that, I wanted to make sure that you were all right.'

For the first time, her voice relaxed a little. The sulky line of the lips moved in a near smile.

'You've been put in charge of me?'

'Of this end of the case.'

There was a pause between them and then Lesley's manner changed again without warning. His dismissal was to be personal, after all.

'You try too hard,' she said, looking at him quietly.

'In what way?'

'To be nice. To persuade people that you are. As if you think they would never believe you otherwise. It's a mistake.'

'Yes,' he said, resigning himself to the criticism, 'I daresay it is. But I can still understand something of what you must feel. I can manage that without trying. Let me know later on if there's anything I can do.'

When she accepted the suggestion, her voice sounded neutral enough to mean anything.

Hoskins checked his watch and thought of Harold Moyle. He drove along the muddy-shored esplanade of Harbour Bar with its Starlight Room dance-hall and its steamer jetty, the little Edwardian shops and snack-bars, the new blocks of yellow-tile flats. He timed his approach to the wider suburban avenues of brick semi-detached so that he was there at four o'clock.

Shackleton Comprehensive. They were streaming out through the double gates, an army of children, for the most part in dark and nondescript uniform clothes which were not in themselves a school uniform. He drove slowly along the route, looking in the first place for a single adult male walking near them, possibly carrying a camera. He saw no one. Several women with bags or shopping-trolleys, nothing more.

Circling, he drove round the block at the top of the hill and back again towards the school gates. A red bus was loading with children. A flock of their bikes swept past him, coats flying like wings, heads down and pedals spinning like a junior Tour de France. Presently Hoskins was rewarded by the sight of Elaine Harris.

A few of the girls at Shackleton Comprehensive were precocious in the smartness of their clothes. This one was blatant without being smart. There was not the least difficulty in seeing what it was that might attract her admirer. She had a costume of innocence on an appearance of hard-boiled knowingness. The broad oval of her face was framed by the lank fair hair worn on her shoulders. The mouth was thin and the dark eyes narrowed as if in suspicion. The white blouse and the striping of the school tie suggested innocence. But the grey schoolgirl skirt with its pleats was worn short to show the robust pallor of her legs just about to the top of the thigh. It seemed to Hoskins a wonder that she had only one hesitant fancier and not half the unemployed males in Harbour Bar.

He drove past carefully. She tossed her fair hair, striding aggressively among the other girls, and directed a shout across the traffic at a group of older boys on the opposite pavement. Hoskins winced. The energy and volume of the adolescent lungs seemed abrasive enough to bring plaster off the ceiling.

But still there was no sign of the follower. No sign, indeed, of an adult male anywhere.

He turned by the school gates and drove up the hill again. A breeze caught the little skirt at the back and lifted it sufficiently to show white elasticised underwear. Hoskins guessed the kind of home life that produced such a vision. Parents out to work at eight. The girl last to leave the house in the morning, in a costume that would never have got past the front door if her elders had been present. First home in the afternoon, she had ample time to change and appear as a conventional daughter of fifteen by tea-time. One day, there would be shock and incomprehension at the signs of her adolescent pregnancy. More likely, it would be the indictment of a man who had 'enjoyed' as the law termed it felonious and unlawful carnal knowledge of this adolescent apprentice to the vice trade.

She turned in at the garden gate of the house, where she or an admirer of her own age had painted her name on the brickwork. No one had followed her. Elaine walked down the short concrete path between the ill-nourished flower borders and let herself in through the front door. So far as Hoskins could see, not a lace curtain had stirred in the bay windows of the semi-detached houses she had passed.

He drove back to Shackleton Comprehensive and found Harold Moyle in his room.

'Nothing,' he said. 'Not a sign of a man with a camera after her. Not a sign of any man at all.'

Moyle rolled the edge of his moustache comfortingly between finger and thumb. Behind glass and securely locked, a row of silver cups and a shield no longer competed for stood like the gravestones of middle-aged self-esteem.

'One of your uniform blokes out there on Monday, Sam. Panda car ticking over on Tuesday. Not likely that anyone'd chance it again yet. Still, supposing I'm right about him, that proves it. If he was innocent and had a reason to be walking the same way as her, he'd still be doing it, police or no police. Eh?'

'I don't know, Harold. But no one saw anything. Nothing. No sign of a face with a camera at any of the windows. Not even a face. And even if he stands in his window looking out as she goes by, there's nothing I can do. It's not on, Harold, unless he's flashing or something.'

Moyle sat back in his swivel chair. Behind him on the wall hung several framed photographs of rugger teams with dates painted white on an oval ball. Darkened by time and the strong light, the 1st XV of 1948 seemed ancient as the figures of chivalry.

'So that's it, Sam?'

'I'll get a man out here again, Harold. Soon as I can. Best for all concerned if we can discourage a schoolgirl wallah from being in the neighbourhood at all. Supposing that's what he is.'

'Thanks,' said Moyle.

Hoskins leant forward. 'Between these four walls, Harold, what about Robbo Smith's young woman?'

'The piece he lived with in Arran Street? She used to be in one of the houses just down the hill. Tried for a job here once. Didn't get it.'

'Anything about her would be appreciated, Harold. Between ourselves. She's got to be eliminated. Just to show that she wasn't likely to have had him shoved off that cliff.'

Moyle pursed his lips and blew thoughtfully.

'Not her style. She was into women's rights and all the rest of it. She collected protest badges like a little boy collecting stamps. But rather snooty and snobby with it. Not a lot of money. One day she packs a case and leaves the barnyard. Ditches romantic bliss, cool as custard. No reason that I can see except she fancies a new thrill with a new man. And so to Arran Street.'

'She'd been screwing around?' Hoskins tried not to let a particular interest show.

'Not that anyone knew, Sam. Could have been easily enough. Certainly seemed to think it was up to her to do what she liked with herself.'

'Was there much reaction round the neighbourhood?'

Moyle grinned slyly.

'Most of them thought it was a rotten shame. The men because they wished they'd had a slice off her while it was going. The older women said it was disgraceful, walking out on her boyfriend again like that. My better half thought the young baggage deserved to be put over someone's knee for a damn good spanking. That conjured up a picture or two in the old middle-class male, I can tell you!'

'You've been reading those books under the desk again, Harold,' said Hoskins cheerfully. 'Thanks, anyway.'

Moyle stood up.

'Nothing for you there, Sam. When that lot get desperate, they vote SDP or carry the banner. I don't see her doing murder. She'd just walk out and live with someone else again.'

'She doesn't even seem to have done that.'

Hoskins drove back through the busy traffic of Orient, past the little shops improvised from terraced housing. Against the five o'clock stream of cars from the city's administrative buildings, he followed the Mall to the headquarters block and took the lift to his room. He had just closed the door when Sergeant Chance knocked. It was evident at once that Jack Chance was in excellent humour. He held out a sheet of paper.

'Couple of things for you, Sam. The girl at Shackleton School and the man following her. Plain-clothes jack – well a jill, actually – got a sighting. Since we put a constable in a pointed hat up there, the chap you want has taken to his wheels. Following her round and round in his car from school to home. WPC Pumphrey managed to get his number.'

With an expression of earnest helpfulness, Chance handed over the slip of paper. Hoskins looked at the car number on it and glowered.

'Prat!' he said furiously. 'That's me!'

Chance beamed. 'Right, Sam. But you've had that Cavalier a month and personnel don't know.'

'They were bloody well told two weeks ago at least.'

'There's a stack of paperwork down there, Sam, and they're short-handed. And what's more, no one knew you were chasing off to Shackleton School this afternoon.'

'I was just passing,' Hoskins said helplessly.

'And passing,' Chance grinned, 'and passing. And passing again. . . . You want to watch your reputation, Sam.'

But he gave the impression of one who was keeping the best until last. Hoskins gestured at the folded print-out.

'Cadillac? Fleetwood Brougham?'

Chance nodded.

'Complete check. Not many metallic gold. Eight in the city and fourteen within a twenty-five-mile radius. Most of it's dead lead. But there's one here you are going to enjoy, Sam. You most certainly are.'

He handed over the folds of flimsy paper.

'The list for the city proper,' Chance suggested. 'Try the one that's three from the bottom.'

'Peninsular Trucking?'

'Right, Sam.'

'That's Carmel Cooney!'

'Right again.'

Hoskins turned and looked out of the window, unable to make any connection that stood up to logic. He turned to Chance.

'If Ripley or anyone asks for me in the next hour or so, I've been called out suddenly and you don't know where. See?'

'Alone?'

'Yes,' said Hoskins thoughtfully. 'Just this once, I want to see him alone. Mind the shop, my son. I'll be back before eight. And perhaps we'll have Mel Cooney at last with the old gyves upon his wrists. Should liven up the city council elections next week.'

CHAPTER EIGHT

The death of Robbo Smith appeared a crime of unexpected simplicity. Either that or the roller-coaster was through the buffers and into the sea. Carmel Cooney had murdered Smith. It remained only to establish why. Hoskins glanced at his watch as he edged through the slow cars and custard-yellow buses filtering home through Victorian semi-detached Canton. Beyond the suburban expanse of Connaught Park, traffic lights at the foot of the incline marked the beginning of Hawks Hill.

Thirty minutes, the average detection time for murder. He might still do it. If not, it would be the fault of the traffic.

Turning off the main drive, away from the avenues of houses in cracked stucco that led down to the tall chimneys of the power station and trading estates, he followed the axis of the Hill. Along Godwin Road the lime trees were in pale leaf, shading the gardens of white flat-roofed houses. Through close-textured privet hedges there was a glimpse of lawns and swimming-pools, modernistic lounges with curved corner windows. It was a world of old-fashioned wealth. There were cocktail cabinets and the moist rattle of ice before dinner, grand pianos and photographs in silver frames. Godwin Road had become the Canton of solicitors and specialists in disease, accountants and auctioneers, built in the last prosperity of the 1930s. Men and women to whom London was as remote as New York lived in the provincial ease of department-store affluence.

Some distance from the crest of the Hill, the warm evening tranquillity of Challoner Road turned off to the left. The houses had been expensive in Godwin Road. In Challoner Road they were very expensive indeed. Their date and design were similar but they had been enlarged and more widely spaced. Several of the gardens had the appearance of a small park. Walls and tall hedges of cypress or rhododendron gave privacy and silence. Like Highlands Avenue, above Ocean Beach, most of the gates were electronically controlled from the houses. To Hoskins' knowledge, there were enough surveillance-patrol contracts in Challoner Road to keep two local security firms fully occupied. The concealed houses suggested original oil paintings and collections of jade, rare editions of prints and the deep luxury of furs. There might be a servant problem in Godwin Road. No such difficulties existed here. Every house had its staff, the casual young who were rewarded by cars of their own and companion holidays in the Seychelles or Malibu.

Carmel Cooney's gates of dove-grey steel were set between dry-stone walls. Hoskins pressed the illuminated plastic panel and gave his name to the mouthpiece of the grille. The steel wings opened with an electric purr and closed again behind him. Raised above the level of the road, the house was faced by windows of tinted glass. At the front, it looked out across the city to the blue glimmer of sea somewhere near Ocean Beach. To the rear there was an inland view, towards the beginning of the valley and the Victorian fairy castle with its conical turrets built by George Gilbert Scott for the first Lord Dyce. A sprinkler cast its rainbow arc of water over the deep green carpet of Carmel Cooney's lawn.

Hoskins stopped his car. He saw a girl walking towards the house. Cooney had plenty of them. He had married one of them, thirty years ago. Enid Cooney, then a blonde torch-singer in the post-war clubs of Ocean Beach and Canton, had been the most expensive toy that money could buy. No doubt she still was, living out her fifties in Barbados or Florida. There had been no divorce. Rather quaintly, Carmel Cooney was a gangster with religious scruples. But the shopgirls came and went, lured and rewarded by their chance of tinsel stardom on the bandstand of the old Winter Garden.

Hoskins watched this one enter the house. He recalled seeing her several times in the perfumed air and deep carpeting of the Royal Peninsular Emporium on Atlantic Wharf. A casual model to display furs or costume jewellery for individual customers in the mirrored cathedral hush of the upper floor. Sian with her rather pale red hair and very fair skin. Not a stunner by any means. Not at all the stuff of which showgirls were made. But she had a certain promise of depravity and perversity in her looks. Enough, Hoskins supposed, to get Cooney into the saddle.

Of all the girls he had known Cooney to pick, Sian was the first redhead. There was a natural bud-like pout to the sensual young lips, though the glossily lipsticked mouth itself was too large for beauty. The cheekbones were rather flat, their points wide as the chin was narrow. The jaw was a little long and there was an openness to the blue eyes that somehow conveyed the opposite of frankness. They hinted at a coveting of pleasure, a sensual greed, desire and stupidity combined. But however stupid, this one must surely guess that there was no future for her on the bandstand of the Petshop. She was not tall enough to be elegant. The first suggestive weight had begun to gather on her hips. Perhaps it was enough for her to wear the jewels and furs, to feel the luxury of Cooney's bed and close her mind to the man who shared it with her. At twenty-one or twenty-two, Sian had already passed from red-haired nymph to the wanton with the swaggering rump. Precisely her master's taste.

'Mr Hoskins!' It was like a shouted rebuke rather than a welcome. Cooney had been in the garden all the time and was coming towards him. Two other men whom Hoskins did not recognise were walking away in the other direction, still in conversation.

'A long time, Mr Hoskins!'

Carmel Cooney carried his age and his weight badly. He had scarcely changed the style of his clothes since his teens, though they were now more expensively made. Even his newly-cut suit had a 1950s antiquity. He looked as odd as he might have done in a wing collar and spats. But spats had never been his style. Hoskins still thought of him as an aged and overgrown razor-boy.

Cooney's body was no basis for a fashion plate. The pale grey suit was far too tight a fit. He wore his jacket open so that, with the old-fashioned waistcoat, his stomach had the shape of a football under the buttoned flaps. It swelled like a deformity or a growth on a figure that was not otherwise less than fat. His legs appeared too slight for the burden, tapering down so that he had the air of a tadpole walking on its tail. He came across the lawn in a lurching manner, like a gross old woman whose hips were partially dislocated by the weight of such a belly.

'Mr Hoskins!'

He held out his hand. Hoskins, with a desire not to do so, took it. Cooney's face was round as a moon, like a man on a regime of cortisone. The blue eyes twinkled, but it was the twinkle of winter ice. The bluff voice had a ring of confident and jovial insincerity common to the racecourse tipster and the three-card trick. It was edged at present with a knowing sneer that came from Cooney's habit of not moving the corners of his lips. He spoke as if holding an invisible cigarette at one side of his mouth.

And yet the voice was Cooney's foremost asset. When he used it to persuade, it grew smooth as a silk choker and rich as cream stout. The voice had been trained, its natural insincerity tuned to a world of financial manipulation where total honesty bred contempt. It was a voice that people liked and even believed in, despite the pricking of caution. It conveyed the reassurance of a rogue who made common cause with you because your interests and his were indivisible – and you were exhilarated to have him on your side rather than against you. There was a moment, even for those who were subsequently to count their losses, when they smiled at one another confidently in the knowledge that they had Carmel Cooney fighting for them. Municipal contractors, land agents, children's charities and brothel touts had all worn that smile at one time or another.

'A private word, if you don't mind, Mr Cooney,' Hoskins said. 'Just a matter of routine.'

Cooney led the way through the French-window entrance into the main lounge. The silver-grey curtains and pearl-tinted hangings made the reflections of the evening sun fall cool and neutral as a gleam of water. Crystal pendants of a modern chandelier broke the aqueous light on ceiling and walls into shimmering lozenges of green and blue, red and violet. Beyond the glass tables and the cushioned chairs, a Steinway grand stood polished like liquid honey. Its lid was open. Hoskins could almost imagine the scents of wood and velvet, the cool precision of the keys and their notes. He noticed a score of Schumann's *Carnival* on the music-stand.

'Still like a bit of music, then, Mr Cooney?'

Cooney smiled like a cut melon. The smooth head seemed to enlarge with the distortion. Then he sighed philosophically.

'I like a tune last thing at night. I don't sleep as good as I did, Mr Hoskins. There's this girl, a music teacher that can't get work on the concert platform. I sub her to come and play to me of an evening. Suits us both very well. I like the one on the stand there. Old Schumann. That's primo, that is. A real top-notcher. If a man works hard as I do, Mr Hoskins, he's a right to a bit of soothing and relaxing after it. You really won't have a drink, I suppose?'

'I won't, thanks,' Hoskins said, 'unless it's a glass of water. I wouldn't say no to that. It's just a matter of your car. The Cadillac . . . the Fleetwood Brougham.'

Cooney heaved himself out of the chair and pressed a bell. He half-raised a hand to silence his visitor as the door opened and Sian came in. She stood, watching the chief inspector with a casual curiosity in her widening blue eyes. The red bud of her mouth was half-open to suggest that she was unable to care for anything in the world. Hoskins noticed that the pale skin was tighter and more pinched on the bones of her face than he had supposed.

'A glass of mineral water for our guest, sweetie,' said Cooney. The melon-smile was thinner this time.

'Good,' he said, rubbing his hands and frowning with

concentration as the girl closed the door. 'I wondered when I'd be hearing about the car.'

'Hearing about it?'

'Yes. About Bank Holiday Monday and what happened.'

The ground did not open beneath Hoskins' feet. Rather it was a sensation of the roller-coaster soaring higher still above the slicing gears of the machinery. His fingers slipped a little on the treacherously smooth metal.

'The paint,' he said, fending off Cooney's self-assurance for a moment. 'I'm talking about the paint on your car.'

'I'm not.' A shadow of annoyance contracted Cooney's face. The ringed fingers locked together and tightened. 'What the devil's paint got to do with it, Mr Hoskins?'

'Robin Royston Redlitch-Smith,' Hoskins recited the name like a poem. 'Robbo Smith of the *Western World*, in other words. He was killed on Bank Holiday Monday when his bike was run off Highlands Avenue and over the cliff near Ocean Beach.'

'Then I don't get you,' Cooney said. 'Just a minute.'

The hand went up again to command silence. The pale redhead entered with a glass. She stooped to pick up the chromium-plated stand from Cooney's elbow and transfer it to Hoskins. As she did so, Cooney stroked the fuller shape of Sian's bottom in the denim of the jeans and stared at Hoskins with amusement at the proprietorial display the policeman must watch. It appeared like the indulgent affection of an owner to a docile cat. Sian behaved as if she had no opinion one way or the other upon what was happening. Cooney dropped his hand and watched her go.

'There's nothing like a girl of eighteen for men of our age, Mr Hoskins,' he said with a smile that was mostly a sneer. 'You try it some time. Like a transfusion of youth. A right little princess, that one. Now then, we were at cross-purposes about the car, I think.'

Hoskins decided to go for the knock-out without preliminaries.

'After Robbo Smith was pushed over the cliff, the bike he was riding was examined. The impact caused a dent on the nearside pannier. That dent was further examined. Where the impact had occurred, there were traces of three layers of paint from a car's wing. Primer, undercoat, topcoat. They were compared at the forensic science laboratory by an electron-beam microscope.

None of the paints is British. That precise combination was used only on the imported Cadillac. The Fleetwood Brougham. Very few of them in that colouring. Fewer still in this area. You own one of them.'

Cooney opened his mouth in a silent 'O' of comprehension. Then he smiled.

'You overestimate me, Mr Hoskins. I've never been fortunate enough to own a Caddie. I shouldn't think the tax laws would approve it. I don't earn enough to justify such expenditure, sir. I wish I did. Now, what would you make in a year? Just between old friends.'

Hoskins repressed a shudder.

'I don't waste time counting.'

'I bet it's more than me,' said Cooney philosophically. 'Earn more, I daresay, and pay more tax. No, my friend, I couldn't run a Caddie. Peninsular Trucking owns the car, to be perfectly accurate. But it was here at the Bank Holiday weekend, if that's what you mean. Parked out there in the drive.'

'Any car,' said Hoskins sharply, 'that could have caused the death of Robbo Smith has to be eliminated. Yours included.'

'When did the poor fellow meet with this accident?'

'Almost exactly half-past seven on Bank Holiday Monday evening.'

Cooney killed his smile as easily as turning off a light switch. He tightened his mouth again at the seriousness of it and passed a hand over his grizzled crop.

'Then he could easily have been killed by the Cadillac parked in the drive, Mr Hoskins. Unless you have some new evidence, neither you nor I can eliminate it. I knew of Smith – never met him personally. He was a contemptible little tyke in his views, though they never touched me. But as you must be well aware, Chief Inspector Hoskins, I am probably the only person in the whole of Canton and Ocean Beach whom the police already know to be innocent of any involvement in that man's death.'

Hoskins waited for Carmel Cooney to play the fifth ace. His stomach grew heavy with foreboding. Though he searched the other man's face for mockery, the suspect now appeared to take the matter very seriously.

'It was about half-past seven when I went out into the garden,' Cooney said. 'Before twenty to eight I had reported the theft of the Cadillac. They must have overcome the steering-lock somehow and pushed the car without starting it until they were near the gates. I can't think it was a job for one man. Of course you can check the time with the Traffic Division. Sergeant Anderson was the officer on duty. Ten minutes after that, he very kindly phoned me here to check the engine number, which I hadn't got to hand when I first reported the theft.'

The roller-coaster, Hoskins thought. Through the buffers and into the sea. Quite definitely. The entire provable case against Mel Cooney was coming apart in his hands like drifts of cotton-wool. And yet he would have bet thirty years' pay and his pension that Robbo Smith's death was a stroke Cooney had pulled. If a car that belonged to Cooney was used to kill an enemy, Cooney was the driver. That was the logic of Cooney's reputation in Canton. It was worth one more try. One more try before he went back and enquired who in hell's name had concealed from CID the alleged theft of Cooney's car.

'You'll be asked to substantiate all this,' he said gruffly, unable to hide his discomfiture. Even as he spoke, routine calculations were performing themselves in another compartment of his mind. It was impossible for Cooney to have driven back from Ocean Beach in less than half an hour or forty minutes, depending on the traffic. If Robbo Smith was killed at half-past seven, which was supposed by medical and circumstantial evidence to be beyond doubt, Cooney could not possibly have been back in Hawks Hill at twenty to eight when the theft was allegedly reported, nor ten minutes later when the duty sergeant phoned him back.

There was a trick. What it was Hoskins could not decide. A car phone that answered to Cooney's number in Hawks Hill was a possibility. But fifteen or twenty miles was a long range. Perhaps Smith had somehow been killed earlier and dumped over the cliff at half-past seven. No one had seen the collision. It was possible that he had died as the result of an impact half an hour before. Cooney might then have driven back to Hawks Hill while one of his minions got rid of the Cadillac and arranged to have Smith and the bike rammed from the cliff. No doctor could time Smith's death within a few minutes or even within half an hour.

Hoskins tried to imagine how such a story would sound to a jury by the time that a good defence lawyer had swung the axe. But it would never get to court on present evidence. The prosecution service would see to that.

'You want proof of those calls, Mr Hoskins? Let's try.'

Cooney got up and lumbered to the bell again. When the young redhead answered, he was back in his chair.

'Find the answering tape for Bank Holiday, dearie. Run it on the player and put it through the speakers here. The call we made to the police about the car.'

Hoskins watched her as she stood receiving her instructions. There was something about Sian which reminded him of a case several years before. He had been to a house to make an enquiry and had seen the most beautiful blonde girl of five or six with wide eyes and a fair translucent skin. He remembered that beauty still. Only when she opened her mouth and uttered the first grunts and cries did he realise that she had been born with less intelligence or self-control than a cat or dog, less power of utterance than a pig or a monkey. There was something of that in Cooney's redhead. A defect of some kind. In her case, it was linked with a visible will to promiscuity or perversion that matched Cooney's own tastes. Cooney patted Sian's behind again, ostentatiously for Hoskins' benefit, as the girl turned to go.

'You know better than I do, Mr Hoskins, the pitfalls that attend a man in my position. I have to be exact. I have to keep a record of what's said to me. There've been threats of murder at times. Not that I take those seriously. All the same, conversations on this line are recorded automatically.'

There was a brief sound of static and then the room filled with Cooney's voice talking about his car. Someone replied to him. There was no doubt whatever in Hoskins' mind that the first voice was Carmel Cooney's and the other Sergeant Anderson's. The voices were clear. There was nothing to suggest a car-phone fifteen miles away; the background had the padded silence of Cooney's own house.

'Now,' Cooney said enthusiastically, 'I could have made that call from anywhere, of course. But listen to the next one. It was made to me in this very room about ten minutes before eight o'clock. Ask your sergeant.'

Hoskins listened. The sound quality seemed identical. He knew that when examined the voices would be authentic, from the burr of the ringing tone and Anderson's opening query to the last word spoken. But an indistinct tape might be doctored by an expert until it sounded as clear as this one. Cooney knew more experts than any man alive.

'May I have the tape?'

Cooney raised an admonitory finger.

'By arrangement with my lawyer, Mr Hoskins, you may have a copy of it made by him in your presence. Of course you may.'

'If necessary, I can take the master-tape without an arrangement.'

'But you wouldn't like to, Mr Hoskins. You wouldn't like to in the least. If you was to take it now, my man would be down at police headquarters complaining to Mr Ripley even before you was back there. You've got your own records, Mr Hoskins. You don't need my tape to prove them. Ask your sergeant to look in his occurrence book. And besides, Mr Hoskins, you jump the gun! I'm not saying it was my car that hit the poor young devil. It might have been – or not. I haven't seen it since – nor have the police, they say. So how can I tell you? I never liked Robbo Smith, nor his ways, nor his views . . . nor his methods. But I don't kill men for that.'

'I'll need a statement,' Hoskins said.

'When the attorney says so, Mr Hoskins.' There was a gleam in Cooney's pale blue eyes, the instinctive pleasure of battle. 'You'll remember that I bought a good deal of trouble some years ago by making statements ill-advisedly to the police and having them selectively edited and quoted back at me. That was the late Inspector Roberts. A vicious little bastard, if ever there was such, Mr Hoskins. The worst enemy the police force ever had. Corrupt, too. He died just in time to save himself a heap of trouble. He was on a weekly take. Round the knocking-shops in Martello Square. Still, you don't need me to tell you that.'

'I'm not here to discuss Roberts,' said Hoskins quickly.

Cooney returned him a smile that came pat as a flick-knife.

'I discuss who and what I like in my own house, Mr Hoskins. Many years ago I was ill-advised, being innocent of that conspiracy business. I thought the police would be honest. So when Roberts read out to me the whole rigmarole of the charges, public corruption and fraud, I was devastated. I said straight, "You can't pin this on *me*, Mr Roberts!" meaning someone else may have done it but I am innocent. And I was, as the jury found. But when that little shit Roberts was in the witness box, he reads it as, "You can't pin *this* on me." Meaning there's a lot else you've got me for in the past – but not this time. That shiddle-come-shite nearly did for me. Cancer was better than he deserved. I know better than to make statements, my friend. I was innocent then – and acquitted. But I learnt my lesson. I was here when Smith was hit by a car twenty miles away. That's the truth and I know it. If you think you can prove a case against me, Mr Hoskins, you go ahead and prove it.'

Hoskins watched the sudden animation of the moon face. Cooney in a rage was like an ecstatic undergoing torture for his faith. The pulling of the mouth was slight but uncontrolled. The eyes rolled as if seeking to avoid those of the man he talked to. But it was not deviousness. Cooney had never been more sincere. He slid one foot in front of the other meticulously, along the tightrope dividing reason from criminal mania. The eyes had looked like this at eighteen, Hoskins thought, when a boy from a rival gang was held down for Cooney to insert a razor in the corner of the victim's mouth and drag it back through the flesh of the cheek until it reached the ear-lobe. On the whole, he preferred Cooney bad to Cooney mad.

'All right,' said Hoskins philosophically. 'So, you were here alone that Monday evening?'

'Alone in the next room, doing the books, until about half-past seven. But the girl and a couple of the helpers was around; I could hear them talking. I never saw them and they never saw me. I don't have an alibi, Mr Hoskins. Except the tape. And except the call your sergeant made to me here.'

'Seeing is believing,' Hoskins said coldly. 'Hearing is something less. Who's your lawyer this time? I'll need that tape.'

Cooney chuckled.

'This time, Mr Hoskins? You're trying to rile me, aren't you? But I don't rile easily. Not over you, Mr Hoskins. Not over any of you. Speak to Jack Cam, he'll answer for me. Come up one evening and have a drink and listen to the girl that plays my piano for me. But don't come to me with fucking rubbish about that little fool Robbo Smith bleeding for humanity. Don't do that again. Will you, Mr Hoskins?'

Ten minutes later, Hoskins walked away to the car without the tape. As he approached the electronically controlled gates they seemed to open automatically. If that were so, a thief could drive out the car unimpeded. But there was no thief. If Cooney's car was a murder weapon, Cooney was number one for being the driver. How he had been able to make it appear that he was speaking from Hawks Hill when he was still at Ocean Beach was the trick that would destroy him in the end.

And there was a trick. If Cooney was involved, there had to be. Hoskins knew it.

CHAPTER NINE

Later that evening, Hoskins was standing in his office, confronting Sergeant Chance.

'Why in hell weren't we told?'

'We never asked,' Chance said. 'No reason we should. And in any case, Cooney's name's not down in the Traffic Division list. That car belonged to Peninsular Trucking and the name that goes with it is Benny Stevens, transport manager at PT. I daresay Cooney's in the file as having reported it, that's all.'

'Thanks to them, I made a bloody fool of myself with Cooney,' Hoskins said bitterly. 'He sat there like an overgrown choirboy, up to his neck in this, somehow. I swear he is. For half an hour he sat there grinning and touching up that red-haired tart of his in front of me – asking me if I could prove anything against him.'

He sat down and slapped his hands on the desk.

'We ran through the list of owners of Fleetwood Broughams,

Sam,' said Chance, placating him. 'There's not another name that means anything. Nothing on CRO. Not even a breathalyser. Cooney's is the only Caddie that's missing in the area. And it was really stolen, so far as we can see. Genuine report. No news of it being sighted since.'

'I won't have it,' Hoskins said, still grumbling. 'If Robbo Smith was killed by Cooney's car, Cooney had a hand. Of course he'd say it was stolen. Wouldn't he? It's probably at the bottom of the railway dock by now, with the silt closing over it. And there might be someone inside it.'

'You'd have to prove it wasn't Cooney that Bill Anderson spoke to on the phone, or else that the call was somehow re-routed. It doesn't sound likely.' Chance sounded anxious on Hoskins' behalf – anxious and unconvinced.

'Nothing that Cooney does ever sounds likely. This one could be either a car-phone or a re-route of some sort. Run a check on the Telecom engineers' office. They do re-route calls for people, after all. And see to it that someone keeps us in the picture from now on.'

Jack Chance sat down and Hoskins stood up, like opposing figures in a child's clockwork toy.

'That's the other thing, Sam,' Chance said uneasily. 'You don't want a real to-and-fro with the traffic people in front of Ripley. If that happens, Bill Anderson and the rest reckon they'll say it's no business of ours – or yours. Traffic had no cause to tell you. Ocean Beach Division is where Robbo Smith was killed. They know all about the Cadillac being stolen. A list of missing cars went to them. Vehicle licensing didn't say anything to me because they don't list stolen cars. And I'd forget Cooney anyway, Sam, if I was you. The Ripper wasn't best pleased to hear you'd gone off to Challoner Road without a by-your-leave.'

'I don't need a by-your-leave, my son.' Hoskins thrust a thermos flask into his briefcase and prepared to go home. 'For all Ripley knows, if a mug like Cooney killed Robbo Smith, he could be preparing to do the lady-friend in Lantern Hill next. See?'

'There again,' said Chance quietly, 'there's a feeling in the Ripley family, after this afternoon's little exercise, that some of us could spend more time in the Division and a little less in Lantern Hill.'

'Then he can come and tell me so,' Hoskins said in controlled defiance.

With a sense of affronted self-righteousness, he went down in the lift, reversed the Vauxhall from the parking-lot and drove home. In his case, home for the past ten years had been a purpose-built 1930s apartment in Lamb's Chambers, held on a long lease. It was the last of the main Canton streets, across the river bridge and not quite into Orient. But the city centre smartness of the 1930s now looked out on the decay of St Vincent Street with its two commercial bars and the paving-stones stained by splashes of vomit. That was how Hoskins had been able to afford it in the first place. The Georgian-style sash-windows were fabricated in concrete and surrounded by soot-grimed brick. From the street, the blocks of 'chambers' that had housed barristers and doctors fifty years before were now as fashionable as a stranded whale.

But as Hoskins put down his briefcase and turned on the sitting-room light, the hidden amenity of the flats was revealed. At the rear, their windows looked out upon the turf of Lamb's Acre, the Memorial Ground of international rugger, the tour matches of Wasps, Harlequins, London Welsh and a litany of famous names. In the darkness the girders of the main stand were half-visible by reflected street lights, stark and gaunt as a half-built ship. On the far side, the concrete ramps of the new terraces were like the shadowy fortifications of a deserted frontier. The Memorial Ground after dark was the ghostly arena of Hoskins' boyhood heroes, the roar of dead crowds in caps and mufflers on winter Saturdays, the stands rising to sing 'O God, our help in ages past' before the annual Barbarians' game. Remembrance Sunday when, by tradition, the pitch was empty and the crowds in the stands stood bareheaded on the stroke of eleven as the Lambs remembered their dead of the World Wars.

It was in the functional cream-walled sitting room with a square-looking three-piece suite inherited from his father that Hoskins lived his secret life. He neither boasted nor even spoke much of his enthusiasms. Heating up the packaged meal from the refrigerator, he ate it quickly, made himself some coffee and settled down to his private pleasure. He needed a sharp razor most of all. And then the tube that smelt of pear-drops. Thin card and matches, and the balsa in sheet and block. He drew the curtains. Across the vast darkness of the Memorial Ground the lights of other windows glimmered distantly as the opposite shore of a lake.

Those who wondered what Hoskins did with himself on such evenings were apt to be surprised and a little irritated when they found out. He was a builder. He had built the Ocean Beach Gaumont with its modernistic Venetian windows and its sun-terrace café. He had built the nearby Odeon with its white-tile facing, flat-roofed tower and red neon. In reality, the white tiles now had the ivoried dullness of old teeth. After fifty years they were discoloured by weather and time like an unloved marble headstone. But Hoskins built the Odeon modern and new, as Anna Neagle had opened it half a century before.

His latest creation, about two feet high, was the Paris Hotel on Canton's Atlantic Wharf. The big square in front of the railway station, where the line on its embankment divided the city centre from the docks, had long since ceased to be a wharf. But it had a feeling of space and sea-wind that suited the name. Next to the Royal Peninsular Emporium and the suggestive chic of Madame Jolly Modes, stood the Paris Hotel. It had been built for a turn-of-the-century bourgeoisie, coal-owners and iron-masters, in the boulevard style of the French Empire. For the past two months, with several photographs beside him, Hoskins had traced and cut, measured and glued. He was working at last on the tall mansard roofs of grey slate, the pale gold sandstone and lines of long windows with their Persian blinds that might have looked out on the Avenue de Wagram or the Boulevard St Germain.

It had occurred to him in the past few weeks that he might do the whole of Atlantic Wharf, add figures and vehicles in the style of the 1930s and photograph it. One day he might finish the whole of Canton city centre and bring to life his childhood vision of it through photographs. It was the past, his boyhood rather than the architecture, that he sought to recreate. As other men devoted themselves to Chartres Cathedral or the Doge's Palace, Hoskins worked to midnight and beyond on the Ocean Beach Odeon or the department-store classicism of Jones and Gower. He lived in the culture of Canton and Ocean Beach. It was nostalgia that mattered to him, not history.

Lost in his vision, he forgot Carmel Cooney and his kind. The building of the past had been entirely therapeutic. But for almost a week the dedication of the builder had been overlaid by images of an arrogant and self-possessed young woman. Worse still, in his thoughts he was beginning to hold conversations with her.

It had crossed Hoskins' mind quite often that he was passing a point of decision. From now on, a second marriage became a diminishing possibility. This did not greatly concern him. Used to his own company, he had become jealous of his solitude and independence. To take on another man's children he regarded as a recipe for grief. But there was an unease when he thought of Lesley. A challenge to his prejudices, perhaps. He was painting the pillars of dark red marble on the Paris Hotel brasserie when it struck him that he was not frightened, after all, by the dangers to his career of his feeling for the young woman. Far more frightening now, absurd though it had appeared, was the thought that he might never see her again.

Hoskins frowned at this. With the razor-blade he began to square off the opaque celluloid pieces that would form windows for the Brasserie Magenta. He thought about career and pension, prudence and reserve. It was prudence and reserve that had got him where he was – a middle-aged widower cutting up pieces of a modelling kit, late at night in a room on his own. He was like the members of a handicraft class he had once seen in an open prison, except that in his case the extra sentence of solitary confinement had been self-imposed. For the first time in his life, it seemed to him that he knew the risks of ill-considered conduct and cared nothing for them.

CHAPTER TEN

At first, Hoskins could not bring himself to go back to the terraced house in Arran Street without a pretext. Sometimes he thought he must avoid a return indefinitely, then he promised himself that he was only delaying it, like a treat being withheld from a child to increase the excitement. There was every reason to go, but very little pretext. In his mind's eye, the image of Lesley grew from an interest to an obsession. At night, working on the brasserie of the Paris Hotel, he returned repeatedly to the thought of her no more than three miles away in a room on her own. Or perhaps not on her own. He could have driven over and found out within twenty minutes.

In other circumstances he might have gone to her and tried, as he thought of it, to get her out of his system in the most obvious way. But misconduct with a potential witness – even a potential suspect – was probably the worst felony known to Canton 'A' Division. His prudence returned to haunt him like an unquiet ghost.

For almost a week after the interview with Cooney, Hoskins and Sergeant Chance drove the length and breadth of Canton, searching the usual dumping grounds of stolen cars for the missing Fleetwood Brougham. Maxwell Ripley considered, as a matter of convenience, that it was somewhere under the silt at the bottom of the railway dock. He begrudged the time spent in the piled graveyards of family saloons. On the fourth morning, Hoskins and Chance drove out to the edge of the Mount Pleasant estates where the last of the city hills looked towards the opening of the valleys.

An area of 1960s high-rise blocks had been flattened and the new houses not yet started. The cleared site was uneven and patched with wild grass. Rutted mud, left by the new year's earth-movers and diggers, stretched mile after mile like the landscape of the moon.

'Your first visit up here, is it, Jack?'

'This part, yes,' said Chance defensively.

Hoskins chuckled. 'All the parts up here are the same, my son. Mount Pleasant estates. Where stolen cars go when they die.'

'Meaning?' Chance enquired.

But Hoskins merely whistled to himself as he drove along the roadway of cemented slabs between the building sites. There was not a shop to be seen anywhere on the estate, and its few pubs were the single-storey bunkers with block-concrete roofs like air-raid shelters. Where the next phase of demolition was to begin, the ground dropped away. Towards the foot of the slope, an empty apartment tower with ply-boarded windows awaited its destruction. On the rutted grass above it were several shells of abandoned cars, wheels and glass gone, ripped seats spilling out through their open doors. Further down lay two more, twisted and blackened by fire. As Hoskins drew up, several small boys who had been playing in the derelict car bodies scattered towards the nearest flats.

'Bloody hell,' said Chance despairingly. 'There's two of them burnt out.'

'Of course they're burnt out,' said Hoskins cheerfully. 'They're firebirds. You spend too much time feeling collars round the drinking clubs and skin-parlours, Jack Chance. Up here is where real life happens. If you were twelve years old and lived up Mount Pleasant, being an enterprising lad, you'd be into the firebirds.'

'Would I?'

'You certainly would, my son. Off down Hawks Hill and nick a couple of fancy cars from the driveways of the wankers that live down there. Fetch 'em back. Get 'em to the top of the slope up here and aim their noses at the wall of the flats down there. Start the engine, tie the accelerator down and vrroooom! Door open – jump at the last minute. See them hit the wall of the flats and explode. They don't always, of course. Still, it's worth a try. A real beauty of a Merc or a Jag, belonging to some bastard that's richer than you'll ever be, going up smash! In a ball of fire like a home-made nuclear blast. More fun than I ever used to have at twelve years old.'

They got out and walked down towards the wrecks. Neither was a Fleetwood Brougham.

'Best take the numbers, Sam.'

Hoskins grinned. 'Look closer and you'll see they've gone. The kids take the number-plates. They flog 'em to their big brothers, the ones that nick cars to sell again. Nothing here for us, my son.'

Already several boys and two girls of ten or twelve had emerged from the shelter of the flats and were moving stealthily towards the empty police car.

'I'm going back before they wreck the last Fiesta in the motor-pool,' Hoskins said. He bellowed at the children, who answered with a salvo of shrill obscenities before taking to their heels. Then he led the way back up the slope to the road.

As they sat in the car, Chance flipped through his notepad.

'Let's face it, Sam, the bloody thing could be at the bottom of the railway dock after all. There's bugger all else left to try.'

Hoskins grunted. 'I'm not having a great big news story on police dredging the dock. Not at this stage of the game.'

'That could be a mistake,' said Chance firmly.

'Shut up and do the driving, Jack,' said Hoskins with a tolerant yawn. 'Drop me off in the car park. I'm going out to see Harold Moyle after lunch.'

'Schoolgirls again, Sam?'

'Just drive.'

Sergeant Chance drove. He dropped the chief inspector in the car park and turned off to the motor-pool.

During the past week Hoskins had made a habit of taking a detour through Lantern Hill when he was going westwards from Canton. Usually he found time to drive up or down Arran Street. But so far he had seen no sign of Lesley. On that afternoon, as he had told Chance, he went to see Harold Moyle. The visit yielded nothing. Moyle thought the fancier was also watching the girls from the fence during hockey practice. But still there was nothing that could be proved.

Hoskins was driving away again and had turned on to the spine of Lantern Hill where the double-fronted red brick houses were bordered by low garden walls and neat lawns. It was the more expensive end of a shabby suburb. The young woman walking ahead of him with two or three bags of shopping looked like Lesley. Then he saw that it was her. It was close to the road where she had lived in what Moyle called romantic bliss.

He stopped just in front of her and walked back, smiling.

'Let me give you a lift.'

'I thought it must be you,' she said, her voice almost eager to please by contrast with the previous coolness. 'When the car stopped, I thought so.'

He took the shopping bags and put them in the back.

'It doesn't look much like a police car,' she said sceptically, noticing the litter in the boot.

Hoskins laughed, in the hope of something like happiness.

'It isn't. We use our own most of the time. There aren't enough cars in working order to keep the Division on the road.'

As they drove past the resort shops and cafés of Lantern Hill centre, he watched her from the corner of his eye: the plain high-crowned cut of fair hair, the moody look of mouth and chin, the cool indifference of the blue eyes under the parted fringe. In combination, they detonated an excitement in Hoskins' heart and loins that he had not known for years.

Having performed the easily rehearsed opening exchanges, he fished for the right topic. But it was Lesley, uncharacteristically, who broke the silence between them as they drove.

'You were right,' she said casually. 'It's easier when it happens all at once. The message. The accident. The end of it all. Robbo and I were trying to make a partnership work. It wasn't exactly Tristan and Isolde. But we wanted to try. People think a woman must be a bitch to act as coldly as that.'

'I doubt it,' Hoskins said with a chuckle. 'Not these days.'

'They do here. I left someone else for Robbo. That's why.'

'A nine days' scandal, in a place like Lantern Hill.'

'What happened to you must have been much worse,' she said presently. It was the first comment he had heard her make which showed sympathy or even preoccupation with someone other than herself. From this, he drew encouragement.

He parked the car and carried two of the shopping bags into the hall. She was thinly dressed for summer in black cotton trousers and white sweater. Hoskins watched the firm thighs and the erotic rounding of her hips as he followed her in. He felt no twinge of conscience. Sexual passion of this intensity was rare enough in his experience, but on those rare occasions it developed

73

with improbable speed and from the most unpromising circumstances.

'I'll make some coffee,' she said, taking his acceptance for granted.

He continued polite conversation in the kitchen, wondering if she was aware of his eyes in their caressing appreciation of her. She could hardly fail to be. In that case, he wondered whether she minded. Unless he was mistaken as never before, there was enough anticipation in the air to chill the spine with excitement. He felt a brief and wild conviction that the whole thing might be a sexually baited political trap, to discredit the police. But the possibility no longer deterred him. There would always be a way out, if he needed one.

Handing him the cup, Lesley stood close enough to be touched or embraced, though she bowed the high crown of her head as if to hide her face. Hoskins, in any case, needed to steady the cup. They went into the front room. He sat down on the settee. Lesley with a neutral casualness chose the floor, her back against a padded chair. Even in her childlike informality there was a new suggestiveness. It was going to be all right. Hoskins could not have said why, but he knew it was so.

'I wanted to ask you one thing,' he said, mainly for the sake of conversation. 'Did Robbo have an interest in Carmel Cooney, so far as you know? A political interest in him, perhaps, as an enemy?'

Lesley made a sulky movement of her mouth and shook her head.

'Not so far as I know.'

He had made the mistake of trying too hard again, asking a question as a pretext. But the damage was soon undone.

Presently she put down her cup and went out, as if to the kitchen. Hoskins waited a moment, collected the cups and followed her. He was a little too early. Lesley stood barefoot by the table, on which lay the sweater and the trousers. She was dressed only in a plain pair of black cotton briefs.

'I thought,' she said, 'I'd surprise you.'

'Oh, you did,' Hoskins admitted. 'No two ways about that.'

'I mean come into the other room and surprise you. Without the knickers.'

'Don't let me prevent that,' he said encouragingly.

The relationship between them had never been predictable. After the coldness at first, they were both on the threshold of laughter.

'Here?' he asked facetiously.

Lesley brushed her fringe with her fingers and was, momentarily, the fastidious ballet pupil.

'Upstairs, I think,' she said softly.

She closed the distance between them, stepping forward and looking up. With the technique learnt from so many cinema matinées in his youth, Hoskins put his arms round her and kissed her on the mouth.

Then without waiting for her instructions he bent, scooping her up under the knees and round the shoulders.

'Which way?' he asked, smiling again and trying not to giggle.

Lesley pointed impatiently. The stairs were rather too narrow for what he had intended but he carried her safely to the top. In the relaxed weight of her body and the ease of her arms about his neck, he sensed her contentment and acquiescence.

In all the books he had read, it was an inventory of the woman's body and the details of the room that came first, leading to the act of love. This was quite different; it was only afterwards that he had time to take in his surroundings. Without ceremony Lesley drew her feet, one by one, free of the black cotton briefs. Hoskins shrugged off his clothes and they lay down together on the covers. There was a moment, several minutes later, when she drew her face from him and said breathlessly, 'The house rules.'

At first he thought she was going to pull away from him, that it had been a trick after all. But she was pushing him so that he turned on to his back and Lesley became the instigator of passion in her turn. Then with a long sigh she slid down upon him.

At last Hoskins took his bearings. The bedroom consisted of two small rooms knocked into one with an arch between them. Pink quilting and pale wood make up the colour scheme. Several framed prints of paintings that were generally familiar to him completed the interior. Surreptitiously, now that she lay sleepily against him with eyes closed, he made the more important survey of Lesley herself. She was nearer thirty than twenty but that, in

Hoskins' scale of appreciation, was to the good. His gaze took in the plain style of the fair hair, the pale shoulders and the curve of her bare back. There was a smooth pallor about her which suggested that she had never sunbathed in her life. It gave off a sensual air of afternoon nakedness upon perfumed cushions with the curtains closed against the sun. Her breasts and loins, like her thighs and her bottom, had the same firm and smooth coolness. For the moment she seemed content to lie there and let herself be caressed by hands that ran easily over her as skates on ice.

They lay together, talking of trivialities and avoiding by any means the subject of Robbo Smith. The sun had gone down far enough to be shining directly into the window when Hoskins said, 'You used to work for Eve Ricard.'

'Yes.' Lesley propped herself on her elbow and watched her own finger stroking his jawline. 'Is that a policeman's question?'

Hoskins laughed. 'No. I shouldn't think she's ever broken the law in her life.'

Lesley leant over and breathed in his ear, 'Don't be too sure about that; she seduced me.'

At first he thought that he had misunderstood or that she meant something else.

'Politically?' It was a foolish question but perhaps the only one.

'Of course not!' Lesley turned on her back and stared at the ceiling. 'When I was living with someone before Robbo, Eve and her partner came to dinner. A boy called Hendrique. After the meal, the two men went into the kitchen to get coffee and started talking about cars or something. Eve never said anything really, just held out her hand and led the way upstairs, as if it was the most natural thing in the world. Which it was, in a way.'

'Really?'

'Yes, really. Does it shock you? Or perhaps offend your virile pride?'

Hoskins smiled at her.

'I spent a year with the vice squad. I stopped being shocked after finding two of the city fathers in a Martello Square knocking-shop in pinnies, rubber aprons and masks. Virile pride lives on narrow escapes from yobboes down the Peninsula with a good eye for a kick to the balls. For a year I read the dirty picture books and saw the skin-flicks that were brought in. I'm not shocked by much that two people can do.'

It seemed to disappoint her. Hoskins had in mind a far more important question.

'Come and have dinner in my flat one night.'

'No.' She shook her head slowly, as if refusing on principle.

'Then, will I be invited back here?'

Lesley squirmed over towards him.

'Of course, so long as you don't insist that this afternoon gives you rights of possession. But if I come to you it looks odd. It seems normal if you come here. Supposing I'm still here myself. I might go away after what's happened.'

'Handcuff you to the bed?'

She hesitated and he waited to see if he was to be rebuked.

'Visitors would find it a little strange,' she said.

For the first time, Hoskins knew that it might work. Despite everything. He caressed her for a while longer, then let his hand fall in a light slap on Lesley's bottom. Still dignity was not outraged.

'I must go,' he said. 'I was only supposed to be paying a routine call on Harold Moyle at Shackleton Comprehensive.'

She turned on to her stomach, tensed her buttocks and swung her legs up from the knee, each in turn, as if performing a gymnastic exercise.

'Will you come back tonight?' she asked, turning her gaze aside to watch his reply.

'Where else?' he asked, pulling himself up. 'I'm off watch at eight. I'll take you to Nono's on the Cakewalk.'

But it would not do.

'No,' she said, 'here. Going out might be compromising. There's plenty in the kitchen.'

'Compromising?'

Lesley sat up and searched for her fallen briefs on the carpet.

'Yes,' she said, with the same impatient shake of her fringe. 'I imagine you could probably be sacked for what you've just done.'

CHAPTER ELEVEN

'There's this one about Eve Ricard, see?' said Sergeant Chance amiably, letting in the clutch as the Osborne Road traffic lights changed to green. 'One day she has a change of heart and applies to join the Force.'

'Keep to West Drive,' Hoskins said. 'No need to go into Lantern Hill.'

'Anyway, they take her on as a probationer and her first job is patrolling a beat in a nudist colony, all right? So she says she'll do it. They explain she won't actually be allowed to wear clothes on the job, so she agrees to that and they send her off to the old flesh-farm. But in the end she has to give it up and resign. Know why?'

'She couldn't find anywhere to keep her whistle,' Hoskins said. 'You don't half fall for old Dudden's whiskery jokes, my son. I've heard that one fifty times over the years, with everyone from Betty Grable to Mrs Thatcher in the title role. Keep straight on here. I want a quiet look round the area where this fancier lives. The one that Harold Moyle reckons is following young Miss Harris. Walks the same way as her after school.'

'Just the frogs'-legs makes me walk that way,' Jack Chance murmured.

For some reason that Hoskins could not guess, Chance was in high spirits.

'And Harold thinks he's watching the hockey practice through the playing-field chicken-wire. The old story. A feast of bare thighs, short skirts and knickers when she bends over to bully off. Keep on to Shackleton Comprehensive and I'll take it from there. We think we know where this merchant hangs out. I'd like a sight of it after working hours.'

Jack Chance crooned to himself, then said cheerfully, 'Few more years, Sam, and we might be feeling your collar at the hockey-field chicken-wire . . . if this keeps up.'

Hoskins took a sideways glance at his sergeant in the driving seat. But the remark was innocent, he thought. Chance could hardly have discovered about the visits to Arran Street.

They were on the hill that led by way of West Drive past Shackleton Comprehensive. Below them and beyond the flat line of the Peninsula in the dusk, two freighters, hull-down in the twilit water, waited for the tide. The massed lights at their derrick-heads blazed like a showboat.

'If I was a blackbird . . .' Sergeant Chance warbled.

'Delta control to all mobiles!' Through the rice-crispie static, Hoskins heard the nasal command.

'I'd whistle and sing . . . I'd . . .'

'Shut it, Jack!'

'Mobile Four-Niner-Niner at Dyce Street and Monmouth Terrace. Tango Four to rendezvous.'

Hoskins put his hand over the mouthpiece.

'Turn this thing round, my son. They've seen Cooney's car.'

As Chance performed a careful loop, Hoskins spoke into the radio.

'Tango Four, Chief Inspector Hoskins to control. Proceeding as advised. Maintain observation but do not approach until ordered. Repeat, do not approach. Report change in location as necessary. Don't lose them.'

Sergeant Chance flicked on the whooping siren and full beam as they took Osborne Road back to the city centre.

'It'll have to be the long way round from here, Sam. City centre, Great Western Street and down the Peninsula from there.'

'Switch that thing off before we get close enough for them to hear it,' said Hoskins morosely, 'supposing they're still there.'

Several pedestrians looked up at them as Chance carved his way through the traffic on the Longwall bridge. The Town River at slack water had dwindled to a murky stream between mud-flats that shone lipstick-pink in the sunset. Past the plate-glass display windows of Great Western Street, Chance switched off the siren. They caught the traffic lights at Atlantic Wharf and turned back parallel to the way they had come, taking Balance Street and its bridge towards the Peninsula.

'Just watch it,' said Hoskins quietly. 'I want the monkeys driving that car even more than I want the car itself.'

Back over the river, closer to its mouth, the long stretch of Dyce Street marked the beginning of the Peninsula proper. It began under the plate-iron grey of the railway bridge where the road dipped down between high pavements to give more headroom for trucks. The rivets of the Victorian steel plating were neat as a seamstress's stitching. But the graffiti in spray-paint owed everything to middle-class radicals and nothing to the dockland streets. 'Dead Men Don't Rape,' said the bridge in uneven white lettering, and then in black, 'Bored and blue? Nothing to do? Kill the rich! Smash their cars!'

Just beyond the bridge, an Edwardian street-corner gin-palace marked the junction of Dyce Street and a grimy dockland terrace called Monmouth Road. At the far side of the crossing, the wide angular grace of the Fleetwood Brougham was unmistakable. It had the elegance of a Rolls while managing to be long and sleek as well. How the devil no one had spotted it before today, Hoskins could not understand. Even the number-plates remained unchanged.

The car had pulled in by the kerb alongside the Skipper, as the pub was known. Several youths were talking and lounging where the walls were tiled in sea-green glazing with amber round the doors. The frosted glass of the Edwardian bar-room windows had been set like ecclesiastical leaded lights.

'Where's the cavalry?'

'No sign, Sam. Someone must be around somewhere. But you did ask them to leave the job to us.'

'Right. Take it easy round the corner into Monmouth Road and stop.'

Chance slowed the motor-pool Fiesta at the corner. As he did so, the driver got out of the Cadillac and walked round in front of it.

'The little bastard!' said Hoskins indignantly. 'It's the Mouse!'

'Which one, Sam?'

'There! Driving it! Neville the Mouse. Right, so long as we know who we want, let's go after him. Put the hooter on and let the others know we're here.'

Jack Chance reversed the car and prepared to come back out of Monmouth Road into Dyce Street again. It was the suddenness of the movement that caught Neville's attention.

'Bloody hooter's stuck!' Chance worked it madly with one

finger. 'What the hell's wrong with the sodding thing?'

'Never mind the hooter, Jack. Get after him.'

There was a glimpse of the lithe dark figure and the shaven head as the Mouse vaulted back into the driving seat of the Fleetwood Brougham and gunned the engine. Before Chance could get clear of the junction, the Cadillac had taken off with a keening of rubber on tarmac and a wild swerve.

'Keep after him!'

Speeding was likely to be the least of the charges. The Mouse accelerated down Dyce Street, the central division of the Peninsula, making for the pier-head.

'Don't let him get clear,' said Hoskins savagely. 'I want to tidy away that half-smart little bugger!'

By the Anglo-American café with its patched cloths on rickety tables and cups of coffee untasted and cold, a woman scampered back on to the pavement as Chance spun the wheel to avoid her. Men and women from the dilapidated streets of dockers' houses were coming out to watch.

'I still don't see the cavalry, Sam!'

'Nor do I,' said Hoskins irritably. They were passing the twin-towered mission church, its ornate romanesque a tribute to the first Lord Dyce's attachment to Anglo-Catholicism. 'Just try not to kill anyone, Jack. Especially me.'

At that moment, Chance pulled in hard to his own side to miss an oncoming bus. The tyres of the Fiesta screamed against the kerb where a fortress-like public toilet in grey stone stood padlocked and condemned beside the long blank concrete of the railway wall. Ahead of them, Neville the Mouse skidded, hit a parked car with a glancing thump and regained control.

'Tango Four. Chief Inspector Hoskins to all mobiles. Am following a stolen Fleetwood Brougham C948 XAP westward, junction of Dyce Street and Natal Road. Require assistance in heading off and apprehending driver. Believed to be Alexander Morant Neville, otherwise known as the Mouse.'

But Hoskins could see the fiasco that was developing. Beyond the railway wall with its patches of lettering for cinemas and music halls long since closed, lay an industrial wilderness. If the Mouse could once get into that, he could lose them in the maze.

Mile after mile, there were workshops in red brick and tall sheds with corrugated roofs painted the colour of warships. A holocaust of broken cars rose in a pile from the Western Reclaim scrapyard. To the meanly dressed children of the Peninsula the motorised hulks were a paradise of easily energised dodgems.

'Don't let him beat you to the pier-head lights, Jack. You'll lose him down Colenso Road!'

The anxiety in his voice turned to pleading. But Chance was in his element, driving the Fiesta like a champion and closing the distance. Hoskins' heart leapt. At this rate, the Mouse was beaten. He still saw no sign of the cavalry but, so far as he could make out, there was only the Mouse and one other person in the car.

'No contest,' he said for Chance's benefit.

Ahead of them were the traffic lights and the open sky above the pier-head. Dyce Street ended in a two-hundred-yard commercial prosperity of the bonded warehouses, graving dock and the Edwardian Customs House that reproduced Calais town hall in cerise brick.

'Watch it!' said Hoskins sharply. 'He's turning the other way, into Martello Square.'

'Then he can't get out.' Chance sounded uneasy. 'We've got the little sod.'

'You've boxed in the car, Jack. You haven't got the Mouse. Not unless you can run an Olympic half-mile after him.'

Martello Square with its banks and ships' chandlers was a one-way traffic system round the vast Edwardian pile of the Coal Exchange at its centre. Deserted since the closure of most of the collieries, the Exchange resembled a grand hotel or casino with flights of steps and balustraded terraces in darkened sandstone. When the commercial life of Dyce Street ended for the day, Martello Square was little more than a thunderous and reverberating assault course for BMX riders from the high-rise wilderness of Peninsula's Colenso Estate.

The Fleetwood Brougham, taking the corner too fast, mounted the pavement and came off again. The Mouse straightened it up, seemed to lose control and spun the powerful car straight at the skittle-shapes of the street-level balustrading. Hoskins saw the metallic gold of the Cadillac hit the stone rail and bounce back with an impact audible above the engines. The bonnet sprang up and the doors flew open. From the upper terraces of the derelict Exchange, the youth of Martello Square and the little streets scrambled down to see the fun.

Sergeant Chance pulled up, almost touching the rear bumper of the crashed Cadillac, just as the Mouse and his companion stumbled out to either side. They were dazed but otherwise showed no injuries. Chance turned off the engine of the Fiesta. By some mechanical freak, this sparked the defective siren into life. The whooping of the police presence surged and echoed across the square.

'Stop that bloody thing!' Hoskins shouted, opening his door. But Chance, wrestling with the switch, swore and could do nothing. The Mouse was pulling away like a born athlete, sprinting towards the deep and empty concrete tombs of the dry docks beyond the Square. Then he and his companion stopped, screened by the line of young men in jeans and scuffed leather. To these teenagers, the sound of the police siren in their own streets was like a call to battle.

'I can't shut the damn thing off!' Chance bawled.

'Never mind! Reverse out of here and follow the little sod.'

Chance slammed the Fiesta into reverse and took his foot off the clutch. Almost at once, Hoskins was thrown forward by an impact from behind. Two boys in a scrapyard wreck, its front bumper trailing noisily on the tarmac, had driven into the back of the patrol car. There was now no way that the Fiesta could move, either forward or back.

A crowd of fifty or sixty youths, black faces and white, had gathered from the terraces of the Exchange. Hoskins knew a dozen of them by sight, adolescent sniffers of solvents or smokers of dope. Most had been caught at one time or another, daring the devil before admiring friends in corners of the Colenso Road multi-storey car park. Casual in dress and suspicious as feral cats, they represented the last word in street-wise.

And still the whooping-crane siren advertised Hoskins and Chance for what they were. The enemy. Fair game.

'Never mind the Mouse and never mind the Caddie, my son,'

said Hoskins quietly. 'Sit tight and wait for the cavalry. They must be able to hear us. Lock your door.'

He held the radio close and spoke with deliberate clarity.

'Tango Four. Chief Inspector Hoskins. All mobiles in Canton centre and Peninsula proceed to Martello Square at once. Utmost urgency. Crowd now estimated fifty plus.'

They were coming towards the car, a lumbering and shuffling line of malevolence in jeans and scuffed leather jackets, canvas shoes and stained singlets. There was no hate or malice in their faces yet. Merely a slack and slightly amused indifference towards the two prisoners-of-war, a curiosity to watch the secret moments of men suffering and dying. Several of them were grinning, as if to assure the two policemen of the injuries intended and yet exhorting them to accept their pain as an irony of fate. It was nothing personal. Just the way the dice had rolled.

'Keep that door locked, Jack,' said Hoskins quietly.

An arm went back on one of the balustraded terraces above and a flying bottle shattered on the bonnet of the Fiesta. The concrete corner of a broken paving stone hit the door panel on Chance's side and bounced off. The first of them were round the car now. Young faces, some childishly smooth and some scarred by skin eruptions, lank hair being tossed back as they stooped and peered through the windows. A few were still grinning and others tight-mouthed.

'Come on, come on,' said Chance, encouraging the absent squad cars.

A muffled but forceful thumping began on the car roof and the side panels. It was not systematic, not a concerted plan of attack. The boots and sticks that dented the bodywork were random and impulsive. Then the windscreen was darkened as bodies and faces covered it, several of the leather-jacketed Chains peering in at the two men. Hoskins saw a fist thump on the glass symbolically. Then a six-inch blade was drawn lovingly from a sheath. A boy of fifteen or sixteen performed a balletic jump, seeming to fly sideways and kick the car door with both feet in succession before landing agile and upright again. The Fiesta rocked to and fro under the pressure of their bodies as they began to heave it over.

'Keep still,' said Hoskins quietly. 'Just keep still.'

But now the heaving had stopped and he saw that two other cars, commandeered from the streets or the Western Reclaim scrapyard, were being trundled towards them. Their doors hung open and younger children were helping their elders, shoving at the rear wings and bumpers. The others drew back and the battered cars came to rest on either side, so close that no door on the Fiesta could be opened.

'What's this?' said Chance, his plump self-confidence fading in the ominous silence of the crowd.

Hoskins had a good idea of what was intended but thought it better not to say. The cavalry would be there in a minute. But, in the extreme, if Jack Chance were to die, better that it should be quickly and unexpectedly rather than after an agony of anticipation.

'They're just arsing around, my son. Sit still.'

Two of the BMX bikers in crash helmets were standing by the windscreen with improvised wooden clubs to discourage a break-out through the glass. From the rear of the Fiesta, Hoskins heard a metallic thud. Someone was using a steel rod to force off the filler-cap of the petrol tank.

Chance squirmed round in his seat and saw the Mouse behind the car with a cigarette lighter and a twist of paper. The mean young face was drawn into lines of earnest concentration.

'Bloody hell!' said Chance. 'They're trying to light the petrol, Sam. For fuck's sake get the Division again!'

There was another thud and the grinding scrape of the cap being forced out of its thread. Sergeant Chance snatched the radio.

'Tango Four to control and all mobiles. Get here! Martello Square! Alexander Morant Neville and his friends! They're going to fry us in our own petrol. Get here!'

'Listen,' Hoskins said. 'They'll have to draw clear before they light it. As soon as those two bastards with the clubs move from the windscreen, smash it out. Use the car extinguisher. I'll try and kick it out this side.'

'It won't shatter, Sam!'

'It will if I tell it to.'

Chance started the engine and began to ram the Fiesta to and fro, as if to force his way backwards by budging the wrecked car at the rear. Apart from a few jolting impacts he achieved nothing. The Mouse's followers were loading the car behind with broken paving slabs to weight it down. Beyond the shouting crowd of teenagers Hoskins saw, with the curiosity of a dreamer in a nightmare, an adult audience from the new estates around Martello Square. They had gathered on the far pavement in a few small groups, watching the preparations for murder. But not one of them would interfere. They knew better and, in any case, the two men in the car were no friends of theirs.

'It's mad!' Jack Chance said, frightened but almost laughing at the insanity of it all. At that moment, for no apparent reason, the car siren ceased its lugubrious whooping. In the sudden quiet, Hoskins heard triumphant laughter as the petrol cap came clear. The first octane fuel spattered on the road. The mineral odour of it reached Hoskins' nostrils. Then there was a crackle from the radio.

'Delta control to Delta Four. Delta Two and Delta Five reported at junction of Dyce Street and Natal Road.'

'Thank God!' said Hoskins piously. Twisting in his seat, he tried to see the entrance to Martello Square but the wrecked car behind blocked his view. Then there was a scampering outside. The twist of paper in the Mouse's hand flamed and vanished. The Mouse vaulted the balustrading and disappeared among the crowd. The rest withdrew in a running patter of canvas shoes, only to regroup on the far side of the Square. Hoskins waited for the explosion and knew, after a moment, that the flame of the burning paper had guttered in the open air. Perhaps it had been intended to. Perhaps, after all, it was never meant as more than pretence at collective vengeance.

He looked over his shoulder. The first of the uniformed figures appeared round the wreck of the car behind. But it was not the cavalry to the rescue. Several uniformed patrolmen were moving warily in the shelter of the cars. Like the warning rocks of an avalanche, stones and bottles began to thump and bounce on the bodywork of the marooned Fiesta. The far pavement, under the sodium glare of the street lighting, was now packed with Peninsula adolescence. To one side of Hoskins several of the patrolmen were dragging aside the scrapyard wreck to free the passenger door of the police car. Someone shouted at him.

'Get out and get back!'

As he forced his way out through the widened gap with Chance following him, something the size of a match-flame arched through the night air and fell short by twenty feet. With a sudden breath of flame, the bottled petrol exploded in a pool of running fire.

'Get back! Get back!'

Doubled and running, hearing the stones thud and bounce behind them, Hoskins and Chance followed the uniformed men. The entrance to Martello Square from Dyce Street was now blocked by two patrol cars and a police Land-rover. Hoskins recognised the uniform of Chief Inspector Tom Nicholls.

'Sam? What in hell happened here?'

'Stolen car,' said Hoskins irritably, 'driven by Neville the Mouse. We followed him down Dyce Street, into the Square, and ran right into this.'

'On your own?' Nicholls looked at him as if he thought Hoskins might be lying.

'There was supposed to be back-up, Tom! Our friends were supposed to be right behind us, not having a twenty-minute cat-nap. We were called up over on West Drive and sent after these little bastards!'

They drew back behind the police vehicles. The shops on the far side of the Square were leased to engineers and merchants, profile cutting and pulley blocks. There was a ships' chandler, a wholesaler of fire extinguishers and a pin-ball-machine manu-facturer. Hoskins heard the first of the shop windows smashed in. The looting-on-principle began. Another bottle of petrol shattered and flamed near the abandoned Fiesta. But the stones were sporadic now, clattering and bouncing well short of the improvised road-block.

Nicholls was at his shoulder again.

'I hope you've got a winning way with you, Sam, when this comes before the committee. For your sake. We'll be lucky if this stops at a bit of smash and grab. With the petrol that's running loose round here, they could burn down half the Peninsula.'

Hoskins peered through the gap between the cars. The stones and bottles had stopped altogether. Another window went in and the clattering cacophony of an alarm burst across the Square.

'Instead of worrying about committees, Tom, get yourself some more law down here. Quick as you can.'

'I did that, thank you, Sam. Quite some time back.'

But the energy of communal hate subsided as quickly as it gathered. The friends of the Mouse were content to stand their ground, jeering and laughing. A third window went and a second alarm jangled with the first. Even so, the real fun was over and they knew it.

'Put a cordon round the bank!' Nicholls shouted as the first of the minibuses pulled up. Behind them, where Dyce Street ended at the rotting wooden galleries and pontoons of the pier-head, the National Westminster Bank looked out over dredged channels and shining mud-flats. It was a monument to the lost prosperity of Edwardian trade, a place of marble halls, pillars and vaulting, a semi-circular staircase fit for a grand hotel. The banking hall, its pillared windows lit day and night, was lined by internal columns with a Grecian fresco picked out in lilac and gold paint.

Despite Nicholls' concern, the crowd was beginning to break up.

'Just let them go, Tom,' Hoskins said gently. 'We'll find the Mouse when we want him.'

It was over, for the moment. The Mouse and his friends had no interest in the pier-head branch of the National Westminster when the contents of the Martello Square shops were there for the taking. Nicholls kept his road-block on the Dyce Street approach while Hoskins and Chance walked away towards the clean wind of the pier-head railings. It seemed absurd that fifteen minutes ago on this quiet and dull Thursday evening they had feared sudden death.

'Months of boredom, punctuated by a few minutes of sheer bloody terror,' Hoskins said philosophically. 'The classic definition of the job.'

They stood back from the pier-head breeze in the bulb-lit entrance of the Realito Club. The Realito was a disused Victorian chapel, its barley-twist pillars and doorway arch now painted in discotheque blue and white and orange. The drama of Martello Square had passed unnoticed by Dyce Street. A deep beat of music and flashing lights came from within the club, where the girls from Barrier and Mount Pleasant met the eyes of their clients.

The photographs of the stage dancers in the showcase showed one familiar face. Hoskins stared at the round saucer-eyes of the soubrette, the dark hair slicked back and the bold features painted like a doll. In a short matador jacket with spangles, long black stockings and short lace pants, the pale and plumpish shape of Louise reminded him of Bank Holiday on the Cakewalk.

'Appearing by courtesy of the Mouse,' he said.

On the opposite side of the doorway was a case of photographs advertising other services. A coffee-skinned girl with a sharp-nosed Egyptian profile, tall-browed and almond-eyed, posed trimly in an expensively embroidered white bikini. She was displaying to the adventurous Canton female the erotic investment potential of Madame Jolly Modes.

'One thing about villainy,' Hoskins pointed Chance's attention to the showcases, 'it's a smaller world than most. The Mouse's girl and Carmel Cooney's boutique proprietress winking at each other across the doorstep of the same club. I'd like to ask the Mouse how much his friend Mel paid him to dump the Cadillac where it wouldn't be found, speaking gently as I wind the old regulation issue thumbscrews up another notch.'

CHAPTER TWELVE

'I think we're going to have to play this one as it comes, Sam,' said Superintendent Maxwell Ripley, rubbing his chin as an aid to thought. 'Mind you, however you look at it, it puts us in a spot.'

He turned the copy of the *Western World* on his desk so that Hoskins could read the tall black headlines on the front page. POLICE STONED IN DOCKLAND RIOT: *Car Chase Brings Looting and Arson in Martello Square.*

'Arson!' said Hoskins furiously. 'I don't suppose they mention that it was me and Jack Chance they were trying to burn!'

Behind the Ripper's head the window framed a cyclorama of blue and lightly clouded sky over the red tiles of Hawks Hill in the distance, splashes of yellow laburnum in leafy gardens.

The superintendent sighed. 'Sam, for God's sake! You know I'm behind you as far as I possibly can be. My people in this Division come first; they always have.'

'That's nice,' said Hoskins bitterly. 'A known criminal is seen in a car that was probably used to commit murder. Jack Chance and I go after him. Not one of the bastards who's supposed to be backing us up is anywhere to be seen. We get set upon by fifty or sixty young yobboes. They try their best to burn us to death – in the execution of our duty, of course. The back-up arrives a quarter of an hour late because Tom Nicholls can't find his own backside in the dark. Someone's got the petrol out and lit the paper. Five minutes more and Jack and I could have died screaming in agony at the hands of a lynch mob. And now I have to defend myself and ask people to stand behind me – apologise for still being alive? Bloody hell, Max! What kind of a fuck-up is this?'

Ripley's mild blue eyes took it all in and were unmoved.

'It's this kind of fuck-up, Sam,' he said, picking up the newspaper and reading: 'Community leaders in the Peninsula were critical of police methods, described by Councillor Adams and Dr Leroy as insensitive and precipitate. Mr Adams, while condemning the violence in Martello Square, insisted that the high-speed chase down Dyce Street and the manner of the police arrival in the Square was bound to seem provocative to the young people of the area. He added, however, that press reports had exaggerated the number of youths involved and the extent of the looting. Police are today assessing the damage to their vehicles, believed to run into thousands of pounds.'

'Sodding rubbish!' said Hoskins defiantly. 'The manner of the police arrival was due to the fact that the car hooter came on and wouldn't damn well go off again. Perhaps that bloody abortionist Leroy might care to say something about the state of vehicle maintenance in the divisional motor-pool.'

'And it's also this, Sam.'

Ripley stepped back, pressed a button and brought a picture to the television monitor in the corner of his room. Hoskins recognised the CN logo of the early morning Coastal Newsdesk. The face was that of Eve Ricard, complete with blue eye-shadow and dark hair in a little-boy shortie. The slightly nasal and classless voice was dealing well with the invisible interviewer.

'But you do condemn the violence on the part of the mob in Martello Square?'

'In the first place, I prefer to think of people and not mobs. . . .'

'But you condemn the violence perpetrated by them, the attack on the police, the looting. . . .'

'I'm not in favour of violence.' The expression on the composed young face was almost that of piety, Hoskins thought. A bloody nun in Max Factor paint.

'But in this particular case?'

'In this particular case, what we saw in Martello Square is the tip of the iceberg.' Hoskins imagined how many of Canton's male proletariat must have been longing to get back into bed that morning and take her with them as she fluttered her mascara'd lashes a little. 'It's part of years of inadequate housing, run-down schools, insensitive policing, provocative restrictions. We bring these outbursts upon ourselves. But I condemn all those things. I always have done. The true violence is all of them put together.'

'Bloody little cow!' Hoskins was incredulous in his rage. 'Bringing it on ourselves! It's me and Jack Chance that it was brought on, not her! We were the ones that smelt the petrol, while she was probably having it off somewhere with one of her young dykes!'

The phrase 'speechless with rage' had never meant much to him until that moment. Now he was silent with an anger beyond expression. Ripley switched off the monitor.

'I'll back you, Sam. Committees or inquiries, I'll back you. But that's what we'll get on the Police Committee; that's what I'm up against. I have to go to them very soon and ask for more money. We need more transport in the division – need it desperately. I can't do that and, at the same time, tell them that Ricard's a stupid little dyke with a sponge where her brain should be. I may not like it, Sam. I might prefer to blast them with both barrels. But you and the others would suffer more than me.'

Hoskins shook his head, the gloom gathering like mist about him.

'Roll on death, Max, demob's too far away.'

'Not for me it isn't, Sam. Two more years and I'm Bournemouth bound.'

They stood in silence for a moment.

'Look,' Ripley said, 'I'm going to suggest a press statement to the Chief Constable. Our officers acted perfectly properly. We will not tolerate violence from any section of the community and will defend ourselves against it. On the other hand, we are conscious of the special problems of areas like the Peninsula. We should welcome the setting up of machinery for community liaison. So on and so forth.'

'Very nice,' said Hoskins laconically. 'Should go down a treat with everyone except me.'

'But you don't have to argue for the money that pays your wages, Sam. Do you?'

There was another pause.

'If that's all, Max, I'll get on with the business of the Fleetwood Brougham and the forensic tests. Charlie Blades, for preference.'

'Do that, Sam.' Relief and approval were nicely balanced in Ripley's voice.

Hoskins spent half an hour luxuriating in the fantasies of what he would have said to Eve Ricard if anyone had ever given him the chance. He was still doing this when there was a quiet knock at the door and Ripley came in.

'Ah, Sam. There's another matter. A call from the infirmary. I'm afraid we shan't be seeing John Stoodley again.'

Hoskins guessed but had to ask. 'Why's that?'

Ripley sighed and sat down.

'They had trouble yesterday, where the shard from the plate-glass window went through and pierced the gut. For some unknown reason a haemorrhage began. They couldn't stop it. Last night it got out of control. They tried another patch-up and it didn't work. He bled to death on the operating table.'

Hoskins waited. 'What now?'

Ripley pulled a face.

'I think most of us would like to give something towards flowers or a wreath. The funeral will probably be late next week because of the need for a post mortem. Requiem, I should think; Stoodley was an RC. It used to be fifty pence each maximum for flowers, but I think we might raise that to a quid. Under the circumstances.'

'Sure.'

'And though I'd rather have Stoodley alive,' the Ripper said thoughtfully, 'Ms Ricard won't find much public support for attacks on the police just now. Not with the television showing uniformed officers carrying the coffin of a comrade killed on duty. Protecting a member of the public.'

Hoskins stared quietly past Ripley, towards the window.

'So that makes two unsolved murders, Max, committed on the Bank Holiday Monday that was unmarred by violence – according to Ricard's pet news editor. How many people have to be slaughtered before Coastal Radio decides that it adds up to violence?'

But the Ripper shook his head and sighed again, as if despairing at such an incorrigible old cynic as Sam Hoskins.

CHAPTER THIRTEEN

Hoskins lay amongst the sheets that were still perceptibly warm from the young woman's sleep. He stared at the tiny geography of plaster cracks in the ceiling.

'What I hope,' he said thoughtfully, 'is that if I'm very good, when I die I'll go to the Odeon, down the Beach. I had a smashing time there when I was a kid. Absolute magic. Great big screen and long electric curtains lit the colour of apricot. Even the disinfectant smelt like California Poppy. And the carpets used to be thick and soft as sponge-cake. Couple of afternoons a week I used to nip off there. *High Noon* and *Samson and Delilah*, *The Big Sleep* and Rita Hayworth doing the dance of the seven veils in

Salomé. And all that in one school holiday! The Odeon down the Cakewalk had a theatre organ with great big colour-flushes either side that went through every shade in the spectrum while the chap played. Bloody marvellous it was. They had Reginald Dixon there for the season, one summer. You'd have been too young.'

Lesley stood before him, still dressed after breakfast. Hoskins had arrived from night watch just as she finished eating. Now he lay amongst the disordered sheets and hoped. She shook her fringe with the familiar little gesture of impatience.

'About seven or eight,' she said. '*Cinderella* or *Snow White*.'

'I was a fine young fellow by then,' Hoskins yawned behind his hand. 'Acne and nicotined fingers and a nice Brylcreem gloss.'

'The boyhood of Samuel Hoskins,' she said disdainfully.

He watched her unbuttoning her blouse and pulling down the zip of her jeans.

'And then there were the magazines,' he said with a chortle. 'Always had titles like *Spick* or *Span*. Sometimes you could get *La Vie Parisienne* or a nude sepia thing called *Paris Hollywood* down the little streets behind the Parade. But mainly it was the little English ones with healthy girls in snug white shorts and tight sweaters looking like friendly gym-mistresses. And one artistic nude in a woodland glade so that all you saw was half a bum and a sideways view of chest.'

She looked up at him, hopping a little as she drew off the jeans. The firm jaw and cool eyes meditated disapproval.

'I can't say the boy Hoskins sounds exactly engaging.'

He chuckled again. 'They did more for growing lads than the stuff the dirty squad pulls in. Nowadays it's ladies showing the lot in full colour glossy close-ups. About as sexy as a medical textbook.'

'The boy Hoskins never played doctors and nurses with little girls?'

By then he was too impatient to argue. Lesley turned away and stooped to put the jeans on a chair. Hoskins considered the suggestive shape of her, the fuller curves of the pale bottom seen through the utilitarian seventh veil of the tights.

'I may bring my camera,' he said, stroking her lightly and knowingly. 'There's a "Rear of the Year" competition in the

Western World that's just crying out for an entry like this.'

She turned upon him, tall and fair-skinned in nudity, with half-comic exasperation.

'You are a pig, Sam Hoskins. You really are!'

But she lay down and moulded herself to him.

'So they tell me,' he said contentedly, 'and a happy pig too. An endangered species in this city.'

Lesley raised her head and looked down on him, the flick of her fair hair and the line of her mouth suggesting a concession.

'Yes,' she said. 'Certainly a brave pig. Certainly that.'

The heat of the day grew quickly in the curtained bedroom. Here and there, where their skin touched, Hoskins felt the slight dampness of her exertion. The energy of desire was as much Lesley's as his. For all her reserve there was a greed in her affection that was more marked than in any other woman of his experience. It overcame reserve and disdain, self-possession and assurance. He did not doubt that it sprang from a need to be restored and comforted after the turmoil of the past weeks.

In their closeness, Hoskins was conscious of her other life, the suburban domesticity subordinated to her own hunger. There was nothing admirable about Lesley and nothing admirable in the sexual vindictiveness that other men and women felt towards her. And this, for some reason that he preferred not to explain, excited Hoskins all the more. Until it was time to get up and improvise a kitchen lunch, neither gave the other much respite.

At the moment when she turned on her side away from him, Hoskins stroked her from nape to hips and hips to knees.

'Better than Ms Ricard?' he enquired facetiously, kissing the high crown of the soft fair hair.

Lesley did not even turn her face to him.

'That's something you will never know.'

'Why?'

'I intend to make you want *me*,' she said, 'not pictures of me and another woman in your mind, like *Paris Hollywood* or whatever it was.'

'The boy Hoskins is not to be gratified,' he said sadly.

'I should think not.'

Perhaps it was the combination of youth and maturity that

made her so appealing to him. She was proud and yet eager, the complex young woman who hurried the children to school and hurried her lover to bed. He wondered, in Robbo Smith's case, whether the perversely plain beauty and distant manner had been cultivated to deny or provoke. But that, like the sexual technique of Eve Ricard, was something he was not intended to know.

In a little while they were sitting at the kitchen table, the scrambled eggs eaten and the coffee cups emptied. As always in rooms of this size, Hoskins was conscious of his bulk, a large man with tinted spectacles and flattened greying hair who occupied more than his share of the limited space.

'I don't belong to people,' Lesley said quietly. The firm pale features were still resolute and only the eyes seemed troubled. 'I made up my mind last year. I won't be anyone's wife or child-minder. I won't be owned.'

'You won't go back?'

'Not even to be the child-minder,' she said. 'You see? A complete bitch, deserving whatever it is that bitches deserve.'

'Deserving the attentions of someone like me.'

There was a moment of silence between them. Hoskins stroked her back reassuringly and slid his hand round her flank as if trying to get it under her.

'What do you think?' Lesley asked, brushing a troublesome hair with the edge of her hand. Hoskins knew that the terms of his appointment were being laid down. And he was being given his chance to refuse them.

'I keep thinking,' he said, 'what a lucky old bugger I am.'

The negotiations were concluded and she began to laugh, moving a little so that the hand might make its intimate but awkward progress under her. When she got up, it was to go into the front room and return with a cardboard folder and a small desk diary.

'I want you to have these,' she said. 'They were Robbo's.'

Hoskins took them and opened them on the table.

'Cooney?'

'Yes.'

'But why now and not before?'

She slid the table back a few inches and sat on his knee so that he had to balance her with one arm round her waist.

'Because I trust you now. Robbo said that there were policemen in Cooney's pocket. There had to be. There was one called Roberts who died a year or two ago.'

Hoskins tickled her through the smooth tautness of denim.

'He was bent – but not in Cooney's direction so far as I know. He was taking money off pimps and brothel-keepers down the Peninsula.'

She shifted a little and tightened her arm round him.

'Cooney's a gangster, Sam. Everyone knows that. I thought if he had anything to do with Robbo, it might be one of his paid policemen who came out here. If he killed Robbo, why not me or even his kids? There wouldn't have to be a body. We might just vanish and never reappear.'

'Fair enough,' said Hoskins gently. 'No one's going to argue with that. But Cooney's not so much a gangster, more of a dishonest local businessman. There aren't many hit artists in his sort of organisation. He scares people who don't know him very well. But there's a Cooney or two on a good many local councils. You'd have been safe with me.'

'I didn't know you,' she said, chiding him a little. 'Now I do. You may be one of nature's bottom-pinchers, but you're not bent.'

'Flattery,' Hoskins said. He opened the folder and found a pile of quarto pages covered in uncorrected typescript.

'That's the trial,' she said. 'When Cooney and the others were tried for corruption, the *Western World* court reporter took down a lot of it in shorthand. They only used part of it in the paper. Robbo was putting together the rest of it from the shorthand notes. He thought he was on to something. And there's everything he could get from the registrar of companies about Canton Coastal Construction. The diary has notes about people he's seen and conversations with them. He never got to Cooney himself.'

Hoskins turned the pages of transcript doubtfully.

'You can't get a man for conspiracy once he's been acquitted. And that's what this is about. Conspiracy to defraud the public purse. Cooney wouldn't be daft enough to kill a man for threatening him where he couldn't be threatened.'

'What was Cooney supposed to have done in the 1960s?'

Hoskins pulled a face.

'He was in the business of the Mount Pleasant estates, when the flats were built up there. There was no housing up there before, just grassland where the punters used to keep little girls' ponies and that sort of thing.'

'That was before I knew Canton,' she said. 'We moved here after the building.'

'Officially,' Hoskins said, 'it was agricultural land. But there hadn't been agriculture there for years. There was a move to get a grant from the Wilson government to create employment in the area. Cooney had two friends on the council. One was a solicitor and the other was a Labour parliamentary candidate. One or both tipped him off. He bought Mount Pleasant just before the land was rescheduled for industrial development. Made him a fortune.'

'As easily as that?'

'A few hundred thousand grand. But it didn't stop there. As soon as they announced an industrial estate for Mount Pleasant there was hell let loose in Hawks Hill. All those posh houses fenced in by jam factories and saw-mills. The Canton Civic Trust appeared from nowhere. They briefed counsel to fight the proposal. And who should be the leading light of the Trust but Enid Cooney – Mel Cooney's missus! Just then, Cooney was on the council for Taylorstown.'

'But that's almost derelict housing, surely?'

'Right,' Hoskins said. 'Cooney went in on an Independent Conservative anti-black and anti-immigration ticket. He won by several hundred votes. A right upset, that was. Held the seat for three years.'

'And then?'

'The council backed down over the industrial estate proposal. Elections coming up. Apart from Hawks Hill, there were too many Labour middle-class votes in Connaught Park and even Clearwater who didn't want light engineering and cardboard-box makers down the end of their road. So the plan was scrapped. As soon as the election was over, the planning committee re-scheduled the land for housing development and made a cool half-million for Carmel Cooney. Ten times what it would fetch as agricultural land. All owned by Mount Carmel Ground Rents.'

'Cooney?'

Hoskins nodded.

'The council bought it for building flats. Compulsory purchase, of course, with the price fixed accordingly. But two of the fixers were his mates on the council – one of them on the planning committee. And half a dozen others on that committee suddenly got lucky. One OBE for public services to a man who couldn't keep his hands out of the choirboys' pockets. Another gets a juicy chairmanship of the twinning committee that was planning to make friends with Canton in China. All expenses paid and an office with a municipally stocked cocktail-cabinet. That was the worst council membership we ever had in the city. You could smell their meetings clear across the water in Harbour Bar.'

Lesley eased herself off his lap and stood up.

'So they called the fraud squad?'

Hoskins grinned.

'But you can't prove that Enid Cooney didn't oppose the industrial estate for good reasons. If she gave five thousand quid to the Civil Trust to fight a legal case, she was entitled. And you couldn't prove all those nods and winks and understandings. At least, that's what the jury thought. And worst of all, Cooney took about ten per cent of his winnings and did good. My God, he did good! The Carmel Cooney children's ward in the infirmary. He bought himself in as patron for charities. Spina bifida and famine relief. Leukaemia because he was supposed to have had a child died of it. He never did. The Carmel Cooney bus for Bangladesh – that was a kick in the balls for the people calling him a racist. Ready to go, full of food and a couple of nurses, with a pair of his tarts from the Petshop posing on the bonnet in knickers that wouldn't cover a new-born baby. The *Western World* had two pages of pictures.'

'He got off at his trial.'

'He got off,' Hoskins said, 'and he can't be tried for it again. They buggered it up, the mob from the Fraud Squad. Cops from the flicks that go round calling their inspectors "guv'ner" and the suspect "chummy". They'd never met anything like Carmel Cooney in London. It's strictly amateur there, compared with him. They'd sent down this whiz-kid superintendent, all of thirty years old and a real rat-face. Apparently, the day it all came to pieces he actually cried in Ripley's office. Makes you almost proud of the local talent.'

The sulky look returned to the line of the mouth, the fretful little girl in the dancing class line-up.

'There must have been something.'

'Oh, there was,' said Hoskins quietly. 'Plenty. But nothing that would satisfy a jury, then or now. If Robbo Smith was going back into the trial, he was wasting his time. Cooney was acquitted. He's not going to have a man run off a cliff for being interested in that.'

Lesley stood close, pressing against him.

'Robbo didn't think he was wasting his time. He was sure that he wasn't. You'd better read these.'

'I will,' Hoskins said, 'tomorrow night on duty, when it's quiet. If there's anything in it, I can go to Ripley. And don't worry about Cooney. He's a fat middle-aged businessman. Personally unpleasant and dishonest, but probably not much different from a fair number of local worthies. He won't come banging on the door with a sawn-off shotgun.'

'And Ripley?'

Hoskins shrugged.

'I have moments when I think someone ought to prefer charges against him for impersonating a policeman. Ripley's all right. He's dim as a curry house light bulb. Spends most of his time trying to wipe the Police Committee's footprints off the seat of his pants. But he's not a crook, he wouldn't know how. Don't worry about him.'

He got up, kissed her and led the way to the door.

'Come back tomorrow,' she said in a tone that suggested rather than commanded.

'Promise me I won't meet the talented young Ms Ricard in the bedroom.'

The blue eyes under the long parted fringe stared at him curiously.

'Something you'd better know,' she said. 'It was Eve that got me to make the break. After that casual evening, I wanted to be with her. I wanted her that much.'

Hoskins gave it up.

'I don't get enough sleep,' he said gently, 'to lose any of it over that. See you tomorrow.'

Aware of a movement in the street, he patted her surreptitiously like a coded message of intimacy between them, and turned to the car.

CHAPTER FOURTEEN

From the window of Ripley's office there was a long view down the red tarmac Mall to the dove-grey Edwardian dome of the museum and the flying Parisian chariot in black bronze. Half a century before, a shipowner's eccentric philanthropy had filled the long cream-lit galleries with a splendid collection of surrealist art.

'I like a day of admin from time to time,' Ripley was saying. 'Clears the system and tones one up. Like a dose of salts.'

Behind him the sprays of gum-pink confetti-blossom on the trees of the Memorial Gardens patterned an evening sky whose thunder-clouds were heavy as smoke.

'We can't ignore it, Max,' said Hoskins firmly. 'Cooney's car killed him. And if this means what it says, he'd got a knife at Cooney's throat.'

Ripley turned the pages of Robbo Smith's desk diary, closed the book and put it down.

'What you can't do, Sam, is go back over the trial evidence again. The minute you try to question Cooney over the land deal for Mount Pleasant, Jack Cam or some other smart-arsed lawyer of his will have you by the shorts. Cooney and the other two were acquitted on all charges at the Crown Court. End of story.'

Like a terrier with its teeth locked on a trouser-leg, Hoskins hung on.

'It's not the land, Max. Read it. Robbo Smith's evidence is about the contract for the Mount Pleasant flats. Canton Coastal Construction got the contract. In the architect's specification each floor of each block of flats was supposed to be reinforced by steel corner-joints and girder-ribs at floor level. The girder frame of the buildings was prefabricated down at Peninsular Steel. Old, old story, Max. When the steel-erectors put the frame together, the holes for the rivets at the corner-plates didn't match up in a lot of places. The Ronan Point syndrome. And like Ronan Point, CCC wasn't going to waste money re-erecting. They slapped concrete over and left the rivets out. Any of those blocks on Mount Pleasant would have come down like a pack of cards if there'd been trouble.'

Ripley thought about this.

'Even if it's true, Sam, Cooney must know he's got a defence. Blame the foreman and the supervisors. You can't expect the company chairman to be responsible for every rivet. He'd hardly kill Robbo Smith for that.'

'There's better than that, Max. Robbo Smith says that the floor-level girders of the frame were supposed to be reinforced with concrete and aggregate. They never were, according to him. Cooney's men left them hollow, except for the odd cigarette packet or chip-wrapper thrown away in them.'

'Did Cooney know?'

Hoskins sighed contentedly, having the Ripper's full attention at last.

'There were accounts submitted for dredged aggregates in large quantities. Cooney bought them and never used them – or rather he used them on another job. That's the story.'

Ripley turned and stared out of the window where the thunder-cloud above the deep-water anchorages was mingling with the summer dusk.

'And who was supposed to be minding all this for the city architect's department?'

'Torrence,' said Hoskins grimly. 'Remember him? Glasses, grey flue-brush moustache. Shabby mac, scuffed briefcase and greasy trilby. Retired about three years later. Dead almost ten years by now.'

'Not much use as evidence, then, Sam.'

There was no mistaking it, Hoskins thought; the Ripper was relieved.

'If Robbo Smith was right, Torrence was on the take. For God's sake, Max, it has been known! An awful little bugger like him with nothing to hope for but a silver watch, five years' retirement in the bowling club, and then the cemetery. He was ripe for it.'

'Was he, Sam?'

'Yes,' said Hoskins firmly, 'he bloody was. Imagine what was dangled in front of him – not just money. Winter holidays in Bermuda. Half a dozen of the best-looking girls in Cooney's clubs clawing at him and whimpering for a taste of his beautiful little body. Champagne for dinner every night. Whatever he wanted. You could buy old Torrence for that, a no-hoper like him. Bloody hell, Max, you could buy most of the jacks in this building!'

'I doubt it,' said the Ripper bleakly. 'And if I were you, Sam, I wouldn't go to the prosecution service with a story like that. Let alone a jury. Even the prosecutor's office wouldn't believe Cooney was likely to take all that trouble for £10,000 of aggregate.'

Hoskins stared at him.

'You really don't get it, do you, Max? Never mind the dredged aggregate; that's just a load of pebbles. What Robbo Smith was on to was the money Cooney saved by skimping all round – and the fortune he saved in wages. He did the job with half the workforce and half the equipment. Getting those rivet-holes adjusted was budgeted for. About £100,000 for structural alignment of the prefabricated parts. And he was paying money to workmen who didn't exist – in other words, back into his own pocket. That's the story Robbo Smith was telling. Out of a budget of three million, there was half a million tied up in this swindle altogether. This isn't a bit of villainy on the side, Max. This is probably the biggest stroke of Carmel Cooney's life!'

'All right, Sam. We'll check it.'

'And,' said Hoskins finally, 'if Cooney knew what Smith was uncovering, he'd be more than pleased to ram him off that cliff.'

'Not the most subtle way of shutting him up, Sam.'

Hoskins chuckled.

'Bit of luck there, Max. Cooney had to act very fast. The flats on Mount Pleasant are coming down. As it is, the city's just glad to get rid of them. No one's looking closely. But if Smith had ever got his story out, then they'd take every girder apart and screw Carmel Cooney. He didn't have time to be subtle. Smith could have blown the story next day.'

'We'll check it, Sam,' Ripley said again. 'I'll be in tomorrow morning and book a quiet word with the city architect. They'll need an inspector up there. In any case, I'd want some of the construction material looked at by our own people.'

'Fair enough,' Hoskins turned to go.

'Just one thing, Sam,' the Ripper said gently. 'We are not going to foul up anybody's murder enquiry. Whether Cooney did or did not murder Smith is a matter for the people at Ocean Beach. All I want to know is whether he committed fraud. That's all.'

Hoskins nodded and went out. It was dark now and the view from the uncurtained windows was of the city by night. Hawks Hill with its detached houses and leafy gardens was almost black apart from a beaded stem of street lamps up Godwin Road. It was across Orient and Barrier that the lights were massed and twinkling, slashed here and there by coloured neon. Presently, he heard the Ripper's door open and close, then footsteps fading down the corridor towards the stairs.

Hoskins stretched, yawned and settled down for the long night's work. There was a backlog of reports from the Department of Health and Social Security dating back several months. In the ice and snow of February, council workmen had been called out to attend to bursts and leaks in houses occupied by clients on the dole. These unexpected visits revealed that the houses were derelict and the clients living with relatives elsewhere, while continuing to claim their weekly allowance of six pounds as householders in their own right. It was the kind of investigation that came Hoskins' way when he was being punished by the Ripper for some outburst of truculence.

He pushed aside the pile of forms and opened his thermos flask. To hell with the DHSS and its clients, who weren't actually killing anyone. By eight in the morning, he ought to be able to map out the first steps in the Robbo Smith investigation. Torrence. There was a girl whom Cooney had given to the shabby little man. Hoskins had not seen it that way at the time but now it was clear. He tried to recall her. Tracey. Lived in the labyrinth of the Redland council estates across from the Peninsula. She had worked at the time in one of the jeans boutiques that specialised in clothes for teenage girls. Bermuda and champagne must have seemed like fairyland to her and, after all, Torrence was hardly in a condition to make excessive or perverse demands. A sugar daddy with a flue-brush tickler and money to leave.

Where the devil was she now? Hoskins could recall her at sixteen or seventeen, one of those tall willowy nymphs with a veil of long fair hair and tight cream Levis that showed off her long graceful thighs and hips. Small wonder that old Torrence's blood pressure had gone through his skull after a few months of it.

The girl must still be around. He had seen her some years later; her figure was still good but the features of the young face had soon grown hard, the nose and jaw prominent, the hair drawn into a short pony-tail so that there was a display of crude jangling earrings. Tracey would have to be put through the wringer, no two ways about that. Here and there in Robbo Smith's notes there were references to what an unnamed 'she' had said. Tracey Torrence, or whatever she called herself now, was number one for that.

Hoskins was still meditating this at half-past nine, preparing to unwrap a sandwich, when his phone rang.

'There's this call, boss, from one of the Evenings,' said Sergeant Beatty on the main desk. 'They've found a girl in the storm drain near the Balance Street outfall. She's on file over an incident in Ocean Beach, if she's who we think she is. In that case, Inspector Nicholls wonders whether you might know her. Something to do with having seen her before. He won't move her until Dr Maggs and the photographer have been down. There's a car going in about ten minutes. Mr Nicholls says, could you just take a look?'

'Why?' said Hoskins belligerently. 'Why can't Mr Nicholls handle it on his own?'

'Don't know, Mr Hoskins. Only he asked. You said something to him, apparently. Made him think you might know who we're looking for. Whoever it is can't have got very far.'

Hoskins grunted. 'I'm having my coffee and sandwich first. I don't fancy the Balance Street outfall as an appetiser.'

'Ten minutes, he said, boss,' Beatty reminded him.

'Then perhaps I shall miss the treat after all.' Hoskins slammed the phone down. He bit into the soft bread and found the sleek ham. Sod's law had been operating with an inflexible rigour just lately. The body in the storm drain would be Tracey, he was sure of it. It was enough for him to think of a potential witness for her to be eliminated from the case – and from life. All his euphoria from the last visit to Lesley had gone. Sam Hoskins was in a thoroughly grumpy mood by the time he went down to the car.

With a sense of occasion, the uniformed driver switched on the siren and the blue flashing light as he turned out into the Mall.

'Shut that bloody thing off,' Hoskins said ungratefully. 'It's less than a mile, the star of the show isn't going to run away and you, my son, are going to obey every traffic regulation as if on road test.'

They drove in hostile silence down the dark and deserted spaces of the Mall, past the lines of custard-yellow buses at the makeshift terminus in King Edward Square, then along the plate-glass displays of the department stores in Great Western Street towards Atlantic Wharf.

At half-past five the metal grille came down like a portcullis over every entrance to the covered shopping precinct. The stores on the main streets had an embattled air and the pavements were empty of window-shoppers. When the business day ended, Canton shopping centre was given up to arpeggios of spray-can graffiti and a symphony of kicked beer-cans.

The driver pulled up near the pedestrian underpass where Great Western Street joined Atlantic Wharf near the railway station. Hoskins saw that Nicholls was waiting for him.

'Thanks, Sam,' said Nicholls hastily, cutting off Hoskins' moroseness by his gratitude. 'I wouldn't inflict this on you, except that I think you may know the person we're looking for.'

'If I do, Tom, you'll be the very first to hear.'

The modern underpass was faced by ceramic tiling, patterned with sailing ships and bales of goods from the city's former prosperity. Uniformed police with white tapes had blocked off public access at either end. Half-way along, the steel inspection door that led to a warren of telephone tunnels and drainage channels had been unlocked. Hoskins followed Nicholls through into a vast unseen city that lay twenty feet below the streets and department stores of Canton proper.

'You'd better have a pair of these,' Nicholls said.

Hoskins noticed that Nicholls himself was wearing the black galoshes issued for such investigations. The tunnel was well-lit by caged light-bulbs and there was a collection of the rubber boots. He undid his shoes and tried a pair for size.

The storm drain was most easily reached from this point. A pre-war addition to the main sewerage system, the drain collected storm water from the low-lying districts of Barrier and Cathay, channelling it to this outfall. The water flowed out down the mud-bank and into the Town River just upstream from the Balance Street bridge, joining the Peninsula to the city proper.

Twenty yards along the main passage, a steel grille inspection gate gave a view of the drain. That gate too had been unlocked and now stood open. Beyond it, the storm drain was a tunnel lined by dark and shining Canton brick. There was a narrow concrete walkway above the channel on the near bank with just enough headroom for a man to stand upright. Hoskins entered with a familiar feeling of gloom and helplessness at what he was about to find. Ahead of him, someone had already run black strands of cables along from the generator to the arc-lamp. A fierce white light illuminated the rest of the tunnel to the opening of the river outfall about a hundred yards away, somewhere under the banks and investment brokers of Dingwall Street.

'Up here, boss,' said the uniformed man who was now leading the way.

Hoskins could see very little at first, blinded by the brilliance of the arc-lamp. Then he passed beyond it and his heart sank.

She was lying in the channel of the storm drain, though the concrete on the upper curve was dry during the fine summer weather. Her face was hidden. Those who had dumped her here had wedged her between the curve of the channel and the concrete overhang on the far side of the drain.

Hoskins saw the red hair and thought of the voice on the Cakewalk screaming at the uniformed men who held her: 'Take your hands off me! Get your fucking hands off!' He recognised the black scuffed leather of her jacket with its frills and 'property patches' that showed she belonged to one of the riders of the Chains. The partnership of 'Digger and Angie' embroidered on the back of the jacket put her identity beyond question. Below the waist she was white and naked, either as a derisive challenge by the Hot-Rodders to the Chains, or else because that was how she was when they killed her.

Hoskins turned away. It was worse than Robbo Smith. There was nothing womanly or stimulating about the way the redhead had been undressed. The mute helpless pallor of Angie's hips and legs had a passive and childish air. For all the banner headlines in the *Western World*, she and the other 'women' of the Chains were seldom more than sixteen or seventeen years old.

He stood for a moment, seized by the malice and futility of it all.

'She's the one,' he said quietly to Nicholls. 'No question.'

In his mind he heard another voice, slack-lipped and sneering: Neville the Mouse. 'You should've let us have her, Mr Hoskins . . . You always have to go and spoil people's fun. Still, I 'spect we can always find her again when we want her.'

He did not doubt that Neville and his friends had wanted her and had found her. Contrary to expectations, the Mouse had not had his fun spoilt after all.

Dr Maggs and the photographer were picking their way cautiously along the concrete walkway from the grilled inspection gate.

'Any idea who we might be looking for, Sam?'

'The Hot-Rodders, Tom. It's their style.'

'That's a tall order, Sam. There might be a hundred of the little bastards to choose from. I was rather hoping you might be able to point the finger at a name.'

'If I do, Tom, you'll get a nod and a smile first.'

'And if it was the Rodders, Sam, how come there's no sign of her boy? They'd want him more than her.'

Hoskins sighed. 'I daresay he's around, Tom. Lying in one of the main drains or on the municipal refuse tip.'

There was no mistaking Nicholls' disappointment, but Hoskins was unmoved. He doubted that the girl's death had anything to do with the Hot-Rodder cult. This was the Mouse and his friends.

Vengeance had been taken in one of the Mouse's rooms down the Peninsula, courtesy of soundproofing or a gag. And in consequence, the Mouse was going to get Hoskins' undivided attention. Once arrested and facing a murder charge for the death of Angie, the thumbscrews would tighten to a notch never before attained. The difference between five years for youthful manslaughter and a minimum twenty-five for murder preceded by multiple rape and wounding. That was how the thumbscrew ratchet wound up the thread. The Mouse emerging blinking and pale at fifty years old. At that prospect, the entire story of Cooney and the Fleetwood Brougham would come tumbling out, faster than beer from a St Vincent Street drunk.

As Hoskins was driven back to the city police headquarters, he saw his way forward. But first, on returning to his office, he picked up the phone and called the night desk of the *Western World*.

'Mr Roskill,' he said patiently. 'I've got something for Mr Roskill.'

There was a bleep, a pause and then a fat well-fed voice.

'Hello, Sam, my friend, what've you got for me then?'

'Just this,' Hoskins said. 'Petrol bombs on the Cakewalk. Bank Holiday Monday night. Female suspect arrested, brought before the magistrates next morning. Bailed in custody of social services. Right?'

'Right-o, Sam.'

'*Western World* reported the case.'

'Right.'

'Including the girl's name, address, where she could be got at.'

'What the hell is this, Sam?'

'What this is, my friend, is bloody simple. You put a tag on her. If the Rodders wanted vengeance – and an hour or two of unwholesome fun into the bargain – you told them exactly how to start, where to find her.'

'Sam, for God's sake! We reported the normal details. You can't put a name without an address in case there are two people of the same name. A right little libel tangle that might be. And you can't report a case with an unnamed defendant. Not unless you want the system run like bloody Russia. So what's the problem?'

'The problem,' said Hoskins quietly, 'is in the storm drain. You needn't worry about libel. She's dead . . . and half-naked. And the last hour or two of her life is something I'd rather not think about.'

Roskill was peevish.

'What do you expect me to do about it, Sam?'

'Tell your shitty magistrates' court reporter at the Beach that he can expect some very special police harassment from now on. If he so much as pauses on a yellow line, I'll have him in aerial ballet supported by piano wire round his appendices. And if any of you stupid bastards ever again puts in details like that in such a case, I'll see you done for aiding and abetting any harm that comes of it.'

'Don't be a prat, Sam. You can't do that.'

'I've just come back from viewing her body,' said Hoskins bitterly. 'Don't you fucking well tell me what I can and can't do to stop that happening again.'

For the second time that night he slammed down the phone. He had done nothing except ensure a complaint from the editor of the *Western World* to Superintendent Ripley on the subject of press freedom. But Hoskins was unmoved. He had probably accomplished nothing and yet, for the first time that day, he felt a lot better. Then he looked at the stack of reports from the DHSS investigation service on social security fraud and gave a belligerent groan.

CHAPTER FIFTEEN

'Candlewick,' said Dr Blades wearily. 'A lilac Restall counterpane, to be precise. They sell by tens of thousands; British Standard serial number in the book.'

'We paid a call on the Mouse.' Hoskins walked across to the window and stared at the boiled-sweet colours of neon coming out in the dusk the length of Ocean Beach. 'No sign of the little bugger. All the same, I'll check the inventory of linen.'

'No two ways about it, Sam. The fibres were spot-on. Found flecks of them on the front of her leather jacket and in her bush. She must have been lying on her face on a candlewick bedspread, with nothing on below the waist. Willing or not. Have a drink?'

'Not willing,' Hoskins said firmly. 'The path lab report lists a post-mortem flush on either wrist consistent with being tied to separate sides of the bed. A belt, they think, not a cord. I'll have a splash, Charlie, if you're pouring anyway.'

Blades winced, tall and cadaverous. After so much trouble with his missing stomach, he was apt to anticipate a twinge by this grimace without waiting for the spasm to grip him. The two men were standing in his office at the top of the new forensic block, looking across Bay Drive and the shopping centre in the summer twilight.

'Sorry about the overtime, Charlie,' Hoskins said amiably.

Blades pulled another face, dismissing sympathy.

'Way of life, Sam, with the bills I pay for her two little bleeders. She's got ideas about a private school.'

'Still, she's half your age, Charlie, and fit and frisky with it. Must be something in all that.'

Blades opened the drawer of his desk, took out the bottle and looked sourly at the darkening scene below them.

'I struck lucky, Sam. Bloody marvellous. Walk into that bedroom, you'd have thought it was the hottest bit of a Swedish film. Staying lucky is another thing.'

The green neon arrow on the New Pier stabbed out and out across the dark water to the bright palace of the funfair pavilion. Slot-machine arcades burst into life with a crazy jumble of letters that suddenly went black and then began again. Still the green arrow strove eternally and in vain towards a dark and undefined point of the channel sky. At the shabbier end of the Cakewalk, the roller-coaster in Ocean Park swooped and soared in a ribbon of brilliance. Automated casino signs blazed for Lucky Penny and Golden Mile.

The cork squeaked in the bottle as Blades opened it and took two glasses from the drawer. He poured a tot for Hoskins and a splash for himself.

'Got a notion then, Sam?'

Hoskins raised his glass in salute.

'A word with Neville the Mouse at close quarters. That's what I want.'

'Little bastard!' Blades touched the glass to his lips. Hoskins stared at the last pink fleece of daylight above the tide.

'I'm too old for it, Charles, my friend. When I saw her wedged in like that, I just wanted to quit. Just that. Let some other clever bugger get on with it. You could offer me a troupe of Balinese dancing-girls at the moment, and the old nerve wouldn't even twitch.'

'Ah,' said Blades scornfully. 'It'll pass.'

'I do hope so, Charlie. It's the Mouse, I suppose. Down the Division, we're all supposed to think he's a bit of a rogue, a fancy spark, a witty villain, Jack the lad. Have to arrest him now and then, but can't help taking to his ways.'

'It's the game, Sam.'

'He's a cruel, vicious little bastard, Charlie. There's nothing else in him. You ever want a concentration camp guard and gas-chamber attendant, you dial Neville the Mouse. And I'll give him a reference. I've cleared up his messes after him for years. The marks he's left on people and the tears he's caused! But I, Charlie, am supposed to act as if he's just a genial little car-thief who nicks some wanker's Sunday limo for a bit of a joy-ride.'

Blades put down his glass and winced again. 'It's the job, Sam.'

But Hoskins was not to be put off.

'The red-headed girl, Angie. Before they shoved her face in the pillow and suffocated her, they did everything you could name. Not to mention the Mouse's strap. I'd like to exterminate the bloody lot of them, Charlie. And if I feel like that, I reckon I should quit.'

Blades shrugged. 'Drink your scotch and stop feeling sorry, Sam. There's worse to come.'

'How's that then, Charlie?'

There was a folder on the desk. Blades opened it.

'Forensic report on Cooney's Cadillac. Yes, it bashed Robbo Smith's bike and it hit the railings in Martello Square. And there's no fingerprints inside the car.'

Hoskins looked at him, waiting for an explanation. There was none.

'Don't talk bloody daft, Charlie. There must be.'

Blades drew his mouth tighter.

'There's the Mouse and Breaker Weekes, his pal. We got them from criminal records. What I mean, Sam, is that's your lot. There's not another print anywhere on the interior surfaces.'

'Not Cooney's?'

'Not anyone's, Sam.'

'That's mad, Charlie. The Mouse nicks a car and wipes off all the prints inside but leaves his own and Breaker Weekes?'

'That's all we found.'

Hoskins stared at the masthead's electric blaze on a container ship waiting for the tide off the railway dock.

'Who was in that car that we weren't supposed to know about? And how much did Cooney pay the Mouse to dump his Cadillac after Robbo Smith was nudged off the cliff by it? That seems to be the form.'

Blades corked the bottle and returned it to his drawer.

'I'd find the Mouse if I was you, Sam, and pull his fingernails out until he tells you. I'm going home. She gets the little bleeders to bed about now; I can go back and have her to myself. I'd give those little belly-achers something to complain about, if they were mine.'

Hoskins picked up his coat and slung it on his shoulder.

'Family life is what it is, Charlie. Backbone of the nation.'

'Backside of the nation more like,' Blades said, and they walked down together.

Jack Chance was in amiable conversation with the duty sergeant. As they stood in the car park, about to separate, Hoskins said, 'Suppose we wanted fingerprints off Robbo Smith's bike, Charlie. Any hope?'

'You could have said before, Sam. It's had a fair bit of handling. We could do something.'

'You'd have to eliminate Robbo Smith's own prints for a start,' Hoskins said. 'He's not on file.'

'Doesn't need to be, Sam. We've got him in person, downstairs in the freezer. Oven-ready, you might say.'

'One thing about your sense of humour, Charlie,' said Hoskins grimly, 'it really cheers a bloke up.'

But Blades winced again.

'Bloody whisky gives me gyp,' he said morosely and turned away towards his car.

Chance was waiting behind the wheel of the divisional Fiesta.

'There's this one about Eve Ricard and Superintendent Ripley,' he said happily.

'The Cakewalk before we drive back,' Hoskins said. 'I want a word with the good Carmel Cooney.'

'Right-o, Sam.' Chance swung the car out of the entrance, past the little hotels and ice-cream parlours of Clifton Hill, descending steeply to the first lamplit ripples of a dark sea. 'Anyway, they decide to put on a civic pantomime, all right? And Ricard and Ripley are the horse. Okay?'

'Turn right at the bottom,' Hoskins said, 'and use the Petshop car park.'

Chance began to snigger in anticipation of the conclusion. 'Anyway, the Ripper being a gentleman and wanting to impress the Police Committee lets Eve Ricard be the front half. Well, the first act goes off smashing and then after the interval they come on as a snake instead of a horse. And someone says, you can't go off as a horse and come on as a fucking snake, it's fucking ridiculous. So Eve Ricard says. . . .'

'I'm not bending over in the front part of the horse until he shaves off that moustache,' said Hoskins wearily. 'Dudden's been peddling that the last three days. Turn right here.'

'Bloody hell, Sam! Talk about the mockers. Charlie Blades say anything about the girders and rivet holes at Mount Pleasant, did he?'

'Nope,' said Hoskins truculently. 'He didn't say because he's not being told. It's a job for a civil engineering contractor, not forensic. City engineer and architect are living up there from now on. Every bloody girder is going to be drilled and every joint inspected as they take it down. You don't need a forensic expert to tell you if a hollow steel beam is full of reinforced concrete or cigarette packets and fresh air. No one's being told except those who have to know.'

Chance parked the car close to the Cakewalk terrace of the Petshop. As he did so, a uniformed figure approached.

'Not here, chief. This lot's all private. You want to park, you find yourself a place on the public road. Oh, sorry, Mr Hoskins.'

'And now you find yourself a place on the public road!' Hoskins said savagely.

As they moved out of earshot, Chance asked, 'Who's that, then, Sam?'

'Old Dougal. Used to be sergeant up at Lantern Hill, where there's more of 'em bent than usual. Resigned in a hurry and got bought up by Cooney as a car minder.'

He pushed the swing door and Chance followed him into the deeply carpeted lobby of the club. There was a reception counter ahead of them with a woman of thirty or thirty-five behind it. At first Hoskins thought she would be dressed in an evening gown of some kind. Only as he approached did he see that she was condemned to the same black bikini outfit as the waitresses, with a bandana over her short crop of tight black ringlets. From top to toe, so far as her skin could be seen, she was pinkly powdered. Her little name brooch said 'Trish'.

Even before they reached the counter, she had drawn breath for her introduction. It was like the liturgical monotone of a tired vicar.

'Good evening, gentlemen. There's a ten-pounds-a-head table charge in the dining area or a five-pound charge for a bar-stool. That entitles you to one free drink. Drinks are served direct to bar-stools only. At the tables, anything you want is brought by one of the young ladies. All right? Last orders for hot snacks at 10.30. All right? If you'd just sign the book here . . . There's a pound charge for the car park, but you'll have that refunded from your first purchase after your frees. All right?'

To one side of them, beyond heavy cinema doors with porthole windows, there was a firework flashing of coloured lights and a vague thumping of music. Hoskins ignored the proffered book and pen.

'I'm here to see Mr Carmel Cooney.'

'Mr Cooney isn't available to visitors just now. If you'd like to leave a name and call back?'

'Tell him,' said Hoskins, 'I'm here to inspect the kitchens. And I know cat from rabbit, as well as Stork from butter.'

The dark-lashed blue eyes gave a startled flutter.

'Chief Inspector Hoskins,' Hoskins encouraged her gently. 'Canton "A" Division.'

'If you'd just like to wait,' the young woman said hastily.

Hoskins turned away and heard her use the house phone. He and Chance took one porthole window each and stared into the former Winter Garden lounge with its ceiling of art deco nymphs and fauns. On a Tuesday evening no more than half a dozen of the dinner tables were occupied and there was no one at the bar. But still the show went on. There were three young women on the stage in abbreviated gym-slips and ties round their blouses, contributing to the St Trinian's fiction that black silk briefs and suspender-belts were regulation school wear and almost constantly visible. Hoskins at last made out the music to which the three dancers were miming inexpertly. It was an old D'Oyly Carte recording of *The Mikado* blasted through the Petshop's amplifiers: *'Three little maids from school are we . . .'* There was a skip, a turn, a flip of the skirts and three behinds arched out at the dinner tables. *'Pert as a schoolgirl well can be . . .'*

Hoskins addressed Chance from the corner of his mouth.

'Did you ever in your life see anything so bleeding ridiculous? No wonder Harold Moyle's got trouble with punters fancying his sixth form.'

'Nothing ridiculous about raking in ten quid a throw, Sam. There's two hundred sovereigns sitting at those tables, even before they start getting in the drinks and snacks.'

'The middle one of the three girls,' Hoskins said, 'that's Maggie from the stockroom.'

'No!'

'It bloody is, Jack.'

'It is too.'

They looked at her again. Her pale blonde hair was fringed and parted on her forehead, worn straight and lank to her shoulders to give her a childish air. But the features of her pale face were hardened and crude. In figure, she was short-legged and therefore rather stocky in appearance, despite shoes with the tallest possible heels.

'Well,' said Hoskins, turning away, 'that's one schoolgirl that's never going to see twenty-five again. Maybe not even thirty.'

'If you'll go up,' said the dark-haired woman behind the counter. She pressed a button and there was an electric buzz of the door-catch at the bottom of the office stairs. Hoskins and Chance went up. Carmel Cooney, the giant pot-bellied tadpole in the tight grey suit, was waiting for them on the landing. The unremoved cigarette muffled his voice.

'Mr Hoskins! You should've said! Could've had a table compliments of the house!'

'Just a word, Mr Cooney. Nothing more.'

Cooney chuckled and led the way into his office. The velvet curtains were closed and the double glazing brought a carpeted hush to the sumptuous leather furnishing. The flush lighting illuminated a desk whose leather surface was large enough to fight a tin-soldier Waterloo.

'Drink, Mr Hoskins?'

'We won't, thanks.'

Cooney put the decanter down again.

'Now,' he said, with his cut-melon smile, 'what the fuck's all this fanny about the kitchens?'

Hoskins sat down uninvited. 'You know how it is, Mr Cooney. Impresses the lady on the desk.'

Cooney's smile grew fuller.

'You don't want to let Jack Cam catch you in my kitchens, Mr Hoskins. He'd sort you for trespass, impersonating a health official, perhaps even breaking and entering, and being on enclosed premises. He's a tartar, is old Jack Cam.'

Hoskins sighed. 'If we could just make progress, Mr Cooney, it's a matter of the car.'

Cooney nodded seriously, held up his hand to interrupt and went across to the other door.

'Like to go out with one of the girls, sweetie? I'll be a bit busy.'

Sian emerged into the main room. She stood and looked at the men, her wide mouth open a little and her pale red hair adorned at the side with a tortoiseshell comb.

'Just a minute,' Cooney said. He spoke to someone on the house phone. Presently, the girl who had finished her number on the stage came up, dressed in her jeans and sweater. Cooney fished in his wallet. He handed three twenty-pound notes to the stocky young blonde.

'Go out and have a bite to eat together,' he said. 'Have a look round the town. Have a bit of fun. I'll be tied up for the minute. Go on, sweetie. You'll be all right with Mag.'

He watched them go out together and then turned to Hoskins.

'Only thing about the Caddie, Mr Hoskins, I'm brassed off at the damage done and I'd like to crucify the two little vermin that did it. It can't never be put properly right. Not what they did to the front end in Martello Square. Mind you, you was a bit too impulsive there, judging from the papers.'

Hoskins felt the blood beat faster but he kept his voice under control.

'A matter of proving a case, Mr Cooney. We need your cooperation. A matter of elimination. No obligation, of course. We'd like your fingerprints. They'll be destroyed as soon as the case is over, one way or the other.'

'My fingerprints, Mr Hoskins?'

Cooney moved and stood over the inspector, as if about to seize him in anger.

'If you wouldn't mind. There's at least a dozen different sets on the car interior. We need to eliminate the ones that would have been there before it was stolen.'

'My fingerprints? But you know who bloody stole the car. You saw them driving it!'

'Saw them then, Mr Cooney. But we don't know who else may have driven it while it was missing. And so we can't prove who actually stole it. All we need is ten minutes of your time down "A" Division office.'

'Then you go on needing it, Mr Hoskins.' There was no mistaking Cooney's anger. 'You saw who was in the car. Arrest the little turds and charge them!'

'I intend to, Mr Cooney. But I mean to know the circumstances of the theft, that's the big one. I want a conviction out of this.'

Cooney withdrew a little and there was a catch of self-pity in his voice.

'I'll be damned if I'll be fingerprinted like some criminal.'

'But you have been, Mr Cooney, haven't you?' said Hoskins

gently. 'Long time back . . . Her Majesty's Military Prison, Colchester. Detention barracks, 1956. Glasshouse. I daresay I could get them from somewhere like that. But if I have to, your Caddie is going to be in the pound for months and the insurance claim will be unresolved this side of next year. And even Jack Cam is going to have to tell you, Mr Cooney, that it's your own bloody fault.'

'Then you talk to Cam about it, Mr Hoskins. That's all.'

Hoskins got up and looked at Chance.

'Your privilege, Mr Cooney. If that's how you feel about it.'

'Next thing,' said Cooney sardonically, 'you'll come out with the crap about two ways of doing it – hard way and easy way. The old police interview-room routine.'

Hoskins turned away.

'Yes,' he said reasonably. 'Still, you'd know about the interview-room routine. Wouldn't you, Mr Cooney?'

Cooney followed them out to the head of the stairs. He spoke closely and confidentially to Hoskins, as if intending that Chance should not hear.

'You done this to rile me, Mr Hoskins. You come here to rile me. I'm the one that's been robbed and wronged. And I'm the one that's got a clean sheet. Not all of your jacks down "A" Division can say that of themselves. There's names going round all right. Houses up Lantern Hill where some inspector or super has a spare fancy woman living. She only got to complain that someone sneezes out of tune and the cars is down there. Uniformed busies laying it on the rest of the neighbourhood.'

'We're not Lantern Hill,' said Hoskins quietly as they went down the stairs.

'Then don't come here and try to rile me, Mr Hoskins,' Cooney said, suddenly quiet and reasonable. 'Don't do that again, will you?'

CHAPTER SIXTEEN

Sergeant Chance started the engine of the Fiesta in the Petshop car park.

'What the hell was all that about in there, Sam? What's this fingerprint business all of a sudden?'

While the engine ran, Hoskins stared at the coloured posters in the glass case. Next week the dark, cuddly and plump Emira harem-dancing in gauze veils – and the Petshop fashion show for Africa.

'Bit of a gag, my son,' he said quietly. 'Whoever nicked that car of Cooney's wiped off every fingerprint inside it. Clean as a whistle. But the dabs of the Mouse and Breaker Weekes are plastered all over it.'

'Wiped off Cooney's prints?' Sergeant Chance let in the clutch. 'What for?'

'Don't ask me, Jack,' said Hoskins wearily. 'All the same, you saw how he took on when he thought his prints were still on it. Took on something cruel, as they say. Drive slowly out of here. Let's see if his girls are going anywhere interesting. Take in the pier and Ocean Park. I bet it's one or the other. It's their style.'

'Sian and Maggie?'

Hoskins nodded.

'I wouldn't be surprised to find Carmel Cooney setting the Mouse up for trouble,' he said thoughtfully. 'There can't be a lot of love lost between them: Cooney getting past it and this young tearaway moving in, cornering the skin trade down the Peninsula. And he'll go on to bigger things, if he's not stopped. By Cooney, that is. The law won't stop him. Give it time, Jack Chance, and all this could be the Mouse's too.'

He made an expansive gesture towards the Petshop and, by inference, the Royal Peninsular Emporium and Mount Carmel Ground Rents.

'Balls,' said Chance.

Hoskins shrugged.

'That's what they said about Cooney at nineteen. When you're an old man, my lad, your local representative on the council may be jovial Neville the Mouse.'

'Sod that,' said Chance emphatically.

'As from next week, you'll be saying "sir" to Councillor Cooney of Hawks Hill. Think about it. There's nothing to choose between him and Neville. Pimps, swindlers, sadists. What we used to call the anaesthetists.'

'What's that then, Sam? Anaesthetists?'

'Inability to feel other people's pain. Jolly young Neville straps that biker's girl Angie, top to toe. No more compunction than if she was a shop-window dummy. Then, time for the fun to end, go out and have a few beers. So, hold the pillow over her face and sit on it until the spasms stop. Out with the boys down the Capstan bar. Not so much as a tremor in the hand that holds his pint of horse-piss lager. That's an anaesthetist, my son. And under the five-hundred-quid suit and the expensive dental smile, that's Carmel Cooney. Don't you forget it.'

On a Tuesday evening, the Cakewalk was quiet. The couples, self-absorbed, strolled beside the low wall and the coloured shimmer of the full tide. As Chance drew in by the pier approach, the machine-shop din of the funfair a quarter of a mile out to sea in the pier pavilion carried fitfully to the shore. The woman's voice was still wailing over the public address system.

> Rosie, you are my posy,
> You are my heart's bouquet. . . .

'What d'you think, Sam?'

'Try Ocean Park. If they were going on the pier, we'd have passed them by now. All it is, Jack, I'm wondering if Cooney sent them anywhere deliberately.'

> Come out into the moonlight. . . .

Chance pulled out into the slow line of cars, the trippers in their motorised armchairs gazing aimlessly and moon-faced at the passing show.

'Rosie, you are my posy . . .' he began.

'For God's sake!' said Hoskins irritably.

Chance was not to be put down.

'All right,' he said cheerily. 'Then there's this Irishman, see? And he's a drug addict, on the needle. And he's sharing it with his mates. And someone says to him, "Bloody hell, Paddy! Aren't you scared of catching Aids?" Sharing the needle and all that. So Paddy says, "No," he says. "I shan't catch any Aids from the needle. I always wear a condom."'

Chance slapped his knee at the neatness of it. Hoskins sat in silence for a moment.

'You know what, my son?' he said presently. 'You're about as depressing as Charlie Blades. Him with Robbo Smith in his freezer. Oven-ready. It's what this town does to people's sense of humour, I suppose.'

Chance shrugged tolerantly, as if to distance himself from killjoys like Sam Hoskins.

Ocean Park marked the eastern and shabbier extreme of the Cakewalk, veiled only by headland and trees from Canton Railway Dock. Bay Drive came to a dead end at this point, circling the park above the last of the sand and sea before turning back on itself. With its metallic din and blazing lights, the amusement park was more like a round-the-clock building site. The dancing letters still rippled and flashed through the darkness for the Lucky Penny machine arcade. In the air above the park the neon-studded chariots whirled like celestial hammers in the dusk. Only the casual street-gangs were here tonight, the drab denim and imitation leather of Barrier or Orient. They were neighbourhood warriors, black faces and white mixed together, serving their apprenticeship in bodily harm at twelve or thirteen. Neither law nor justice was a deterrent to them. As the children of Barrier and Orient saw it, they had nothing to lose, convicted or not.

'How the hell old Harold Moyle teaches that bloody lot, I do not know,' Hoskins said despondently. 'Throw a piece of chalk at some noisy little yobbo in class and you can be done for civil assault. Clip the little bastard's ear or tan his arse and you'd never teach school again.'

'But then,' Chance said, 'old Harold teaches out at Lantern Hill, where all the little girls want ballet classes and the little boys want to build computers. He doesn't know he's born.'

He stopped the car on the opposite side of the road to the park entrance. Below them, the sands were bleached by the twilight and the dark violet sea was cut by a cold June wind.

Chance went back to the matter of the fingerprints.

'Can't see what there was to get Cooney going about the prints. I'd expect to find his dabs inside his own car. And I'd expect to find his redhead's there as well. Odd if they weren't. Who else had to be wiped off?'

Hoskins thought about this. His face brightened.

'Eve Ricard's secret vice. Being done by a male thug like Carmel Cooney in his expensive limo. Her secret shame. Chains and thongs.'

'You been going to the pictures with the dirty squad again, Sam?'

Hoskins sighed.

'Bet you Ms Ricard has something odd ticking away inside. That sort always do. When she blows, she'll really blow.'

After about ten minutes, Chance said, 'Your first bit of luck today, Sam: Sian Jones and her girl-friend.'

Hoskins watched them walking slowly to the bulb-studded entrance arch of Ocean Park. The two young women seemed apathetic and numb, paying no attention to the scene around them and not even speaking to one another. Time passed for them without apparent significance. He slid from his seat and went across the road with Chance following him.

'There's something wrong with that redhead,' Chance said sourly. 'Either a head-case or doped. You could sit her on a red-hot stove and I don't suppose she'd blink.'

The brightness and the din engulfed them, the wheels spun and the games of fortune rattled and bleeped. Hoskins and Chance were following an alley between two rows of stalls when the girls ahead of them stopped to look at a souvenir display. Hoskins put his hand on Sergeant Chance's arm to slow him down.

Sian had picked up a plastic figurine, a comic dwarf, and was staring at it without interest. She transferred it from one hand to the other and then put it back on the counter. Side by side, the two girls surveyed the rest of the display. Then they turned and began walking towards the chariot ride.

'Hang on,' said Hoskins quietly. He walked to the stall and picked up the plastic dwarf by the tip of its ear. The man behind the counter was a breathless heavyweight with a squashed nose and oiled hair.

'How much?' Hoskins asked.

'Six quid. I'll get you one.'

'I want this one.'

'Sorry, squire, we sell 'em wrapped. That's display, marked so's it can't be thieved.'

The stallholder turned away enquiringly to someone else, as if making a point of his indifference to Hoskins. Hoskins spoke quietly but clearly enough to be heard.

'You had the Health and Safety Executive here lately about those cables? The ones running from the stall-lights back to the generator? Right little Spaghetti Junction. Someone might break a leg or a neck tripping over that lot. And those tapes that look like economy-sized band-aid wrapped round them – I reckon they'll have the inspectors giggling.'

The heavyweight drew breath for an expletive.

'Hello, Micky Finn,' said Sergeant Chance cheerfully. 'Remember me? Jack Chance. Canton "A" Division. Little matter of bouncing a stroppy student from the Blue Moon club down the Orient. Arm broken in two pieces.'

'I was acquitted,' the bully grizzled. 'I was provoked.'

'Then don't provoke my friend Mr Hoskins. He's doing you a good turn buying that. That's evidence, that is. He could just take it, give you a receipt and leave you six quid out of pocket.'

'You got no right.'

'I know,' said Chance sympathetically. 'You're a victim of police harassment. That's what you are. And this is where you tell us that it's ratepayers like you pay our wages.'

'I don't pay rates,' Finn said contemptuously. 'All right, take the bloody thing. Where's the six quid?'

Hoskins handed over the money.

'Thanks, Micky,' Chance said. 'See you again soon.'

By this time Sian and Maggie were being spun in the darkness by the chariot ride.

'What you want her prints for, Sam? Even if you could find 'em in the Cadillac, it's only what you'd expect.'

'Not the Cadillac, my son. It's where else they might show up that interests me. Come on, I'm not standing round here any longer. They're not going anywhere special. Ride on the big wheel, Chinese nosh down Rundle Street, then back home to give Big Daddy something special in the old three-seater bed. I wonder if that blonde puts her gym-slip back on to rejuvenate old Cooney?'

'There's a video the squad confiscated last week,' Chance said. 'All about that.'

CHAPTER SEVENTEEN

The sun was still lying in pools of candy-pink reflection on the sleek flanks of the mud channel as Hoskins and Chance parked outside the palatial Pierhead branch of the National Westminster. The tide had ebbed at sunset and the slack water of the dredged seaway was tranquil as a mountain pool. The long daylit evenings made the night-watch more agreeable in June. But on the far side of the street, the fringe of coloured bulbs was fully and unnecessarily lit round the old chapel doorway of the Realito Club.

'Wait here,' Hoskins said. 'If that little prick should happen to be in there, he'll try to do a runner. Fast on his feet is Neville the Mouse. Stand by to trip him as he bolts. You won't catch him otherwise.'

Chance yawned. 'Been on me bloody pins twenty-four hours. I'm not chasing after anyone. Any case, I can't see Cooney letting Neville lie up in the Realito. Not with the good old Mouse being wanted for murder. After all, he's Councillor Cooney now, or very nearly.'

'Not Cooney,' Hoskins scowled in the mirror. 'That punk tart of Neville's. The very charming Louise that he tows everywhere on a dog-leash. She flashes it here. The Mouse's best hope.'

He got out, slammed the door and crossed to the bulb-lit

entrance. A girl who was a stranger to him stood behind the desk in red matador pants, coatee and pill-box hat.

'Now,' said Hoskins reasonably, 'there's a young lady your age been tied to a bed, beaten, raped, suffocated and dumped in the sewer. I'm going in there to have a word with someone on the subject. I don't want to be mucked about and I don't want that phone of yours lifted so much as a whisker. Unless you'd fancy being done as an accessory. Okay?'

Her eyes travelled down to the misty green plastic of the warrant card.

'I think you'd better go in,' she said.

'Thanks.' Hoskins put the card away. 'There's a gentleman across the street in my car. He's watching you just now to see you're all right. And I'm sure he's listening in to that phone of yours.'

With a sense of achievement, he pushed open the baize doors and negotiated the heavy velvet curtain.

The Realito was the Petshop's poor relation. Dockland rats lived snug and undisturbed in its wall cavities and under the floorboards. The kitchen cockroaches went about their business with the panache of an elite cavalry regiment. Stage and auditorium, bar and dance floor were bathed in a subdued red glow. Intended to suggest the perverse pleasures of a satanic underworld, it also served to dim the squalor that might have alarmed its middle-class punters, the insurance brokers and commission reps from Clearwater or Lantern Hill.

Where the chancel and pulpit of the old Baptist Mission chapel had been, there was now a shallow stage. Where the Victorian congregations had bowed their heads on Sunday in the long pews, the dance floor was covered by little tables at which the couples sat. Here and there a man alone or a pair of men were with the club hostesses, the daughters of back-to-back houses in Barrier or Mount Pleasant high-rise. A long bar ran down one side of the room.

As Hoskins entered, the club dancers were lined up on the stage, performing to amplified music. The costumes of the chorus line were cheap and minimal, little more than a display of department-store underwear. He walked slowly and looked along the line for Louise.

She was there, high-kicking for the insurance brokers in her black silk stockings, black knickers that had a gloss like Japanese lacquer and a rosebudded corselette with the ritual suspender-straps. Arm-in-arm with the rest she kicked and grinned, fluttering the lashes of the saucer-eyes while the bold young face maintained its nervous self-assurance like an electrified fence against the eyes of young brokers and reps. The pale plumpness at the top of her thighs shimmered at every jolt. There was the regulation can-can kick that threatened to split the knickers open, the turning and the plump sticking-out of the bottom in a nicely balanced gesture of allure and disdain. The music stopped, there was a slight patting applause and the girls shuffled off as if they had just run a race.

Hoskins walked to the vestry door, as he still thought of it, and through into the dressing-rooms which had once resounded to portly choirs at practice on groaning evangelical hymns.

No one stopped him. No one even questioned him. The girls dressed and undressed collectively, but not one of them took the least notice of his arrival. They were there to amuse the punters. Screeching modesty was superfluous. One of them was naked but for her stockings. She glanced at him and then went on with her conversation. Louise was still in her costume, though the punk style of her slicked-back hair and the youth of her face were now more evident than on the stage. She saw Hoskins and took a step away, looking puzzled as if her memory of him was uncertain. Or perhaps she was not that bright.

'Don't run away,' he said gently. 'I just want a word. One side of the room, out of everybody's road.'

She said nothing, allowing herself to be led with his hand on her bare upper arm, unresisting and suddenly frail as a child.

'Neville the Mouse,' Hoskins said.

'I finished with him!' The interruption was a little too quick to be convincing. 'I never knew it was stolen. Honestly. I never knew the car was stolen.'

She was lying about that, he thought. But Neville had probably not told her of the last hectic hours with Angie. Even Neville could hardly be that stupid – or that arrogant. No point in frightening her with murder now; the Cadillac would do.

'Did the Mouse steal it?'

'I don't know. I'm finished with him. That's all.'

'Pity,' Hoskins said. 'I think he needs a friend. Someone like you.'

'Why's that?'

The blue dark-lashed saucer-eyes, so suggestive on the stage, looked scared and sham in reality.

'Someone who could make him see sense.' Hoskins tried to look wise and understanding. 'As it stands, he's got taking away and driving uninsured. There wasn't that much damage to the car, other than paintwork. But he's getting in deeper all the time. Touch-and-go at the moment whether we add assaulting a police officer, resisting arrest and attempted murder. A bit of cooperation could help a lot.'

'In what way?'

'The business in Martello Square. That could be put on the shelf. Just taking away and driving, he might get six months. Attempting to murder a couple of police officers, he could pull five or six years. You could kiss goodbye to whatever he was going to do for you. Whatever that was.'

He saw the misery blooming in her young face like a growth and regretted his deceit. Then he thought of Angie in the storm drain and the regret was lost. A false move by Louise and she would go the same way after an hour or two of hell on earth, with the Mouse's compliments.

'I don't know,' she said miserably. 'He went home after I saw him last. Four days ago.'

'And suppose he's not at home now?'

'I don't know,' she wailed. 'He might be with Breaker. The one they call Breaker.'

'And suppose Breaker's not home?'

'I don't know!' The first tears and anger shone in her eyes. 'I don't bloody well know! Can't you see?'

'All right,' said Hoskins reasonably, 'fair enough. We'll let it go at that. One thing, though. If you harbour him, you'll be done as an accessory. And that means accessory to two charges of attempted murder. Not six years, I daresay, but three or four. Banged up with a couple of seasoned prison ladies in a cell. Not that you'd exactly go to waste. You'd hardly get a wink of sleep.'

Not for the first time, he had made an old mistake. Threats had no effect on Louise and her kind. There were too many immediate burdens in the life of Barrier and the Peninsula for their people to worry about what might or might not happen after that. In any case, opinion held that the police seldom caught anyone and a good many of those caught got off lightly. And this opinion was supported by official statistics. Louise turned away and sat down on a stool with her back to him. She lowered her head and began to weep. But Hoskins had heard a good many people cry in the course of his duties. The tears of Louise were not of apprehension but the relief of one who has got away with it – for the time being.

He went back outside to Jack Chance.

'Put the word out. Policewoman Sally Barnes and Sergeant Bragg to go in. Cosy plain-clothes drink for two. Young Louise to be followed from now on. Anstey in his taxi starts cruising at midnight. Now take me to the Mouse's gaff.'

They turned off Dyce Street and across Martello Square. Beyond the tomb-like berths of the dry docks, a row of houses in Edwardian stone looked out across the mud-flats and the dredged channel. The door of one of them was open. On closer inspection, the wood near the lock had been splintered by a sledge-hammer. Two cars were drawn up outside and the uniformed driver of one of them was talking into his radio. A pair of men in dark berets, combat jackets and black trousers sat side by side on the low sea-wall. Hoskins nodded at the damaged door.

'Tom Nicholls came calling, then,' he said cheerfully.

'And our little Special Patrol Group.' Chance nodded at the pair of men sitting on the wall. 'Tweedledum and Tweedledee. Wogs flogged by appointment to Her Majesty. Queers bashed while you wait. Never a shot fired in anger.'

'Shut up,' said Hoskins warningly.

Someone saluted as they went through the doorway and up the stairs. The Mouse had occupied the first floor.

'Bugger-all here, Jack,' said Dudden to Chance at the head of the stairs.

'Candlewick bedspread?'

129

'Nah! There wouldn't be, would there? He's not that bloody simple. There's sod all.'

Hoskins pushed past and found the rooms taped off. Two dark-suited men from forensic were going carefully over the carpet and soft furnishings. A uniformed constable was reading out the contents of a drawer.

'One wrist-watch. One Boots instamatic camera. One packet of processed photographs, dated last week. One string of beads. . . .'

'Rosary,' said Hoskins the pedant.

The policeman looked up.

'Bloody hell, boss! Don't tell me he got religion.'

Hoskins grunted.

'Him and Carmel Cooney both. Pupils of Cardinal Vaughan primary school, same as Archbishop Lewis. A long time apart, though.'

The uniformed man sniffed his disgust.

'Hand over those photographs,' Hoskins said encouragingly.

'No good, boss. They were done before she died. Dated ten days ago. Must have been taken a fortnight back at least.'

'Let's have a look, even so.'

'If Mr Nicholls says so,' the man suggested.

Nicholls appeared from the other room.

'All right, Sam. Shake 'em out by the corner of the envelope and hold 'em by the edges.'

Hoskins went downstairs and used the table in the hall.

The pictures seemed to be of the Mouse and his family, whoever they might be. There was an indoor scene, all paper hats and grins. He came to the last two.

'Oh boy,' he said softly to Chance 'cop this pair!'

There was no doubt about it. The photographs had been taken on the Cakewalk. By the look of them the day had been bright but cold, men and women still wearing winter coats. Two of the promenaders were in self-conscious and earnest conversation. One was clear in both pictures as Sian Jones. The other, seen only from the back in the first shot, had been caught unmistakably in the second one as the late Robin Redlitch-Smith.

Hoskins glared at Chance, daring him to say a word. He went back upstairs and handed the packet to Nicholls.

'Nothing here for us, Tom.'

'Nothing here for anyone, most likely,' Nicholls said, 'I don't think they screwed her here or killed her here. Doesn't make sense with people all round.'

'And Breaker Weekes?'

'No sign of him either. Morgan's lot are spinning his drum just now, as they say. I had a quick word. Nothing obvious there. Certainly not the famous candlewick bedspread that she'd got on her jacket and in her hair.'

'No,' said Hoskins. 'Still, they'd burn that first thing, wouldn't they?'

There was too much excitement in his mind just then to talk further with Nicholls. He went out to Chance in the car.

'We're on our way, my son! Confession time is here.'

'How's that then, Sam?'

Hoskins smiled.

'I wonder what Cooney's going to do to that red-haired tart of his when he discovers.'

'Discovers what?'

'That young Sian Jones was singing for Robbo Smith like she was auditioning for Mimi.'

'Who's Mimi?'

'Don't be a prick,' said Hoskins severely. 'That's how Smith did it! That's how he got the gen on the Mount Pleasant swindle. Through Cooney's tart. When she knows that we know, she is going to be the most cooperative witness we ever had.'

'Poor little bitch,' said Chance philosophically.

'The Mouse knows it too,' said Hoskins triumphantly. 'I want that little bugger. All in all, Jack Chance, we've got our story. Robbo Smith gets at Sian, gets the Mount Pleasant story through her. Cooney finds out Robbo's interest, perhaps by courtesy of the Mouse and his camera. Next thing, our investigative reporter is nudged off the cliff.'

'And why doesn't Cooney take it out on Sian's hide?'

Hoskins thought about this.

'Perhaps he did. Then they kissed and made up. Stranger things happen. And perhaps she's the Mouse's next contract, after Angie. Her turn on the candlewick bedspread with Cooney paying the bill.'

'She didn't act scared,' Chance said, 'just rather stupid.'

'Then perhaps she doesn't know,' Hoskins said. But he frowned at the last grey skyline of the day beyond the mud-flats. The final part of his theory seemed not to fit. Chance was right about that. Carmel Cooney did not forgive. By now, Sian ought to have undergone the fate of Angie. Multiplied in Cooney's case to the power of ten. But Chance was right. Sian was alive and well. And she didn't even look scared.

And that bothered Inspector Hoskins.

CHAPTER EIGHTEEN

'There's this one when Eve Ricard gets adopted to stand for parliament,' said Chance, grinning. He pulled out of the car park and turned into the Mall. 'Anyway, she goes before the selection committee and they think she's terrific. Just the job. But when they tell her she's got it, she says, "I think I ought to mention something. I'm a practising lesbian." And the chairman says, "That's interesting. Are you getting any better at it?" See? Practising. Getting better at it!'

'Yes,' said Hoskins tolerantly. 'I think I can just about see that. Through Orient to Lantern Hill. I promised Harold Moyle a look-in.'

'Schoolgirls!' said Chance enviously. 'Young at heart, and all that.'

'Car-to-car for Chief Inspector Hoskins. Alexander Morant Neville and companion, thought to be Weekes, under observation at the junction of Great Western Street and Atlantic Wharf. Please advise.'

With a fierce exultation, Hoskins put the radio to his mouth.

'Hoskins. Received and understood. I want the eight officers on standby to proceed to Great Western Street car park. Two cars and unmarked van. Maintain observation on subject. On no account approach or attempt to apprehend before rendezvous. He's as slippery as a greased monkey.'

Chance accelerated past the parked yellow buses in King Edward Square, down Great Western Street, and pulled into the car park behind Jones and Gower's with a satisfying screech of tyres and a jolt of brakes.

Hoskins put the radio to his mouth again.

'I want the man on the beat direct. Where's Neville and what's he doing?'

There was a pause, a murmur of voices, and then the foot patrol came on.

'PC Ozanne, boss, and WPC Walters. We've got the two of them in view from the coffee stall in the Plain. One's definitely Neville. I think the other's Weekes. They just seem to be looking in the window of the Royal Emporium. Pointing and laughing at something, then looking round at the traffic. Could be they're waiting for a lift. Or waiting for someone else to show up.'

'Keep watching,' Hoskins said. 'If they move off on foot, follow sensibly and tell me. If they get a lift, I want the vehicle number at once. In about three minutes from now, you'll have two cars and a van on watch with you. Don't try to catch those two jokers on your own. The Mouse is a knife artist.'

'Right-o, boss,' said the disembodied Ozanne. 'Another thing, it's after lunch. Looking at it from here, they could be pissed.'

Hoskins glared through the windscreen at the heat of the June afternoon shimmering from the bonnet of the car and the tarmac surface.

The first of the other cars arrived, followed by the plain white van.

'You never said anything about a couple of marksmen, Mr Hoskins,' said Sergeant Driscoll enquiringly. 'They're putting two of them on the roof of the central library just in case.'

'In the middle of a crowded shopping centre?' said Hoskins sardonically. 'Whose flash of inspiration was that?'

'Dunno, boss. Mr Ripley's, I suppose. After all, if Neville's carrying one, we could be up shit-creek without a back-up.'

Hoskins turned briefly to Chance with a face of despair. Then he began his briefing.

'Right! I want DI Grimshaw's crew parked by Balance Street river bridge, in case they try doing a bunk towards the Peninsula. That's most likely. Anything goes wrong with me, DI Grimshaw is in command of the operation. Right? Sergeant Dooley with Crayle and Fleming, British Rail short-term car park. Cut them off the other way. Both lots keep your eyes and glasses on 'em. If you can't see direct, post a look-out. Sergeant Chance, Rutter, Pope, and me in the white van. The van comes down Great Western Street and parks just short of the Royal Peninsular Emporium. I'll give it a minute, then cruise forward. When you see that, close in. Four of us come out of the back of the van and grab them. If they get clear, it's down to the rest of you to head them off. For fuck's sake watch Neville's knife. Now, go!'

'And me, boss?' the spare driver asked.

'Take Sergeant Chance's mobile, the Fiesta. Park across Atlantic Wharf. If you see any vehicle pick up Neville and Weekes – or Neville alone – block it off. If necessary, ram the bloody thing.'

The first two cars were already turning out into Great Western Street as Hoskins and the others clambered into the back of the traveller. Hoskins put the radio to his mouth again.

'Chief Inspector Hoskins to foot patrol direct. What's happening?'

'Nothing, boss,' said Ozanne's voice reassuringly. 'Still there. Larking about with the girl in the store window, by the look of it. I'd say they were well pissed. There's two mobiles passing us here . . . turning on to Atlantic Wharf opposite ways. Just out of sight. You come down now, and that's the cork in the bottle. And there's Desperate Dan in his black macho-suit and telescopics, waving about on the library roof. All he needs is a loud-hailer in case anyone hasn't seen him yet.'

'Boy's Own Sodding Paper,' said Hoskins ungratefully. He turned to the driver. 'All right, let's go before someone gets shot.'

The width of Atlantic Wharf lay across the far end of Great Western Street, like the crossing of a T. By blocking Balance Street at one end of the Wharf and the British Rail approach at the other, Hoskins need only come down Great Western Street itself and the trap was closed. It was so easy that he knew it was not going to work. The Mouse was a great improviser.

The blinds of the department stores were drawn out to shade the pavements from the summer heat. Traffic was moderately heavy in Great Western Street, the bus lane clogged by two double-deckers and the cars moving slowly. The Royal Peninsular Emporium occupied the right-hand corner at the far end, its windows curving round and facing on to Atlantic Wharf as well. On the opposite corner was the Paris Hotel with its Brasserie Magenta and Madame Jolly Modes.

The drab stone of the old Carnegie Library was half-way down Great Western Street, with the coffee stall beside it.

'Pull in here,' Hoskins said.

He looked ahead of them, through the windscreen. The Emporium had been built in the pale stone of the banquet years of Edwardian prosperity and extended in the ivory-white of 1920s modernism. The sweep of its long display windows was rounded at the corners, catching reflected light dazzlingly in the June sun. The glass was set in ornate cast-iron frames with swirls of Art Nouveau and 'Peninsular Emporium' in raised italic script along the base. The 'Royal' had come in the 1930s, during a visit by the uncrowned Edward VIII. High above the sun-blinds, a frieze of attenuated dancers in bas-relief ran above the second-floor windows.

The Mouse and Breaker Weekes were standing by the second window along, kicking their heels, turning in amusement at something in the display and then scanning the street again.

'Right,' said Hoskins into the radio. 'Everyone here? Tango Alpha?'

'Yes, boss,' said Dooley from the station car park. 'We can see 'em. Can't see you yet.'

'You will do,' said Hoskins patiently. 'Tango Delta?'

'Yes, boss. Can't see 'em from here. They're round a corner from us. But we've got the Peninsula route well sewn up and Mac standing out by the railway wall to keep us briefed.'

'Right,' Hoskins said. 'Everyone keep quiet and ready.'

They waited in the fierce glare of the year's first heat-wave.

Chance turned in his seat. 'What's up, Sam?'

'They could be waiting for someone. Give it a minute and see if anyone comes. And tell Ozanne and his WPC to go in the store by the other way, alert the manager and keep watch from inside. I want them there before we move.'

Women in loose blouses and summer cottons made the pavement look cool in the heat. Great Western Street was crowded on a Thursday afternoon but not exceptionally so. Across the broad square of Atlantic Wharf, the railway embankment on Harbour Wall closed the view. The sky above it seemed paler and sun-bleached by the reflected brilliance of light from a calm summer ocean. In Hoskins' boyhood it had been possible to see the masts of Atlantic traders above the railway bank. Now King Edward Dock was empty, apart from fat and shallow container vessels in the Outer Basin. But that afternoon, the air of the Wharf in summer was as he had always known it. It was dusty with a thunder smell of hot metal and coal, overlaid by a fug of boiling malt from Jupp's German Brewery beyond the railway station.

'What the hell's he doing?'

Chance had the glasses trained on the Mouse and his companion. They were grinning and scuffing, staring into the window with its summer fashions on anorexic wax dummies. There was an old-fashioned depth to the windows and an opulence in the goods displayed. A girl with a mane of Pre-Raphaelite ringlets was setting out a display of fashion jewellery among the figures. In her plain jeans and singlet, she was distinguishable only by her hair, her rather bold features and her height.

'Who's that, then?' Pope asked. 'Not one of the Mouse's tarts?'

Chance yawned. 'Fuck knows. Could be. On the game in her spare time. Anyone recognise her?'

'Nah, c'mon.'

'They're winding her up,' Hoskins said. 'That's all.'

The young window-dresser was glancing uneasily at the pair. She returned to her work, only to look round and find the Mouse grinning at her. As she glanced back while stooping, Neville made an upward and unambiguous gesture with something in his hand. The girl flinched and stood up.

'Saucy little bastard,' Pope said.

'What we waiting for, Sam?'

'Let's just see if she's with them. I want the lot of them this time.'

The two young men seemed to lose interest in the girl. She was polishing on all fours round a white display pedestal when the Mouse turned and gestured again behind her, drawing the crotch of his jeans tighter.

'He's bloody flashing at her, Sam!'

The girl looked again at the leering satyr-face, scrambled to her feet and fled from the window.

'Here we go,' Hoskins said quietly into his radio. The van signalled to turn out into the stream of traffic. No one gave way.

'Give 'em a blast on the horn,' Chance said.

'No!' said Hoskins sharply. 'I don't want them looking this way. Just push the nose of this thing out. Smile nicely at that punter in the Volvo.'

'Will you look at that!' Chance screamed. 'The cheeky little bastards!'

Neville and Weekes had moved with a speed that belied their lunchtime drinking. As the girl disappeared, the Mouse pushed open the swing door, entered the store and made for the hardboard door of the window.

'Get over there,' Hoskins snapped.

The Mouse was in the window now, gathering up the fashion jewellery and stuffing his pockets. If the assistants or the customers noticed anything amiss, they averted their eyes. There was no extra pay for wrestling with a Peninsula thief and his knife. Neville came out again to join Weekes just as the white van skidded to a halt. Pope and Chance jumped out first. Hoskins saw Weekes turn, but the Breaker was too late. Chance was on him, knocking him to the pavement and twisting his arms behind his back.

Pope, a dark and heavily built thirty-year-old, made the mistake of grabbing the Mouse by the collar of his leather jacket. The Mouse hardly seemed to move beyond a slight shrug. Pope, holding the jacket and nothing else, lost his balance as the fugitive broke from him. He came down on his knees among the shoppers. The Mouse, in a leisured moment, aimed a kick at Chance's ribs as the sergeant wrestled with Weekes. Chance, evading the second boot, collided with Rutter and lost his grip on the Breaker. What should have been a swift arrest had turned into a loose and panting maul among shopping-trolleys and gently smiling pensioners, looking about them for the arrival of the candid camera team.

Hoskins kept his eye on Neville, aware that Breaker Weekes had bolted somewhere in the direction of the Paris Hotel with Rutter now pounding after him.

Like a greyhound released from the trap, the Mouse sprang forward with Hoskins and Chance in pursuit. Hoskins heard Pope emit a monosyllabic 'Shit!' of pain and snarling frustration and the voice of a shopper raised on behalf of public decency. Worst of all, the Mouse had dodged through the swing doors and back into the Royal Peninsular Emporium itself. It was precisely what the pincer movement had been intended to prevent. As Hoskins raced after Neville he was dismally aware that the headers-off, led by Dooley and Grimshaw, were now running the wrong way.

'Stand back!' Hoskins bawled at the customers thronging the lower floor and, to his surprise, they did as he asked. No one intervened. No one 'had a go'. The shoppers in the Emporium were not the stuff of which George Medallists were made. Chance was sprinting round the far side of the perfume counter under the pale ceiling lights and plastic fans, trying to cut off the Mouse's escape. Hoskins lost sight of the fugitive beyond the white-lit glass signs for Rochas and Chanel.

Then he saw him again, the rangy figure with the shaved coffee-brown head and easy movement. The Mouse glanced and saw them closing on him from two sides. He took a run, hurdled a make-up counter, knocked down the girl behind it and gathered speed on his new course.

'Lock the doors!' Hoskins shouted to anyone who would listen. There was no sign of the manager, nor of Ozanne or his policewoman. Where the hell, he wondered, was everyone?

'Someone grab the fucker or he'll be out the other side!' Chance panted at Hoskins' side. Despite his age, Hoskins was in better condition than his plump sergeant. The creamy confectionery odours of the perfume counters gave way to the chemical tang of new cloth and ammoniac cleaning fluid in the men's outfitting. The Mouse was still in sight, the brown cropped head bobbing easily beyond the staring faces of the crowd.

Then the unbelievable happened. The Mouse caught his foot

and went sprawling. He rolled, sat up hugging his knee and then stumbled to his feet.

'Hold him!' Chance screamed to anyone who would listen. Nobody held him. The Mouse swept a shelf of cut-glass to the floor to impede the pursuit and lolloped onwards. There were smells of meat and warm pastry in the air now. It was the Food Hall and the far entrance on Atlantic Wharf. The Mouse plunged through the doorway and into the dazzling afternoon again.

By the time Hoskins emerged, the fugitive was pulling away across the width of the square towards the incline that led up to the pavilioned entrance of the British Rail booking hall and the railway embankment. As if a second miracle had happened, Hoskins saw that Dooley and his two constables were still with their car outside the station entrance. Why they had ignored the order to close in as the Mouse and Breaker Weekes were grabbed, he had no idea. But now the Mouse found his route blocked by the three men, of whom Dooley was known to him at once. He hesitated, looked back and saw Hoskins, then turned aside and began to run straight at the railway bank. Hoskins, with boots of lead and jacket flapping like a sail, breathed deeply and raced after him.

The Mouse vaulted the fence at the bottom of the bank and began to scramble up. Hoskins jumped at the top of the fence boards, caught hold and heaved himself up with an effort. Chance was somewhere behind him. So were Dooley and his crew. There was a shout above him and he saw that Breaker Weekes was already at the top of the incline, encouraging the Mouse to follow. How the Breaker had managed to get clear so fast was something Hoskins never learnt. The Mouse was up the bank as well, standing beside the welded track of the high-speed rail. He looked at Hoskins, turned and began running down the line with Weekes, towards the bridge. It crossed the Town River parallel with Balance Street.

Once across the rail bridge, the Mouse and his friend had only to shin down the bank, into the little streets of Peninsula or the flats of Dyce Street, and disappear for good. Hoskins made one last effort.

The four tracks of the main line to London crossed the bridge in two pairs, flanked by the heavy studded girderwork of Victorian Meccano. Weekes and the Mouse were still ahead at the bridge, following the double track with a breast-high steel-plate wall either side and a gap before the metal fence of the up line to Paddington. As if to demonstrate his dexterity, the Mouse put his hands on the roll top of the dividing steel wall, preparing to vault it and run along the narrow alley between the metal fences of the up and down lines.

Disaster came so aptly and quickly that it was almost comic. Perhaps the Mouse had been drinking at lunchtime, after all. But it was natural to assume that a pebbled space lay between the two sets of tracks. Hoskins had no idea whether it did or not. Only as the Mouse vaulted over did he realise that the up and down tracks were two separate bridges. Where Neville expected to land on an intervening path, there was nothing but a drop straight down to the dark river-water twenty or thirty feet below.

The Mouse fell without a cry and the splash came faintly as if from a great distance. There was a shout from behind Hoskins and he knew that Dooley had seen the accident. Breaker Weekes stood dumbfounded, staring down with a look of mesmerised horror. But it was Hoskins who was nearest.

He turned and clambered over the wall at the station end of the bridge, skidding and slipping down the bank towards the water. The cocoa-coloured tide of the Town River was slack just then but the approach was difficult. Above the mud-banks, the Victorian engineers had edged the river under the bridge with steeply inclining stonework. Hoskins slithered down with a precarious hold. The Mouse had broken surface about thirty feet out, the water streaming from his bare brown scalp.

'Get a rope!' Hoskins shouted and heard one of Dooley's men echo the command above him. Under the edge of the lapping brown water he tested the surface and felt his foot sink into mud that was soft as custard.

'For God's sake, Sam!' Chance shouted. 'You won't get out again!'

The Mouse went under with a look of quiet resignation, then broke surface in a sudden threshing. Despite the distance, the astonished eyes seemed in dreadful proximity to Hoskins' own. The two men looked at one another briefly and the Mouse went under again.

Chance was beside him.

'His leg's caught in metal. Car door or something hinged, I think. You can't get him out this way. Half a dozen steps on that mud and you'll be in over your head. And you can't jump in midstream without hitting a wheel or some other bit of wreckage dropped in there.'

The Mouse came up very slowly and the face looked in mild surprise at what was happening to him. He opened his mouth as if to say something and then appeared to forget what it was. Just as slowly he sank below the brown water again.

'Drop him something to grab hold of! A spar or a wooden pole. Give him something!'

Someone was running from the station platform. But the plan was never going to work. Suddenly the Mouse appeared again, leaping breast high, drawing breath, sinking again. He leapt breast-high once more, like a hooked fish, in a mute and desperate attempt to free himself from the metal of the wheel or car door that dragged him down. Then the water closed and was still.

'Hold on to me,' said Hoskins grimly. Chance held him by one arm but it was hopeless. Within three steps the cool suction of the mud was at Hoskins' thighs.

'For God's sake, Sam! You'll sink in that before there's enough water to swim in.'

'Tie something round me and hold on.'

'Tie what?'

In the confusion above, an angry voice was shouting at the plain-clothes men on the bridge.

'Get off the line! There's a 125 from Paddington due in a few minutes! You'll be pulled into the slipstream if you're anywhere near it!'

Hoskins took a step back from the waterlogged sludge and looked round him.

'I think he's got a rope. The supervisor. Coming down the track from the station. Something coiled. I'm going for it. He's never going to hurry at his age.'

He climbed awkwardly up the bank and began to run along the track the way he had come. Perhaps it was the pain in his own lungs that held in mind the dreadful last struggle in the stinking water of the Town River. The Mouse sinking into the nightmare drifts of mud twenty feet below daylight, holding his breath until the bursting ache in his lungs forced it from him. The first minute was over by now in the cold roaring darkness of the head and the terrible padded silence of the river bottom. Hoskins passed the disused signal box, its windows ritually smashed, running awkwardly on the railway shingle, his trousers wet and heavy below the knees. Second minute, the convulsive and instinctive inhaling, the cold of the water scorching the lungs like fire. Pressed to death. The rosary. Perhaps the Mouse in his sudden peril was trying to remember a long neglected formula of contrition. The last of many swift deals. Third minute. The explosions in the brain like the blowing of one circuit after another. Limpness and blackness.

Hoskins stopped running. The supervisor coming towards him was holding a lifebelt, not a rope. It was no more use now than a block of granite. One way or another, the hope and the horror were both over.

When he reached the station, there were small groups of people on the platform, trying not to look inquisitive. Someone was coming towards him.

'We got the frogmen on their way, boss,' Rutter said helpfully. 'And the supervisor phoned through. He stopped the 3.15 Pierhead local at Taylorstown. And they're trying to hold the London 125 at the Mason's Arms signal.'

Hoskins heard the whooping-crane siren of the ambulance or the fire brigade. He prayed for the Mouse's sake that he was beyond hearing such things, faintly and mockingly above the water that scalded his lungs in a last riot of choking spasms. The only charity for Neville was to wish him quickly dead.

Breaker Weekes was brought back along the track in handcuffs five minutes later. There were firemen in yellow safety suits and white helmets on the bridge and an ambulance close by. Like a traveller without a ticket, Hoskins went down the platform steps and through the tiled subway. Above the exit, greeting the new arrival, was an advertising banner with a grinning and gormless cartoon family of all ages. Jovial and gormless mum and dad, grinning and gormless kids, jolly and gormless grandma and grandpa. 'Welcome to Canton,' the banner said, 'where the Best Things in Life Are Free! And the Good Things Cost Just a Little More from Cooney's Royal Peninsular Emporium!'

Ignoring the ticket collector, he walked out again into the hot petrol-hazed sunlight of Atlantic Wharf.

CHAPTER NINETEEN

'Whichever way you look at it, Sam,' said the Ripper coolly, 'it was not the most professional operation this Division has ever carried out.'

Hoskins sat at his desk in the fluorescent-lit office, while Ripley occupied the space before him.

'We've got Weekes banged up,' he said firmly. 'What happened to Neville was his own doing. He jumped from a bridge into a river. Whose fault's that?'

Ripley curved his fingers and examined the nails critically.

'If he was in terror of his life, Sam, the fault may be yours.'

'Bollocks!' said Hoskins stubbornly. 'A known villain, wanted for the attempted murder of two police officers, car theft, suspicion of raping, beating and murdering that biker's girl. Not to mention involvement in the Robbo Smith case. He does a runner from old Pope and the rest of us. Jumps down where he thinks there's ground and finds there's none.'

'Terrified by you and your thugs. You, Sam, shouting at him, calling him a black bastard, promising him a kicking to put his kidneys out of action for good. He cried out in terror and jumped with you close enough behind him to push him off.'

Hoskins fought against an encroaching cloud of incomprehension.

'I wouldn't be that daft, Max.'

'Breaker Weekes heard your every word. He'll swear to it in court.'

'A car thief and arsonist, also up to his neck in the Martello Square business and the biker's girl!'

'But not charged, Sam. Let alone convicted.'

Hoskins got up, scowling at Ripley.

'Let's see who a jury believes. I'd just done an Olympic half-mile after the Mouse, through the Emporium, across Atlantic Wharf, up a fifty-foot embankment and half-way down the line to Taylorstown. He's more than twenty years younger than me, and fit with it. If I'd been close enough behind him to push him off the bridge, I'd be a biological miracle. And the stuff about black bastard and the kidneys! Be your age, Max! Someone else would have heard me, supposing I'd had the breath to shout the odds while also setting up a world long-distance record.'

Ripley frowned at his nails. 'That's the way it stands, Sam.'

Hoskins piled his paperwork aside, as if preparing to go home.

'Then we'll see who the jury believes.'

'This one may believe Weekes.'

'This one?' Hoskins continued stacking Form 52. 'Got a special jury, have we?'

Ripley checked a small yawn and eased the fingers of one hand with those of the other.

'I'm talking about a coroner's jury, Sam. An inquest. The criminality of these two youths will not be the issue. Your conduct will be. Mr Lobo is representing the Neville family. You are being subpoena'd as a witness. That's what I wanted to tell you. I can't say I envy you.'

'Lobo?'

'Yes, Sam. He will no doubt remind you that Neville was technically under arrest after Pope apprehended him. A suspect under arrest is entitled to certain forms of protection, even against his own suicidal urges. He is not to be hounded into the path of high-speed trains or forced to jump to a watery grave. I'd say, Sam, that your most prized appendages are now laid out on the chopping-board for Mr Lobo's hatchet.'

Against the pale globes of iron lamps in the Mall below them, Hoskins saw the trees toss fitfully in the night wind, like the heads of restive horses.

'I think I can look after Mr Lobo, Max.'

Ripley smiled, pitying such self-reliance.

'I doubt it, Sam. If I were you, I'd approach the Federation for a spot of professional advice. They may not put up a lawyer, but they can tell you how to keep your nose clean.'

'My nose is clean enough,' Hoskins said.

Ripley gave the subject up. But instead of leaving the chief inspector to himself, he sat down on the other chair.

'I mentioned the subpoena as a friend, Sam. There's an official matter, however. I'd rather you heard it first.'

By some means unknown to him, they had found out about Lesley. It was Hoskins' first thought.

'Mount Pleasant,' the Ripper said. Hoskins relaxed.

'Mount Pleasant?'

'You and I have a problem, Sam. The city architect's department has examined every load-bearing beam in the flats that are coming down. All were filled with aggregate to the correct specification. The prefabricated sections were made and fitted with some care. The architect says there's not the least evidence of the frauds that you – or rather Robbo Smith – suggested.'

'Early days, Max,' said Hoskins uneasily.

'Afraid not, Sam. You don't have to take a building down nowadays to examine it. The Civil Engineering Department in the University uses what you might call an X-ray scan. They've been most co-operative. A full survey is now in progress. Indeed, the architects say it's three-quarters over. One or two beams look a bit dodgy, but that's well below par for the course. Certainly nothing corrupt nor criminal. Nothing that Carmel Cooney could be in trouble over.'

Hoskins stood up again.

'Robbo Smith was rammed off that cliff by Cooney's car. That means Cooney's in trouble over something.'

The Ripper shrugged as they went together towards the door. Standing with Hoskins in the corridor, he mellowed quite uncharacteristically.

'Sam,' he said wearily, 'we've worked together a good few years. If you go down, it won't give me any pleasure at all. But they'll break you, if you push that way too hard. With Neville being killed and the Martello Square riots, you are dangerously deep in the municipal excrement, if I may put it politely. Very nearly nostril-deep, from what I hear upstairs.'

The Ripper walked away slowly towards his door. A natural concern for his subordinate was not entirely unmixed with satisfaction at Hoskins' predicament.

Without speaking to anyone, Hoskins went down to the car park and sat behind the wheel of his car. The warm day had faded from a summer glow into the first lamplight. Neither day nor night. What he needed more than anything else was warmth, a bed and the young woman to share it with him. As he turned the Vauxhall Cavalier into the Mall, he had no idea whether she would be at Lantern Hill or if she would be alone. In a cold moment he imagined his arrival and the appearance of another man from the bedroom or kitchen. But there was, he decided, nowhere else to go.

He drove past the length of the brown stone Keep, opposite the shops of Longwall. Through the archways there were glimpses of the parkland inside. A Florentine clock-tower, its woodwork picked out in red and gold, was the work of the Victorian designer Augustus Welby Pugin. Hoskins remembered the name from school. In the twilight, a few joggers were still lurching heavy-footed among the late pale daffodils.

There was no other man. Lesley, unsuitably dressed in a long skirt and boots, was changing a stair-well light bulb by the aid of a flimsy chair.

'I could reach that,' Hoskins said helpfully. 'Give us the bulb a minute.'

She brushed her fringe into place and watched him reaching up.

'I didn't expect you,' she said enquiringly. 'I didn't prepare anything.'

He tested the light switch. 'I didn't expect to be here.'

Something in his voice seemed to make her suddenly ashamed of her objection.

'It's all right,' she said quietly. 'I didn't mean you not to come.'

Without discussing the matter, they went together to the bedroom and sat down on the quilt.

'You may hear some things, or see them in the papers,' Hoskins said, 'about the business of Neville. The inquest could be nasty. His friend is prepared to say that I called him a black bastard, threatened to smash his kidneys, and hounded him till he jumped to his death in the river.'

'But you didn't.'

It was not quite a question and not quite a statement.

Hoskins sighed.

'I'd been after him for about half a mile. He was twenty years old and a sprinter with it. I reckon he'd got about thirty yards ahead when he came to the bridge. Once he was over it, he'd be into the Peninsula and away. I was on my bloody knees by then. I couldn't croak, let alone shout. I went into the mud to try and get him out but you can't do it. That mud is soft as cotton wool with the seepage under it. You have to get across it to the water before you start swimming. But you can't get across it without sinking in over your head. That's how it happened. No ladders and no lifebelts there, because you don't think of people falling into the river from the railway bridge.'

For the first time the defensive and dismissive young face under the long parted fringe of her hair became trusting.

'I know you,' she said. 'That's why it doesn't matter. I don't think you'd go round calling people black bastards.'

He shook his head.

'When I was a kid in school, there were lads with all sorts of names and some of 'em good at high jump or whatever. No one thought about it. It wasn't till years later that I looked back and realised, of course, old Boyd must have been Jamaican or old Noel was Asian. We never thought about it. Now there's so many vested interests that they won't let you think about anything else.'

Lesley stood up, hands on hips, legs braced aggressively.

'Come on,' she said.

The spur-of-the-moment visits were always the best, when they worked. It was Hoskins who undid the blouse and then watched the more complicated removal of the skirt.

'I like the boots on the bare legs,' he said presently. 'That's nice.'

'Male conditioning,' she said with mock disapproval, tugging them off. 'The ladies in the magazines.'

He watched her a moment more. Then he assumed the mask of the Boy Hoskins, with the acne and the nicotined fingers.

147

'Turn round a minute,' he said encouragingly, 'and show us your bum.'

Lesley glared at him briefly, and then turned round.

It was, he supposed, all the tension of the past twenty-four hours that found such release between them that evening. He still could not quite understand why such a perversely plain young woman should inspire the sexual energy in him that Lesley did. Not that it mattered. Hoskins was not complaining. They lay together uncovered in the warm room, while his lips teased her in ways that might defy even Eve Ricard's imagination.

'I'm going to get some supper,' she said at last, impatient and a little ungrateful. 'You must be starving.'

Hoskins chortled at the banality of it. After a while he followed her down to the kitchen. The television was on, flickering in dumb-show, while Lesley in her briefs and sweater emptied a tin of ratatouille into a saucepan.

'You don't mind, do you?' She indicated the silent images. 'Eve's on after the news. Coast Way, Facing Facts. She and your friend.'

'What friend?'

'Councillor Cooney.'

'Bloody hell!'

He went out to the car and returned a few minutes later to find two plates of food ready at the kitchen table. The heads on the screen were already talking.

'But then,' Eve Ricard was saying primly, 'I don't think that Councillor Cooney and I have much in common on the subject. He stands for the exploitation of women's sexuality in ways that the modern world finds outmoded and unacceptable.'

There she was, Hoskins noticed. The little-boy shortie and the blue eye-shadow, the display of icy sexuality and the assured nasal whine of the classless educated voice. The new ruling caste.

'Unacceptable in what way?' The youthfully grey host of the show leant forward helpfully.

'The kind of display that you might see in Councillor Cooney's so-called clubs. The treating of young women as objects, as animals. His support for a tightening-up of the obscenity laws is an insult to the intelligence of the electorate.'

'The Petshop?'

Before Eve Ricard could agree with the host's suggestion, Cooney had intervened. He sat in his leatherette swivel chair, well back and well down, like a portly jovial uncle. The fat that made him repulsive in life suggested geniality in the blander tones of the screen.

'On a point of information,' he said, smiling comfortably, 'I don't own any clubs and I never have. Now, of course, I wouldn't go all the way with Eve, but I expect we've more in common on these matters than she thinks. I don't want to see women exploited or degraded. Course I don't. Where's the pleasure in that? And the people don't want it either. What we as a party have proposed – right from the top, from Margaret Thatcher on – is a law that would censor what is grossly offensive to a reasonable person. Now where's the harm in that?'

'The harm,' said Eve Ricard shrilly, 'is in the degrading display that women are forced to provide for money in the clubs run by Councillor Cooney. . . .'

But he was at her again, the jovial finger-wagging uncle.

'You find a club that's owned by me, Eve, and I will contribute one thousand pounds to any charity you care to name.'

He sat back, smiling at the interviewer.

'The Petshop,' the host said reasonably.

Cooney's melon head gaped in a wider grin.

'I'm a long way from owning that, sir. I have a very few shares in a public company that owns the lease of the old Winter Garden premises. Bought to save a fine building from being pulled down. Part of all our lives, it was. But I tell you this, Mr Grove. If the Petshop was to put on a grossly offensive act of any kind there, I'd sell my shares tomorrow.'

'But it does!' said Eve Ricard sharply.

Cooney shook his head again, rather sadly.

'Now that's the point of disagreement, Eve. I don't see anything wrong with a pretty girl kicking her legs on the stage, if she wants to. I wouldn't even object to a broad-minded joke or two where it's adults only. I'm not a killjoy. What we're after is to stop deliberate smut and violence. I've got kids; I want to know that I can turn the television on and not be embarrassed to be sitting in the room with them. I want to go to the newsagent and not see a row of grossly offensive magazine covers. . . . You see? Now we, as a party, have always stood for the values of family life. There's nothing against a leg-show or a bit of glamour. There's no harm in a bit of fun so long as you don't go too far. But when you have so-called artistic films on family television that's nothing but gilded filth, and really dirty jokes at seven or eight o'clock in the evening, then we say enough is enough. It's public money – and it's public taste. Those that pay the piper shall call the tune. . . .'

The discussion was submerged in a babble of disagreement.

'I don't believe I'm hearing this,' said Hoskins quietly. 'Carmel Cooney's put more girls to work for him on the street than anyone else in this city. The only reason he's not done time for some of the acts in his clubs is that he always had some mug nominee as owner. Course he doesn't bloody own the clubs. That'd be too dangerous.'

'But he's Councillor Cooney now,' Lesley said bitterly.

'Anyone that wants to know can look at the records,' Cooney was saying. 'I've tried to bring homes to people of this city through Coastal Construction. I've tried to bring 'em a few little extras through the Peninsular Emporium. And while we're on the subject of the Petshop, I'm not the least ashamed of its record. We raised money. . . .'

He paused and began to count off the good causes on his fingers.

'. . . for spina bifida. We raised money for the flood disaster in Bangladesh. We raised money for leukaemia. We raised over £4,000 for Ethiopia. Now – wait a minute – wait a minute. We've put almost £100,000 into these charities, thanks to our pretty girls and the kind hearts of the people of this city. And I'm bound to ask you, Eve, how much has your party in this city – how much has your woman's action movement in this city given?'

There was uproar in the studio. Above it, Cooney's voice carried the day.

'No . . . no! Come on, now! How much? That's a straight question! While your women's action group was moaning about the lack of screening for cervical cancer, the boys and girls out the Petshop actually raised the money for it. While you was moaning, we was saving women's lives. Real women. It's not the dance clubs that exploit women, it's the so-called women's groups that's got no interest in 'em beyond propaganda . . .'

'He is an absolute bastard!' Lesley said quietly.

Hoskins nodded. 'One of the finest. Your friend shouldn't tangle with Cooney. It's thirty years since he first learnt how to use the razor or the strap on a girl that crossed him. He's tailor-made for a political career.'

'The bloody hypocrisy!' she said.

Hoskins shrugged. 'Cooney's everywhere. You won't stop him. He's got a porn shop out here in Lantern Hill. The little one with the blacked-out windows at the back of the metro-rail station. That's his.'

Lesley looked up at him. 'You're behind the times.'

'Am I?'

'There's no blacked-out windows now. It was all cleared out a month or two ago. It's a slot-machine arcade. Fruit machines and automatic bingo. The kids go there after school.'

'That's nice,' said Hoskins thoughtfully. 'Well, I don't suppose Cooney would want them wasting their money on someone else's porn, would he? Not when they could be playing his machines.'

The ill-tempered discussion on the television had ended and the ensemble of closing graphics was swimming about the screen like a shoal of alphabetical fish.

'Let's go to bed,' Lesley said.

They went upstairs, she barefoot and Hoskins in his stockinged feet. It was enough to be in bed together, insulated from the world by one another. Just after midnight, he woke her again.

'There's something in the air,' he said quietly. 'Something in this house. In the air of it. I must have smelt it all the time and it didn't register.'

'Something in the air?'

'Yes. You don't smoke. You wouldn't. You're not the type. Did Robbo smoke cigarettes?'

'Yes. But he only did it when he was at work, or in the little room that he kept as his study. Yes, he smoked. Not heavily, but he did. When he was working. When he was under pressure.'

'Thank God for that,' Hoskins said piously and went back to sleep again.

CHAPTER TWENTY

'Ash-tray?' The voice of Dr Blades at the far end of the line sounded more than usually glum. 'Why should we? No one said.'

'They're saying now,' Hoskins murmured. 'Look, Charlie. There must have been a few dog-ends and what-not. Someone must have had a drag in that Cadillac. Somewhen.'

'Oh, they did,' said Blades. 'It's all done up neat in a plastic bag. Filter-tip with lipstick on. The lot.'

'The dog-ends,' Hoskins said. 'Robbo Smith's fingerprints. I can get Sian Jones' too, come to that. See if his turn up first. See if anything turns up.'

'His fingers we've got in the freezer, Sam. No problem. Hers we haven't got. She's still wearing them.'

'I'll sort that out, Charlie. Just see what you can get off the dog-ends.'

'It won't be this morning, Sam. Not a chance.'

'I'll ring you this evening,' Hoskins said, 'before you go home to the little bleeders.'

As he put the phone down, Sergeant Chance shook his head.

'You want to watch it, Sam. We're not supposed to have Sian Jones' fingerprints. Are we?'

Hoskins stared from the window across the full-leaved trees of the Mall.

'What we've got, Jack, is the plastic dwarf from Ocean Park. What we do with that is up to us. Any fingerprints on it that match the fag-ends must be hers. The more I think of it, she's somewhere in all this. If there's one thing that'd rile Cooney more than a journalist investigating him, it'd be that journalist screwing his current tart into the bargain.'

'If that's what it is,' Chance said sceptically, 'first thing he'd do would be to reach for his belt and give Sian the tanning of her life. No sign of that.'

'Not yet,' said Hoskins, patiently gathering up his papers. 'Not yet, my son.'

The inquest on Neville the Mouse was a haphazard affair. Hoskins walked across the Memorial Gardens to the city coroner's court under a sky of warm pearl. The black bronze figures of the memorial – rifles half-raised, bayonets fixed, knees flexed in a posture of defence – guarded their perpetual space among the beds of apricot-coloured roses. The battles on the plaques were long-forgotten skirmishes in obscure Japanese-held jungle or the arid plains of Mussolini's Africa.

He went up the steps to the entrance and walked down the marbled corridor to the coroner's office. A Jamaican woman of about forty with several children was standing forlornly by the stair-well. She was dressed in a black trouser-suit and scuffed shoes. Hoskins guessed that he was in the presence of the Mouse's mother and the younger children. She looked about her wonderingly, as if unable to take in the complexity of her new surroundings. An usher came and spoke to her.

'On in about half an hour, Mr Hoskins,' said another voice behind him. It was Delahaye from the coroner's office. The Mouse's mother looked up at the sound of his name and then turned her head on one side as if ashamed in her grief.

It was almost two hours before he was called. The coroner sat in a court of pale walnut panelling that was scarcely bigger than Carmel Cooney's drawing room. There were four rows in the public gallery, occupied by the Neville family and a few sympathisers. Apart from the coroner's staff, the main area was given up to two tables for legal representatives. Ex-councillor Lobo, friend and attorney to the Peninsula, student Black Panther twenty years before, was there for the Neville family. Of the Mouse's own friends, there was no sign. Dr Strachey, in dark blue chalk-stripe, presided over the hearing.

It was Lobo, grey hair thinning on a tall bronze skull, who went straight for retribution.

'Alexander Neville was at first in custody, Chief Inspector?'

Hoskins took his hands away from the ledge of the witness box and stood upright.

'Yes. Technically.'

'And was allowed to escape?'

'His coat came off as he was apprehended.'

'This boy then ran off, closely pursued by three car-loads of police officers?'

'By two officers from among them.'

'He was chased through a department store, across Atlantic Wharf, up the Harbour Bank and along the railway track to the river bridge?'

'I assumed he was trying to get across the bridge and down into Dyce Street.'

'The fun of the chase, Chief Inspector Hoskins? Three crews of policemen hunting a boy of twenty. No attempt to block him off or head him off. Not one man there who could or did catch him. Hounding him down the track towards the next high-speed train.'

'It was Neville who chose to run in that direction.'

'To escape you.'

'I suppose so.'

'In fear of you.'

'Perhaps.'

'I put this to you, Chief Inspector Hoskins. He would scarcely be running into the path of a high-speed train unless he were in even greater fear of you.'

'He was trying to get away. That's all. And there was no train in sight just then.'

There was a pause. Hoskins stared at the black and gold clock on the panelled wall at the far end of the room. It was a quarter past twelve.

'Indeed he was trying to get away, Mr Hoskins.' Lobo looked up from his papers, took off his gold-rimmed glasses and folded them away in his breast pocket. He leant forward on his hands, as if to show that he now meant business. 'He was trying to get away – was he not? – from the leader of the pursuit. From a man who shouted after him, "You black bastard," and promised to rupture his kidneys with the toe of his boot.'

'Nothing of the kind happened,' Hoskins said. 'No one shouted at him. There wasn't time and, in any case, no one would have had the breath.'

'So the only non-police witness present is lying?'

'No one shouted anything.'

'The dog that did not bark, Mr Hoskins? A pursuit of half a mile, five or ten minutes, perhaps?'

'Perhaps.'

'All carried out in total silence? In all that time, no one shouted? Would it not be the most natural thing in the world for a policeman to shout at a fugitive, telling him to give himself up? Your men pursued this boy for half a mile and not one of them, at any point, shouted at him to stop?'

'Someone may have done. I didn't hear. We were fairly scattered.'

'You didn't hear?' Lobo took out the glasses and studied a paper. 'You were fairly scattered. Presumably out of earshot of one another. That is not what it says in your statement, Chief Inspector. In your statement you were positive that there was no shouting.'

'I'm positive I didn't hear any,' Hoskins said grimly. 'And I didn't call Neville a black bastard or anything else. The first words I spoke to him were when he was in the water and we were trying to reach him from the incline under the bridge.'

'"You black bastard,"' Lobo continued to read from another of his papers, '"I'll kick your fucking kidneys till it makes you cry to use them." Is it not the case, Mr Hoskins, that having given way to expressions of this kind you thought when you made your statement that it would be best to say that no one shouted anything at any time – a story which upon present examination seems utterly absurd?'

'I didn't shout or speak to him!' Hoskins saw the reporters' pens hurrying over their pads. 'I hadn't the breath!'

'"You black bastard . . ." A man who is short of breath, Chief Inspector, may stop for long enough to shout that.'

'I didn't.'

'"You black bastard . . ." According to the only independent witness, you did.'

'I don't go around calling people black bastards. Apart from anything else, Neville wasn't black.'

Lobo looked at him uncertainly.

'He was no more black,' said Hoskins savagely, 'than you are.'

For a moment he felt the satisfaction of the submarine captain seeing the torpedo strike amidships. But Lobo controlled his anger well.

'You are not here, Mr Hoskins, to give evidence on questions of ethnic origin.'

'Fifty per cent of Neville's origins were from Welshpool or Wrexham. He was no more black than a Spaniard or an Italian. If I'd wanted to shout abuse at him, I'd have chosen something more accurate.'

But Lobo's anger was now a match for Hoskins' own.

'And that is the extent of your sensitivity on matters of race, Chief Inspector?'

Hoskins was aware of Dr Strachey drawing breath to intervene. He was going to regret his reply to Lobo later on, but the sheer luxury of blasting him was irresistible. The submariner emptied the torpedo tubes in one salvo.

'Mr Lobo, compared with the ham-fisted, tin-eared, counter-productive antics of certain parts of the race relations industry in this city, I'd defend my sensitivity towards the people I deal with. You can smell the reputation of the community relations experts a long time before you get to them.'

'Mr Hoskins!' Dr Strachey was there at last. 'I shall not tolerate comments of that kind in my court. Being under hostile examination does not entitle you to attack Mr Lobo or his part on the Racial Equality Board. If there is any more of this sort of thing, I shall make it the subject of a report to your chief constable.'

'I withdraw the last reply, sir,' said Hoskins, meeting Lobo unrepentantly, eye to eye. 'But I want it noted that I was asked about my sensitivity on matters of race. I think I was entitled to answer.'

All that afternoon there was an uneasy calm. It was Chance who came in just before four o'clock with the *Western World* evening edition.

'Bloody hell, Sam!' he said, his voice mingling dismay and awe.

It was there on the front page, though confined to the lower half of the last column. *NEVILLE INQUEST: Police Witness Slams Race Policy.*

'That didn't take them long,' said Hoskins indifferently.

'You really said all this?'

'Yes, my son. I said what everyone thinks.'

'They may think it, Sam, but they don't say it. Lobo and his mob must be going spare!'

'I really enjoyed it,' said Hoskins nostalgically. 'For years I've watched him getting fat on public salaries and doing bugger-all to earn it. Expense account and flash car, going round schools monitoring their race awareness and cultural bias. He's stirred up more trouble than half the National Front.'

'I hope the Ripper sees it that way, Sam. Still, if you're lucky, there'll always be a job for you. Out at the Lantern Hill roundabout, wearing a pointed hat and directing traffic. Hope you kept your white gloves.'

Ripley appeared without knocking and Chance went out.

'I did my best, Sam,' he said without anger or preamble. 'They wouldn't take it off the front page, you couldn't expect them to. But at least we've stopped it being in banner type across the top.'

'Good,' said Hoskins indifferently.

'How could you be such a fool, Sam? How could you let Lobo needle you? I don't get it. After all, it wasn't exactly your first time in the witness box, was it?'

Hoskins stood up, his back to the window view of Hawks Hill.

'I don't know, Max. I think, as Councillor Cooney would say, he riled me. Lobo. Smooth two-faced bastard. He's about as black as me with a suntan. But there's money and political prospects in making his clients believe he's one of them.'

The Ripper sat down.

'From now on, shut up about it, Sam! You're in deep enough already to put an end to your career. In case you hadn't realised that. I've spent the last two hours trying to see a way out. And so far I haven't found one. The only good news is the verdict. Delahaye phoned me just now. Accidental death. Jury was only about fifteen minutes. He'd already told the chief constable. Anything worse and you might have been suspended then and there.'

'This is where,' said Hoskins thoughtfully, 'you tell me to take any leave that's due. Hand over diary and warrant card. All the rest of it. Pity. I think I've got the answer to Robbo Smith. Just about.'

The Ripper looked at him, ignoring Robbo Smith.

'Either this thing will blow over or it won't,' he said at last. 'If it doesn't, Sam, you're in the clag anyway. If it does, then it won't much matter where you are. The way I see it, we might argue that Lobo asked you a question in your private capacity. He didn't ask what the police thought about the Racial Equality Board. He asked what *you* thought. And you told him. We might even argue that it was improper for him to put such a question and improper for the coroner to allow it.'

'It's an argument at least,' Hoskins said. In his mind, he could see the Arran Street bedroom. He would have given anything to be there with her at that moment. There were vapour trails in the hazy blue above the gardens and expensive red tiles of Hawks Hill, the glum grey towers of the Mount Pleasant flats. The nation's defenders were rending the sky with their din, flying in low over the coast and following the valley, pretending that Volgagrad or Minsk lay at the end of it.

'Apart from which, Sam,' the Ripper was saying, 'I can't have anyone on leave just now. There's Stoodley's funeral on Friday afternoon. The turn-out we need for that is going to leave us short everywhere.'

'Right,' said Hoskins distantly. Another jet tore the sky, low enough to hurt his ears.

'There's no reason you and Jack Chance couldn't stay as a team for the present.'

'Right.'

'We need a pair of eyes at Stoodley's funeral. For some reason I don't pretend to understand, people who kill get a kick out of watching the funeral. Amazing how often it happens. We need a good pair of eyes on guard.'

'They don't need to go to funerals nowadays, Max,' said Hoskins wearily. 'They can see it all on telly. They can even record it and play it over and over. If that's what it takes.'

'All the same,' the Ripper said, 'you'll be observation car with Chance on Friday. I can't think you'd want to be pallbearer as things are. Not that close to Stoodley personally, were you? And you can't come to much harm just watching. Stoodley dying and the funeral coverage is doing us some good just now.

You ought to be grateful, Sam. You really did.'

He made a ghastly attempt at a reassuring smile and went out.

Hoskins looked at his watch and heard the first hazy roar of the summer afternoon rush-hour. The light across Barrier and Orient had the earliest honeyed tint of evening. He lifted the phone, dialled the code for Ocean Beach and then put it down again without completing the number. God knows who might be listening in by now. Unlocking the drawer, of his desk, he took out a carefully wrapped package. It was the fairground plastic dwarf bought by Sian Jones at Ocean Park. Then he relocked the desk and went out into the corridor.

One or two men from the sergeants' room greeted him in a manner that was just a little too briskly amiable. It was, he supposed, like having Aids or the clap. Or dying of anything at all. The signs of mortality were upon him and everyone was too polite to mention it. Except the Ripper. And except Jack Chance.

To avoid encounters in the lift, he went down the stairs and wondered which road to Ocean Beach would have the least traffic by now. Best on the whole to avoid Lantern Hill.

CHAPTER TWENTY-ONE

'How's it feel to be on page one, then, Sam?'

Blades asked the question without appearing to listen for the answer as he led the way up the stairs to his office. A window arch showed an apricot flush of six o'clock channel sky above the pier and the Cakewalk.

'Not much different, Charlie. All in the line of duty. The Ripper's pissed off. Lobo and Leroy and the Ricard woman are probably going to have his knackers on toast for it.'

'Ah!' said Blades disparagingly. 'Still, you certainly told 'em, Sam. I specially liked the bit about Lobo not being black. He won't live that down in a hurry.'

He whistled to himself and pushed open the door of his office. From its window, the whole of Ocean Beach, super-cinemas and department stores, sands and warm rippling sea was bathed in the same apricot flush of sun. It was like an ambitious stage-lighting exercise. Blades stood in the window looking down wistfully. Hoskins closed the door.

'What have we got on the dog-ends, then, Charlie?'

'Not much, Sam. A few prints on the filter-tips. Cooney's. Probably his girl's. Shan't know that till old Fumblebum downstairs dusts off that dwarf you were good enough to bring us. Lipstick all over some of the filters. Her style, would that be?'

Hoskins had a mental image of Sian's mouth, wide and painted, slack and lascivious.

'I'd say so, Charlie. Still, that's not much without Robbo Smith.'

Blades opened a drawer and took out a cardboard folder.

'Hardly worth having his fingers out of the freezer, Sam. Still, good thing us country cousins out at the Beach aren't all as stupid as we look.'

Hoskins waited expectantly. Blades turned over the loose pages in the folder. He found one and handed it to the chief inspector.

'His underpants, Sam.'

'How's that, Charlie?'

'We went over his clothes. Matter of routine. When you mentioned the dog-ends, it just crossed my mind to do a bit of matching-up with the forensic sweep on the upholstery.'

'Yes?' Hoskins studied the paper, looking for the connection.

'Yes, Sam. His Marks and Spencer cotton Y-fronts, medium size, have several little flecks of reddish fluff. The nap from the car seating of the Fleetwood Brougham.'

'Right!' said Hoskins enthusiastically.

'Other words, Sam, our Robbo must have been having naughties in Carmel Cooney's Cadillac. Unless you think he just used it to change his pants in. And, if he was coupling up in there, Sian Jones has to be number one. Again, unless you think it was Cooney that turned him on. Sian drives off to meet him in a woodland glade or back of the cemetery. Cooney caught them, chased Robbo Smith, rammed him off the cliff. Open and shut.'

Hoskins sat down and pretended to consider this. Through the open window there was a mingled odour of blossom from the trees and vinegar from the fish restaurants. In full sunlight the first neon alphabets were dancing above the Cakewalk. The crooning from the New Pier amplifiers and the fairground organ blasting across Ocean Park filled the petrolled air of the early summer evening.

'Won't do, Charlie. If Cooney was that cut up – if he knew – young Sian'd be going round with a backside tanned the colour of a tomato. Or she'd be missing at the bottom of the railway dock, if he was really cross. And there's no way our people can show he wasn't answering phone calls in Hawks Hill when Robbo did his sky-dive.'

'Not much help, then, Sam?'

'I don't know, Charlie. What I rather fancy is Cooney calling up Neville the Mouse: "There's this pain from the *Western World* screwing my girl and prying into my affairs," he says. "Come up and steal the Caddie; I'll leave the key in the ignition. Find him and wipe him out. Hit and run. And let's have your Giro code so we can drop you a couple of grand for old times' sake. Oh, and by the way, young Mouse, wipe the Caddie over inside so that no one finds the deceased's fingerprints flashing out 'Hello! Hello!'" See?'

'Easier ways,' said Blades sceptically. 'Young Sian finds that Robbo, while stretching her over the car seat, is actually pumping her for Cooney's secrets. Her modesty outraged, she rams him off the cliff.'

Hoskins stood up and together they looked across the glitter of the pale tide.

'Good thing you never thought of joining CID, Charlie. You think Cooney's girls love him that much? Risk a life sentence for him? Not the way he treats them. There's one out the Petshop now: Maggie. Long blonde hair and fringe, like a little girl. Used to be a looker when she was sixteen or seventeen, but getting brassy now. She was number one for a while. And she and Sian Jones go out together. She'd soon tell her that Cooney's arrangements are strictly temporary. Temporary staff don't kill for the boss, Charlie.'

Blades shrugged.

'Right-o, Sam. It's the Mouse. In which case, it's all over bar the funerals. What I can't imagine, though, is in that car. You know. I wonder how they went about it, exactly, in there. He must have had the hots bad.'

'Or she did.' Hoskins saw in his mind the young redhead's slack lascivious look, the blue eyes vacant with a dreamy desire and the glossily lipsticked mouth open a little in expectation.

Blades chuckled.

'Mind you, Sam. There was a time when I'd first met up with Sharon. Nineteen, she was then. Only twenty-seven now. You should have seen the capers in that bedroom! Sometimes, next day, I used to feel quite ashamed of making such a beast of myself the night before. She never said no to anything.' He smiled reminiscently.

'There's a bit of mileage left in you, Charlie,' said Hoskins politely.

'Ah,' said Blades in the same disparaging voice, 'it's just her two little bleeders. There's one thing about this private school lark – if I could raise enough for 'em to board, they'd be well shot of. They could come home at weekends, I suppose, but they wouldn't necessarily have to.'

Hoskins looked round as the door opened. It was Fry, Blades' assistant from downstairs.

'There's a match, Charlie,' Fry said, handing over the plastic dwarf. 'Prints there and on two of the filter-tips. And two sets on the frame of Smith's bike.'

'That's nice,' said Blades, taking the dwarf.

'Anything else, Charlie?' Fry had his hand on the door.

'That's just nice, Freddie. See you tomorrow.'

'Take care, Charlie.'

Fry went out and Blades turned to Hoskins. 'End of story, Sam. Wouldn't you say?'

'Daresay, Charlie. Or else the beginning.'

Presently they walked down the stairs together.

'That biker's girl,' Hoskins said. 'Angie. There was never anything more that you or Aldermaston came up with?'

'Not from what you gave us, Sam. Never found the Restall counterpane, did you? Apart from the post mortem on her, we only had her boots, her jerkin and leather jacket. Jeans and knickers burnt along with the counterpane, I suppose. Still, if it was the Mouse again, you've left it a bit late now.'

'That turned me up more than anything I can remember,' Hoskins said. 'Her in the storm drain. I've seen worse things, including the Mouse in the river, but that one stuck.'

'It's the job, Sam. If you were given an outer, it wouldn't all be bad news.'

They stood in the warm yard in a fragrance from the horse-chestnut trees.

'It's all down to money, Charlie. I don't want to end up like old Dougal, shunting the punters' motors in Cooney's car park. I don't want to be a Jones and Gower's store detective. And I don't want to work for Securicor. Short of being commissionaire at the Paris Hotel or the Odeon down the Beach, that's it. Unemployment black spot, they reckon. Unless you're a villain or a copper.'

He parked the car at the Highlands end of the Cakewalk and walked for half a mile by the sea wall with the tide slopping gently against it. There was another possibility that he could discuss with no one. What if Robbo Smith's notes and investigation had been concocted for Lesley's benefit? What if, behind the interest in Cooney's frauds, there lay only Robbo's itch for Sian Jones? He stopped and stood by the pier approach, staring out across the ripples that were cut by the first colour tones of sunset. In that case, Robbo Smith had made fools of them all. To his surprise, Hoskins rather liked the idea.

He walked back by the Cakewalk terrace. The Petshop was glowing with coloured light. There was music across the terrace and car park. But it was no longer Maggie the blonde schoolgirl of twenty-five sticking her tongue or bottom out at the audience. Posters for next week's *Nights at the Winter Garden* showed toothily smiling couples who waltzed to the beat of a conductor in white tie and tails. Where the adult schoolgirls had provoked and sneered, a throaty contralto was in full voice with Ivor Novello's 'Some day my heart will awake. . . .' National paranoia over child abuse had put paid to over-age schoolgirls. Councillor Cooney was now aboard the evangelical juggernaut.

Still thinking about Robbo Smith and Sian, Hoskins went back to the car. It was a disquieting and carefully edited truth in

Canton or Ocean Beach that most abuse was inflicted on children by other children. If the Mouse were innocent, red-haired Angie at fifteen was statistically most likely to have met her fate at the hands of boys – or girls – no older than she. But press and public preferred the image of a middle-aged man beckoning from a cruising car.

He let in the clutch and drove back along Bay Drive. Through the calm air of the seaside evening, the voice from the Petshop assured him with Novello's warbling optimism that some day the morning would break. For the moment there would be no more skin or schoolgirls on the bandstand of the Petshop. Quarter of a mile out to sea, the neon alphabets on the pier split the twilight to the rattle and bleep and clash of Councillor Cooney's gaming machines. The evangelists of the secular age had cleaned up Ocean Beach.

CHAPTER TWENTY-TWO

'Supposing you bumped someone off, Sam,' Chance enquired, 'would you try getting to the funeral?'

'Nope,' said Hoskins philosophically. 'Then, I never was a great one for funerals.'

They sat together in the parked car within the cemetery grounds, partially concealed from the road by the low stone wall and the laurel hedge that grew above it. The wide wrought-iron gates had been fastened back for the cortège and the gothic mortuary chapel rose spikily against the hot sky. The lines of tombs and crosses were pale against an edging of variegated holly and yew trees.

'One-parent family,' Hoskins said. 'That's Sian Jones' story. Name Jones on the birth certificate and mother's maiden name Jones. That and a discreet little "s" for spinster beside mum's name in the records. Don't think they do that nowadays. Discrimination, it would be. Mum still lives in Orient, down Talavera Street. Visited most days by her loving daughter. I suppose Hawks Hill must seem a bit of a step up from that.'

'Not enough to be worth murder.' Chance was staring at the discreet placing of the television camera by the main gates. 'Girls like her, if they sense trouble, they get the hell out of it. She can't have been that gone on Cooney. No one could. Mind you, I like the idea of her over the back seat in Cooney's limo. I wouldn't mind a slice of that.'

'I told Charlie Blades,' Hoskins said. 'All those girls know they're strictly temporary. Sian must have got that from the blonde one, Maggie. She'd been through the mill already. None of 'em had cause to kill Robbo Smith for love of Cooney.'

'And poor little Sian never even got her break on the bandstand.' Chance shook his head. 'All that for nothing.'

'No,' said Hoskins thoughtfully. 'She never did. Not really the shape for it.'

'Nor's Maggie,' said Chance. 'Too short in the leg.'

There was a stir of interest among the television crew from Coastal News. Far down the road, between the yews and monkey-puzzles, the hot thunder-light gleamed on a smoke-grey Daimler hearse. It moved forward slowly between empty pavements in the quiet suburban roads of Clearwater. At regulation intervals along the route, a uniformed and helmeted policeman came to the salute as the coffin passed. A single wreath of red roses lay upon the pale wood. In the second car, Hoskins could just make out Anne Stoodley and her two teenage children, an awkward looking boy and a frizzy-haired girl.

Chance sighed. 'Poor old John.'

The cortège paused just within the gates of the city cemetery, waiting to take its place behind the bandsmen, most of them borrowed from the Metropolitan Police band for the occasion.

'Anne never wanted all this, I hear,' Hoskins said. 'I think the chief constable had a word. Good for the image of the Force and all that.'

'Handy for you, Sam, as things are. You was lucky not to get a mention on Coastal News. That must have damped the fires down a bit. Nothing worse than a report in the *Western World* evening edition.'

Hoskins shook his head.

'The cream-puffs at Coastal Network couldn't very well

announce over the air that Lobo isn't black. And they couldn't very well report that I'd said the community relations mob had done more harm to race relations than the National Front. Not without the risk of most people agreeing with 'em.'

The band moved forward to strains of the Dead March from *Saul*. Despite himself, Hoskins was moved by the scene. The stately Handelian chords of an eighteenth-century court receded across the shattered tower blocks of Mount Pleasant, the gang-sprayed walls of the Peninsula, the rattle of the Ocean Beach gaming arcades, the rude tongues and bottoms of adult schoolgirls on the bandstand of the Petshop. The last echoes of its Augustan grandeur died somewhere in the hot sky above the vomit-splashed pavements of St Vincent Street and Martello Square.

'You was lucky, all the same,' Chance said.

The coffin was being carried now, behind the band. In its wake walked the black-dressed woman of thirty-five or so and the two awkward children, whose manner suggested that they had courteously taken time off from more important pursuits.

'Is that right about Cooney cleaning up the Petshop?' Chance enquired.

Hoskins clicked his tongue as the procession turned a corner and moved out of sight behind the yew trees and holly. The band stopped playing and he guessed the mourners had come to the open grave.

'It's all Ivor Novello and Old Vienna out there now, my son.'

'Sod that!' said Chance sceptically. 'You think he's serious? Born-again Carmel Cooney?'

'Councillor Cooney. That's all. Him and old Sprat that was Tory MP for the county division. Moral majority and so forth.'

'Sod that,' said Chance again, as if lost for any other comment. Hoskins chuckled.

'You know old Sprat was burgled once. Before your time, I should think. Anyway, we get to the place in minutes, him having a niner through to the communications room. Chaos everywhere. Upside-down. In his office, there's some stuff on bringing back the rope and all that. Very keen hanger. And then there's all these instructional films on the benefits of corporal punishment for young ladies.'

'No! Old Sprat?'

'Too bloody true, my son. All the way from America, they'd come.'

'What'd you do then, Sam? Pull 'em in?'

'Looked the other way,' Hoskins said. 'Instructions from on high.'

'Bloody hell!'

Hoskins grinned.

'Anyway, in the course of conversation, old Sprat says something about American Super-8 films sent him by a constituent for vetting. Never been able to view them, not having an American-gauge projector. See?'

'Shame!'

'Two weeks later, I get the nudge from Bill Walker, the special constable that works for Fields the photographers. They got to send all the way to New York for this replacement shutter-gate for Mr Sprat's projector. Worn out through excessive use.'

Chance slapped his hands on the steering wheel with a hee-haw of laughter at the neatness of it.

'That's nice, Sam! That really is nice!'

'Trouble with this bloody country, Jack, is people like Sprat and Cooney. Either you get full-colour visions of ladies with legs open like next Sunday's joint uncooked. Or else some old bag bellowing down the line every time there's a hint of bum on the telly.'

'Live and let live, Sam.'

'No one does any more, my son. Like John Stoodley. No one let him live.'

From the warm distance, the band struck up brightly and the voices followed, uneven but hearty:

'For all the saints, who from their labours rest. . . .'

'Never exactly thought of old John as a saint,' Chance murmured.

'No,' said Hoskins. 'Still, I don't suppose you'd be that quick to recognise one if you met him.'

They sat in silence while the music finished. In the warmth of the early afternoon, Hoskins closed his eyes.

'Sam! Look at this lot!'

He opened his eyes. Along a narrower path from an opposite corner of the cemetery came a curious procession. Their funeral was over and they were shambling and laughing in a straggling rout. The clothes were sharp but cheap, girls in short skirts and tall boots, young men in long jackets and slim ties. A few were in leather flying-tops and baggy pants. Hoskins stared at them. They looked like the turn-out of an old-fashioned palais de danse or a Fascist rally. Then he saw the troubled face of the older Jamaican woman and the several small children clustered round her.

'Everyone's funeral today,' he said equably. 'Looks like they've been burying the Mouse.'

'What a shower of . . .'

'I don't suppose he had much to leave, apart from his pimping concessions and one or two girls.'

As Chance looked, he saw what Hoskins meant. Louise was there, the dark-lashed saucer eyes, the slicked-back crop of brown hair, the bold young face and the plumpish pallor of her figure. Despite himself, Chance was shocked. She had paid her last tribute to the Mouse by joining the funeral in her boots, black leather hot-pants and pearl-studded coatee.

'At a funeral, Sam?'

'You're behind the times, my son. The Chains usually send a guard of honour when they kill someone from the Rodders. Black leather and swastika badges. Doing the salute. Not this time, though. They didn't kill the Mouse. We did.'

'And there's bloody Weekes! I'll have him, here and now.'

'Sit tight, Jack Chance. You won't get him now. According to the Ripper, the prosecution service can't find a case against him. He was seen in the Cadillac with the Mouse. That's all. Innocent passenger. He was outside the Peninsular Emporium that afternoon and he ran off. According to his solicitor, he thought he was being attacked by a gang. And that's all there is against the Breaker. You couldn't hold him five minutes, if you was to collar him at all. And a runner wouldn't look good across the gravestones in the middle of John Stoodley's funeral.'

'He was with that lot in Martello Square.'

'Innocent bystander, Jack.'

'And he probably screwed that biker's girl before they smothered her.'

'Probably did, Jack. For all anyone can prove, he might as well not have done.'

'Little bastard!'

'And what we don't want just this minute, my son, is anything that looks heavy. According to the Ripley family, I am about nostril-deep in the constabulary excrement. I'd as soon not be nudged in any further.'

'Look at that!'

Louise was on her leash again. Hoskins had not noticed it at first. But she had passed into the possession of the Breaker, who was probably her junior by a year. Weekes' face showed the excitement and uncertainty of an owner with a newly acquired pet, as if he could not quite make up his mind what to do first.

'Little bastard,' said Chance again, more glumly this time.

The television crew were standing easy, watching the Mouse's mourners. There was no more to be done until the other procession returned and the chief constable gave his brief on-the-spot summary of Stoodley's courage and the undischarged debt of the public to the police. Louise walked ahead of the Breaker, squirming ostentatiously as if to encourage him.

Presently, the bandsmen and the others came back from the committal of John Stoodley's remains. The instruments were now carried or slung and the family mourners walked with the chief constable and the lord mayor at the centre of an informal phalanx. There was an air of relief. Tunics and helmets were adjusted. Even Stoodley's friends were glad of an excuse to get back to their duties.

'So much for the murderer turning up to have a giggle at the funeral,' Chance said. 'Unless, of course, you think it was the Metropolitan Police band that chucked him through that window.'

Hoskins nodded.

'Turn right out of here, Jack. Let's have a quiet drive down Talavera Street and a peep at where Sian's mum lives.'

'Right-o, Sam.'

'Charlie Blades reckons the girl'd been on Robbo's bike. He'd been in the Cadillac with his trousers down. The Mouse photographed them together on the Cakewalk. Probably sold the snaps to Cooney. Cooney must have known.'

'Or the Mouse tried it on Robbo?'

'No sign, Jack. Cooney must have known. And in that case, why didn't he teach her a lesson? Always had done before with his tarts. He's razored girls as well as blokes. Not in person of late. Now it's just a word to someone else to do it. No more to him than asking them to take the dog for a walk.'

'Sian had something on him?'

'Then why didn't he keep his promise to let her flash it on his dais?'

Chance shrugged. 'Dunno, Sam. She can come and flash it on my dais any time she's got an evening free.'

He turned past Connaught Park towards the little terraced streets of Orient.

CHAPTER TWENTY-THREE

On the following afternoon, a warm summer rainlight illuminated Atlantic Wharf under an island of charcoal-grey cloud. The entire scene was eerily cast in shadows of grey and mauve. Chance drew in at the kerb.

'One thing, Sam,' he said cagily, 'if this goes wrong and there's a general bollocking in the Ripley family, it's your turn in the barrel. All right?'

Hoskins tightened his mouth dismissively and watched the first heavy drops begin to fall, splattering the size of medals on the hot stained paving of Great Western Street.

'Your trouble, my son,' he said thoughtfully, 'is you worry too much. If I'm wrong, nothing'll happen. There won't be an answer. No problems.'

'Apart from Cooney finding out that you've been into his private affairs and apart from you then having to touch your toes in front of the entire squad. That's all. Not much.'

'Be your age,' said Hoskins grumpily. 'Go in there and have a look round first. I'll sit here; they're less likely to twig you.'

The rain was falling harder now, gathering force with the sound of a tap being opened fuller. Its drops drummed and bounced on the taut canvas of the shop blinds, gathering and streaming in miniature cascades to the pavement below. Shoppers paused and began to gather under the shelter of the blinds, looking up reproachfully at the sky.

Across the width of Great Western Street, where it opened out into Atlantic Wharf, another of Cooney's enterprises flourished. In what had once been part of the Paris Hotel, flanking its foyer, the windows of Madame Jolly Modes were capped by frivolous dome-shaped sunblinds in sky blue with cream frills. The scooped velvet and tight satin of the windows shone with cut-glass necklaces like the booty of an imperial campaign. Slim wax mannequins posed like a frieze of captured female slaves in a conqueror's triumphal procession. The word boutique scarcely did it justice, Hoskins thought. It was the last word in Canton chic and sophistication, its interior dimly lit, evoking a promise of perfume and bare flesh, silk and feminine sensuality.

He sighed impatiently and waited for Jack Chance. Between the shoppers clustered from the rain under the blue and cream blinds, he could just glimpse a girl beyond the cut-glass brooches and necklaces of royal purple or midnight blue on their beds of white velvet. His eyes took in the long slope of her brow and nose, the warm tan of her skin, the enigmatic almond eyes that quelled the glances of the bystanders, the dark hair elegantly pinned up to leave the slim neck and neat ears on show. She might have been Grecian, Egyptian, Asian, Provençal, Caribbean. Any or all of them, Hoskins thought. Madame Jolly Modes was the Canton he had always known. The warm beauty that was a legacy of generations of trade and shipping, the easy mingling of dockland marriages. His childhood had been spent against such a background. That, not Lobo, was race relations to him.

Again he sighed, thinking of the girl's hidden beauty under the singlet and jeans, the trim legs and narrow waist, the satin-smooth tan that was dark in the small of her back and then copper-pale on her bottom and legs. Once, he thought affectionately, he had known such a girl: Connie. He smiled.

'Sam!' Chance's voice was at the open window. 'You gone deaf or just obstinate? That's the third time.'

'Sorry,' said Hoskins amiably. 'I was just having a break.'

Chance slid behind the wheel.

'It's all set up. She's there. If you're going to do it, do it now. And don't say I didn't warn you.'

Hoskins hummed a little tune to himself, mostly to conceal the tension he felt as the time came to test his plan. He had not the least idea whether it would work or not. Pushing upon the swing door on the Atlantic Wharf side of the Royal Peninsular Emporium, he entered the Food Hall. Cooney had indeed brought the good things of life to those citizens of Canton who could afford them. The shelves were stacked with spiced German biscuits and continental fruit juice, Italian sauces and French candy. The freezers and refrigerated shelves were a treasure trove of fresh salmon, prime cuts, Roquefort and Stilton.

He made for the escalator and went up floor by floor, past three-piece suites in square reproduction art deco style, past rows of evening gowns and wax dummies displaying female underwear of a brevity and translucence to have Eve Ricard eating the carpet. Or perhaps not, Hoskins thought. Perhaps the wearing of the suspender-harness was her private vice and secret shame. He doubted it, but the idea cheered him all the same.

At the third floor he stepped off in the rich dark air of fur coats and expensive women. He kept his head down but no one seemed to notice him. There was a glass door to one side with a sign above it proclaiming *Accounts*. Hoskins pushed it open and went through. But instead of going to the accounts window, he turned aside and passed through another door. This one was *Staff Only*.

No one challenged him. He stopped at the next room. It was a general office with a counter. One of the three girls at their desks got up and came across.

'Mr Benson about, is he?'

'He's out to tea,' the girl replied, a note of query and objection gathering in her voice.

'Chief Inspector Hoskins,' Hoskins said, holding up the misty green plastic of the warrant card. 'Matter of some urgency. I want your young lady to put this out on the public address system.

Won't take her a jiffy. I'll wait here for the person concerned, if you don't mind.'

To his surprise and relief her manner changed at once. She made not the least objection as she glanced at the sheet of paper with the message on it.

'Of course,' she said quietly. 'I'll get her to do it right away.'

Hoskins stood back politely and waited. Presently he heard the musical ding-dong of the address system calling the attention of the shoppers to a public announcement. The words came less distinctly from beyond the partition but he caught the gist of them.

'. . . Cooney . . . Miss Cooney. . . . Please come at once to the general office. . . Urgent message awaits . . . Miss Cooney . . . please come at once to the general office on the third floor . . . An urgent message awaits you . . .'

Hoskins stood and listened to the pecking of fingers on keyboards and the clatter of the room about him. The girl repeated the message over the speakers and still there was no response. Chance seemed to be right. The whole plan had come adrift in Hoskins' hands. It was his turn in the barrel, indeed, with Carmel Cooney on the outside.

He released his tension in a long breath. At that moment the outer door of the general office opened. He saw that it was Sian in a pair of smart caramel-coloured pants and a coatee. She was looking at one of the girls beyond the counter and he guessed that at first she could not have noticed him.

'Sorry,' she said breathlessly, the wide painted lips now smiling rather vacantly in apology. 'Sorry, I was in the loo. I suppose the message must be for me.'

For the first time in months, it seemed to him, the trumpets rang out for Samuel Hoskins.

'I think,' he said, taking a step forward into her line of vision, 'I think you and I ought to have a little talk, Miss Cooney.'

He was so convinced of her coming collapse, the breath knocked from her in the moment of unmasking, that her reaction took him by surprise. The young redhead looked at him for a split second. Then she turned and dodged out through the door, slamming it after her. Hoskins felt no more than an irritation at her evasion. He might not have been able to catch the Mouse, but Sian was unlikely to out-distance him for long.

He pushed open the door, not even at a run, and saw her feet flying as she turned round a row of dark sables on their hangers. She might hide among the racks of clothes. That would be the worst thing. But there was only one way for her now. Sooner or later she must give herself up.

At that moment he saw her heading across an open space of carpet by the sales counter. Hoskins spurted after her. She rounded a corner and fled into an alcove with a door. He was there a moment later, ready to burst through it and corner her. There was an engraved notice on this door as well. It said *Ladies*.

Cursing under his breath, Hoskins swung aside to the sales counter.

'I want that girl out of there!'

'I'm just serving this customer, sir. . . .'

The grey-haired woman did not so much as look up from folding a fur stole.

'Chief Inspector Hoskins, Canton CID! I want that girl out of there!'

'I'll see if I can get the department manageress, sir.' She reached for the phone.

'Is there another way out of there?'

She put the phone down. 'Not really, sir. Not another door.'

'A window?'

'Well, yes, sir. Of course there's a window!'

'Leading anywhere?'

'Not leading anywhere, sir. Only to the fire escape. There has to be one there, sir. That's city fire department regulations. Has to be unlocked while the building's open to the public. We had a talk from the store manager about it.'

'Then don't waste time making that phone call,' said Hoskins savagely.

He loped back down the escalators and found the point in the well of the building where the fire escape came down. It must have been as easy as coming downstairs for a girl of her age. Sian would have been clear of the Royal Peninsular Emporium while the saleswoman upstairs was still hesitating with her phone.

Then it occurred to him that Chance might have seen her leaving the building, perhaps even stopped her. He pushed open the swing doors and stepped into the rainy summer afternoon. But Chance was sitting alone in the car, staring wistfully across the broad street at the trim almond-eyed figure of Madame Jolly Modes.

'Well, I suppose you did it,' Chance said presently, in tribute to Hoskins' report. 'Hole in one, I'll give you that, Sam. Don't alter the fact that Cooney's going to shit a brick when he hears about this afternoon's little caper. There's going to be some right bollocking over this. You mark my words. Still, you got the bullseye. Miss Cooney.'

Hoskins dismissed the concession with a twist of the mouth.

'She had to be, Jack. The more I thought of it.'

'Not much family resemblance.'

'No. Still, I can't imagine anyone outside a freak show or a zoo that'd resemble Carmel Cooney. But it had to be, Jack. She was having it off with Robbo Smith in the limo. That was good for a tanning, if not a touch of the carver. But she gets off without a mark. And she's still mixing his drinks and modelling his furs.'

'You reckon?'

'She was up there now. As for sticking her bum out at the punters in the Petshop, of course he wouldn't let her, would he? It's other people's daughters you like to see doing that, not your own. I should have seen it sooner, though. Like Robbo Smith smoking, it's something that must have been floating in the mind. I thought of it once. And then yesterday, for some reason, I was bloody sure.'

'And when you went out there first, he was touching her up in front of you?'

Hoskins shrugged.

'I suppose fathers pat and stroke their grown-up daughters. I don't know. I haven't got any. Never given the subject much thought.'

'Dirty sod,' said Chance disparagingly.

'Cooney . . .' Hoskins followed Chance's line of sight across the road where Madame Jolly Modes was watching the passers-by with feline malevolence. 'I wouldn't put it past Cooney to screw her if he wanted to. He's bent enough to do it. Depends whether you think that's better or worse than the razor, I suppose.'

'Well, fuck that,' said Chance self-righteously. 'I may have been brought up poor, Sam, but at least I was brought up clean.'

'Yes,' said Hoskins blandly, 'anyone could tell that. Come on, my son. Let's go and spread the good tidings to the Ripper. Dust off the old rack and screws ready for a bit of juicy questioning.'

Chance shook his head as if to clear it of confusion. Then he let in the clutch and edged the car out into the wet traffic of Great Western Street.

CHAPTER TWENTY-FOUR

'You pick 'em, Sam! You really do pick 'em!'

The Ripper sighed and turned away towards his window. Above the leafy avenues of Hawks Hill, the cloud had parted sufficiently to allow a shaft of bleak pale sunlight to catch the homeward-bound traffic near Connaught Park.

'It wasn't my idea to shove Robbo Smith off Highlands Avenue,' Hoskins said stubbornly. 'That's all down to Cooney and the girl. Principal and accessory, one way or the other.'

Ripley gave an unhappy little growl.

'Which way round, Sam? Let's not start this until we know precisely which way we're facing.'

'Sian Cooney or Sian Jones, whichever you want to call her. She must be number one. I don't know which came first with Robbo Smith, the screwing or the investigating. I'd guess he began looking into Cooney when the first of the Mount Pleasant tower blocks came down: "Radical journalist reveals all about capitalist corruption." He could have had the evidence, if it had been there. A lot of people thought it was, back in the 1960s. Only thing then was that the buildings were supposed to last for ever, not twenty years. Somehow he got into Sian. Perhaps through the Emporium. Presumably thought she was Cooney's tart. Screwed her and winkled out bits of information at the same time. Perhaps he even found out who she really was. I doubt it, but you can't tell. One day, she finds that all the loving is just a way of destroying her father. He may be repulsive to us, Max. But daughters do get hung up on fathers.'

'Mine never did,' Ripley said glumly. 'And you might give some thought to it being simply a screw that went wrong. One that she didn't want in the first place or resented afterwards. Drop all the other stuff.'

'Wild hysterical scene near cliff,' Hoskins persisted. 'Robbo takes off. The girl goes after him, screaming at him to stop.'

'Was the Cadillac insured for her to drive?'

'Even if it wasn't, Max, people have been known to drive uninsured. She rams him off the cliff a few minutes before half-past seven. That's my reckoning, from where I was standing with Harold Moyle. Panic-struck, she parks the car in the drive of Cooney's cliff-top split-level – takes less than five minutes. Call to big daddy describing how she killed Robbo. He tells her to lie low. Phones Anderson at the traffic department about twenty to eight. Ten or fifteen minutes is long enough for all that, Max. My Caddie's been nicked, he says. Tells Sian to get back on the bus or lie low in his place at Ocean Beach. Anderson phones back for the engine number. Cooney's in Hawks Hill and there's no two ways about that. Ten to eight. With a report like that, Anderson's hardly going to drive out to Ocean Beach and see if the Caddie's parked in Cooney's place there. Is he? So, at his leisure, Cooney gets hold of the Mouse. Lose that Caddie, and there's a couple of grand in the post. But the Mouse, being a flash young yobbo, can't resist driving the bloody thing round for a few days. And so we meet up with him in Dyce Street and there's the set-to in Martello Square.'

The Ripper shook his head.

'It's not the timing or the mechanics of it, Sam. Unless you can show that Sian Jones had a damn good reason for getting rid of Robbo Smith, it's not even a starter. And how do you show that?'

'They were seeing each other. No two ways. The Mouse knew it. Cooney must have known it.'

'But perhaps not until Robbo Smith was dead. In his present

situation, Cooney isn't going to kill a man when he knows the evidence of fiddling the Mount Pleasant contracts won't stick. Why risk murder?'

'He wouldn't,' Hoskins said shortly, 'but he might abet a murder where his daughter was involved. Concealing evidence. Fabricating an alibi. Perjury even. That's what I want Cooney for.'

The Ripper sniffed.

'Yes. Well, Sam, you'll only do that if you can prove Sian Jones nudged Robbo off the overcliff to begin with.'

'That'll suit me, Max. Just nicely.'

The attack squadron began to rend the late afternoon sky again, ripping in from the sea and following the valley to their imagined Soviet targets somewhere beyond Hawks Hill and Lord Dyce's fairy castle.

'What do you want then, Sam? Exactly.'

'A word with Sian Jones. A long and exclusive word. I'd like her brought here for questioning and released, if at all, on police bail – pending further inquiries.'

The Ripper's grey moustache seemed to droop a little.

'You don't think the Mouse could have rammed Smith off the overcliff drive?'

Hoskins shook his head.

'He was down on the Cakewalk an hour or so later. With that tart of his on a lead. Louise. He didn't act as if he'd just killed a man. More important, nor did she. His own car was there. In fact, I passed him driving down as I left old Harold Moyle and went to find out what was burning. I can't see how he could have done it, Max. I'd say he knew nothing about the Caddie at that stage. Sian Jones is the only one it really fits. Unless, of course, you believe it was a total stranger. A casual car thief.'

'A bit neat,' said Ripley sceptically. 'All right, Sam. You can't go busting out there with the cavalry to arrest Sian Jones, even if she's at Cooney's place. All this is just a bit too delicate. I'll make the arrangements. I'll try and get hold of Cooney on the phone. And then, I daresay, I'll have to talk to his lawyer.'

'Jack Cam? That half-smart bugger?'

'Sam,' said the Ripper patiently, 'you don't really think

Cooney's going to let you talk to his daughter except in the presence of his brief, do you?'

'If she was picked up and brought in, he'd have no choice.'

Ripley stared at him, uncomprehending.

'You are hanging by a thread, Sam, after the Neville business. And now you want to haul in Sian Jones on circumstantial evidence and put her through the mincer, presumably denying her the legal right to make a phone call to a relative to say she's been held. And that relative, Sam, is almost certainly going to be Councillor Cooney, now of the Police Committee. There's going to be a row, anyway, over your little stunt at the Emporium this afternoon. That was too clever by half. Just button your fly, Sam, before the curtain goes up on this number.'

'All right,' said Hoskins sourly, 'do it your way.'

'I'll be in touch, Sam.'

Hoskins went back across the corridor to his own office. Chance was sitting in the chair where he had left him.

'Well?'

'We can't arrest Sian Jones. Bloody Ripley won't go to the stipendiary for a warrant. Any other way's too tricky. He's going to try and arrange for us to question her. If that's all right with Carmel Cooney!'

'Huh!' Chance said. 'Mind you, Sam, if you'd come out of the Neville business better he might have taken a risk.'

'I don't know,' Hoskins said.

They sat in silence for a moment. Then Chance brightened up.

'Bit of excitement out at Lantern Hill. According to old Dudden.'

'What's that, then?'

'Couple of the lads on the Force there been going shopping on duty.'

'On duty?'

Chance sniggered.

'Small hours of the morning. Foot patrol. Testing doors of lock-up shops to see all's well. Tobacconists and that kind of thing. Shoulder to the door and extra bit of heave. And, lookee, there's been a break-in. Only thing is, they don't report it till they've done a bit of self-service. Searched their houses this morning. One with enough ciggies to smoke his entire family into the cancer clinic. The other living in a pyramid of Mars bars and kids' fireworks.'

'That's going to do a lot of good round Lantern Hill,' said Hoskins bitterly.

'Yes. Still, you'd know about Lantern Hill, wouldn't you, Sam?'

'Would I?'

'Yes. I mean you working on the domestic end of the Robbo Smith case. Finding out about him smoking and all that.'

'Yes. Well, it wasn't that difficult.'

Chance looked at Hoskins and a grin brightened slowly on his full red face.

'Sam! You haven't been knocking a slice off her out there, have you?'

'Don't be daft, my son.'

'You have! Look at your face! You bloody have! You've been having naughties out there with that girl in Arran Street!'

'She's not a girl. Don't be a prat.'

'Not much she isn't! Not so's you'd notice the difference! You dirty old devil, Sam Hoskins! Old Dudden said there was some whisper round the village there. Car seen parked at funny hours.'

'Don't be bloody silly. She's a witness – or could be if there's a case.'

'Right!' said Chance enthusiastically. 'So, who's being bloody silly? Screwing a witness – a suspect even – means straight out the door. No time to clear the desk nor nothing. Silly? I should say so!'

Hoskins recovered his composure.

'I tell you what, my son. There was never an inquiry yet where the chap questioning the young woman witness wasn't supposed to be having a bit with her too. You ought to hear what old Dudden says about you.'

'Me?' said Chance indignantly.

'Yes. Mind you, he's about as observant as any man with his head up his own behind can be. All right?'

Chance shrugged.

'If you say so, Sam. I don't care what you do to who, personally. All right by me. Bit stand-offish that one looked, anyway. Bit of a nun.'

'Exactly,' Hoskins said, as the door opened and Ripley came in.

'Ten o'clock Wednesday morning, Sam. Councillor Cooney's house in Hawks Hill. That's as close as you're going to get to an interrogation.'

'Wednesday morning? She could be in Brazil by then.'

Ripley smiled understandingly.

'You've seen her, Sam. She could hardly cross the road on her own. Seems she's got a hospital appointment tomorrow. A matter of some importance. And, by the way, you can expect Jack Cam to be there.'

'We need her in here, on her own.'

Ripley nodded. 'I daresay. When there's evidence.'

Instead of turning round and leaving the room, he walked across to the window and studied the view. Presently he faced Hoskins and Chance again.

'That was good,' he said. 'The coverage of John Stoodley's funeral. A lot of goodwill came from that. I had a drink with Tom Mason in the CN bar last night. His people have been getting some very positive responses indeed from their opinion research. The public appeal fund doubled in forty-eight hours.'

The other two made noises of appreciation. Ripley thought for a moment and then walked across to the door.

'Wednesday morning, then,' he said cheerfully. 'It'll need both of you out there. I'd appreciate some news as soon as you get back.'

Chance watched the door close.

'That's the way forward for you, Sam. Straight through the plate-glass window and a slap-up funeral on the telly. None of this schoolgirl-watching and witness-tickling out Lantern Hill. Turns the ratepayers right off the Police Force. Mind you, from what I saw, she did look a bit nice under the snow queen coolness. Might turn really imaginative in the bedroom. But then, if you're not into her, you wouldn't know about that. Would you?'

CHAPTER TWENTY-FIVE

'Fair's fair,' said Chance philosophically. 'I wouldn't mind living up here. Supposing anyone made me an offer.'

He parked the car, got out, yawned and stretched. The summer morning in Challoner Road was a house agent's dream. There was a quality in the air and sunlight that seemed clear and fresh, a stillness among tall hedges and lawns like green velvet. From the oak trees and beeches of the gardens came a sporadic chatter of bird-song and a soft hooting of doves. Light danced on a blue-basined swimming pool beyond a low wall. A girl with skin the shade of honey and an emerald-green bikini raised her arms and executed a perfect swallow dive. She swam back, pulled herself out, shaking the water from her tousled crop of light brown hair, the emerald-green nylon wet and clinging to her breasts and buttocks.

'Takes practice, that,' Hoskins said. 'That's his au pair: German. Claudia, sixteen years old.'

She turned away, moving with careful steps to repeat the dive. The light picked out the delicate bone pattern, the fine shape of her spine under the sleek skin of her wet back.

'Any time she wants to au pair me, I'll be waiting,' Chance said.

Across the alluvial foreshore of Canton, the tidal anchorages off the railway dock and King Edward basin glittered in the strong sun. But in Challoner Road that morning even the powered lawn-mowers had the discreetly muted purr of a Rolls-Royce. The rest of the city, from Barrier to Taylorstown, from Mount Pleasant to Orient, was no more than a distant hum.

'Right, my son. Let's see what the blessed Carmel Cooney has to say for himself.'

Before they could reach the double front door, a man came across the lawn to intercept them. He was tall and thin, in a dapper fawn suit of summer weight. He wore a waistcoat with a fob-watch, its chain looped across his belly like a prosperous Victorian family man. Everything about him was slim and spruce, from his neatly barbered grey hair to his coffee-tan handmade shoes. He had the air of an actor costumed to play the middle-aged dandy in an old-fashioned comedy.

'Morning, Mr Hoskins. Mr Chance.'

'Morning, Mr Cam.'

'We thought we might have our little talk round the side, on the terrace. Mr Cooney doesn't get that much air. Hasn't the time. It's comfy there, too.'

They followed him past the conservatory. The view of Canton dwindled and now they overlooked the beginning of the valley, the sharp-edged hills and the fairy castle half obscured by a haze of heat.

'Keeping well, Mr Hoskins?'

'Staying alive, Mr Cam.'

'Yes,' said Jack Cam. 'Well, that's the most important thing. Got the toe of your boot nicely into Mr Lobo's backside, from what I hear. He's been inviting that a long while.'

'Over and done with now, Mr Cam.'

Cam dropped the subject and indicated an open door.

'You want a slash or anything before we start, there's a place in there.'

'Safe for now, Mr Cam.'

Carmel Cooney, like a hippo surging from its river-bed, got up from his basket chair to meet them as they reached the expanse of the red and white paved terrace. Padded garden chairs had been arranged round an outdoor dining table. There were glasses and a jug of lemon-coloured drink.

'I know you good people won't take a proper drink,' said Cooney, chuckling. 'And being on the committee now, I mustn't encourage you. No harm in a drop of lemon, however, if you fancy it.'

There was no sign of Sian Jones as they sat down. Hoskins began.

'First of all, Mr Cooney, there's some questions to be put to Miss Jones. To your daughter.'

The melon-face surveyed him with a movement of total indifference.

'Mr Cam's here to tell you all about that, Mr Hoskins.'

Hoskins had expected a trick of some kind. Not Brazil,

perhaps. But something the Ripper was going to have reason to regret. Jack Cam opened a folder that lay on the table.

'Miss Jones was examined yesterday by two specialists: Mr Brockenden Brown and Mr Ellis Tolland. She is a very sick young woman.'

'You wouldn't have thought it the other afternoon,' Hoskins said sceptically. 'Not the way she took to her heels out of that store. Down the fire escape.'

Jack Cam frowned slightly, as if at a joke in bad taste.

'Miss Jones was examined at Roseland. By two specialists, eminent in their field, who came independently to the same conclusions.'

'Roseland? Psychiatrists?'

Cam nodded.

'Both Tolland and Brown are of the opinion that Miss Jones is suffering from dissociative reaction, that it is progressive and might under provocation become catatonic. In other words, there is a divorce from reality which if aggravated would cause what I always think of as a brainstorm. She'd spend the rest of her life sitting in a chair, staring in front of herself, seeing nothing and hearing nothing.'

'Two days ago she was modelling furs in the Emporium.'

Cam conceded this with a nod.

'And might be now. It may have been the shock of your appearance and the accusation you made, Mr Hoskins, that tipped her a little more. Don't misunderstand me. I don't hold you to blame, nor does Mr Cooney. You weren't to know. But imagine the effect on a girl in her mental state, of suddenly being confronted and accused of illegitimacy. Of being threatened with exposure before the world for something that never was her fault. Something she could neither deny, evade nor defend herself from. Why, you saw for yourself, Mr Hoskins. You told us just now. She turned and ran in panic.'

Cooney shook his head, the eyes in the melon-face sliding downwards in defeat to fix their gaze on the terrace tiling.

'My little girl's sick, Mr Hoskins. Very sick. It's the great grief of my life. I done all I could to protect and shelter her. But I can't keep her here and watch over her day and night.'

Hoskins ignored him.

'Mr Cam, Sian Jones knew Robbo Smith, the sports reporter who was killed. He'd been in the car, the Cadillac, before it was reported stolen. We think he was in it with her. We also think she'd once been on his motorbike with him. And a photographer took a picture of them together on the Cakewalk. Robbo Smith's bike was hit by that Cadillac when he was killed. Now, whatever the answers may be, you of all people must see that there're questions to be asked.'

Cam bared his teeth and drew breath, as if at the difficulty of it all.

'You can't question a patient who's been committed to a psychiatric hospital, Mr Hoskins. And even if you forced the issue somehow and you did it, no court would accept evidence obtained under such circumstances. There's two opinions now saying that she's not fit to be out and in charge of herself. Let alone give evidence in a court of law. And she could get worse. Much worse.'

The au pair performed another swallow dive, a beautiful pagan goddess soaring against infinite blue. There was a distant splash. Someone clapped and there was laughter.

'She can't be left out of it, Mr Cam. She was having an affair with Robbo Smith, not to put too fine a point upon it. And he was killed by a car that belonged to her father and which she was able to drive. A car he'd been in.'

'How d'you know that?' Cooney's jowls shook a little with indignation.

'Forensic evidence, Mr Cooney, of a kind to compromise Mr Smith.'

'That bastard!' Cooney brought his fist down softly on the table, as if restraining his anger by virtue of grief. 'That degenerate young bastard! To take advantage of my little girl, that's hurt in her mind! To do things like that to her! No one ever done a thing like that to her before, Mr Hoskins. She was so trusting. Always been watched over. And then that fucking scumbag Smith? How could he, Mr Hoskins? How could anyone?'

Hoskins looked at him patiently.

'That's one of the things I'd like to hear the answer to, Mr Cooney. Smith was killed, after all. There could be a connection.'

'Not killed by her, Mr Hoskins! I was here, in this house. You know it, you can prove it. And she was here too, all the time. I could hear her in the next room. And soon as I knew the Caddie was gone, I went in there to tell her. Twenty to eight, Mr Hoskins. You tell me how she could have been with Robbo Smith in Ocean Beach at half-past seven and then back here less than ten minutes later. You couldn't do it in under half an hour. And now you want to question a sick girl that hardly knows what she's saying? Question her about how she could be somewhere she could never possibly be?'

Cam intervened.

'There's no thought of that, Mr Cooney. No one suggests that your daughter was involved in the man's death. Mr Hoskins would never suggest it on the present evidence. Nor would he try to interrogate someone certified as mentally sick by two consultants. Of course he wouldn't. You really have no cause for such distress, sir.'

Hoskins felt his face grow warm as Cam headed him off.

'There are questions to which I want answers,' he said.

Cam nodded, placating him.

'But not from a psychiatric patient, Mr Hoskins.'

'If I have to, I will. I can get an independent examination to decide if she ought to be a psychiatric patient at all. Or if she's just conveniently been put out of the way.'

Cam sighed, the peacemaker thwarted in his efforts.

'In that case, Mr Hoskins, I shall brief counsel this afternoon. An application can be made before a judge in chambers by this evening, restraining you from interfering in the treatment of a patient who is seriously ill in hospital. I shall also make a report of any police interference to such professional bodies as Mind and Mencap. Mr Cooney may be a member of the Police Committee, but his membership ought not to disqualify Miss Jones from having her case mentioned there and on the Women's Committee of the council. Hospitalisation is quite an issue with those ladies already.'

'A man was killed,' Hoskins said. 'Possibly murdered.'

'But not by Sian Jones, Mr Hoskins. You have no evidence to suggest her involvement in the murder. Indeed the evidence, as Mr Cooney tells you, is all the other way.'

'I've got questions to ask him too.'

'Which he will decline to answer, upon my advice, if you pursue this line further,' Cam said smoothly.

The verbal manoeuvres continued for another half-hour. Hoskins got nowhere. As they stood up to leave, Cooney lumbered across to the chief inspector. His feet moved awkwardly under his weight. His face was now puckered as if partly with incomprehension and partly to begin blubbering. He plucked ineffectually at Hoskins' sleeve and spoke in a querulous confidential murmur.

'Why can't you leave my little girl alone, Mr Hoskins? She never done you any harm! She never done anyone harm!'

'I hope that may be true, Mr Cooney.'

The smooth round face brightened at this concession. He plucked Hoskins' sleeve again and gestured towards a trellised enclosure beyond the pool.

'She got her bunnies over there. Had them since she was a little girl. Brought 'em when she come up from Talavera Street. She loves them creatures, Mr Hoskins. She loves every creature. You should see her. Wouldn't hurt a fly. And that's the little girl that your dirty degenerate bastard Robbo Smith soiled and fouled. I'm glad someone had that scumbag put down. But she'd never do it.'

Hoskins sighed.

'Right,' he said. 'Thanks. I'll talk to you again in due course.'

Jack Cam walked towards the car with the two policemen.

'Not one of your pleasanter duties, Mr Hoskins.'

'Not one of Robbo Smith's pleasanter outings either, on that cliff.'

They turned the corner of the conservatory and Canton glittered in the sun.

'No,' Cam said, 'I reckon they'll miss him on the *Western World*. He was coming on nicely, from sport into politics and industrial reporting. He could have gone a long way.'

Hoskins nodded. A bronzed boy of seventeen or eighteen, stripped to the waist, was wheeling out the Cooney lawn mower.

The sprinkler, drawing its veil of droplets across the grass in a steady circle, slackened and died.

'Come to that, not one of your better summers, I suppose, Sam,' Jack Cam said when they were out of sight of Cooney. 'Robbo Smith dead and no one knows the answer. That nasty affair of the girl in the storm drain and not a clue who did it. All that noise down Martello Square. The Mouse in the river. And then the to-and-fro with old Lobo at the inquest. A bit of a bastard all round.'

Hoskins paused by the car door and nodded a curt acknowledgement.

'That's about it, Mr Cam. For all the bloody good I've done since May, I might as well have stayed in bed the past couple of months.'

'Somewhen soon,' Cam said, 'I'll buy you a drink and make up for it.'

He closed the car door for Hoskins and waved them off. The grey steel gates purred open on the automatic signal and Chance turned into Challoner Road.

'How about that then, Sam?'

Hoskins shook his head and sat in silence for a moment. They were heading down Godwin Road, past the crossing that led to the trading estate and the tall power-station chimneys, before he recovered his composure.

'The whole bloody thing,' he said, 'is slipping through our fingers. I can see it. I can feel it. I know how it's happening. And there's fuck-all I can do about it. Roseland. A fancy private loony-bin. Out towards the valley and Dyce Castle. Used to be a hotel at one time.'

'Question her,' said Chance simply. 'Just go ahead and do it.'

Hoskins shook his head.

'Jack Cam's right about one thing. Evidence or statements from her as things are, a mental patient questioned under what looks like duress, would be a disaster in court. In fact, it might be God's gift to the other side.'

'Have her examined by an independent bloke?'

Children were playing a disorganised game of football on the threadbare grass of Connaught Park.

'Not worth it,' Hoskins said. 'Cooney's bought the best two round here: Brockenden Brown and old Tolland. Any case, by the time we got a man in, she'd have been well coached in the symptoms. Thing is, she looks and acts a bit odd anyway.'

'How did Cooney get 'em to commit her, then?'

'I daresay they owe him a favour. He's put a bob or two into their pet charities. In any case, no one's saying she's entirely normal. All a matter of opinion and degree. And anyone could write "dissociative reaction" on a bit of paper.'

'What's it mean?'

'Long-winded way of saying someone's out of touch with reality.'

'That's half bloody "A" Division,' Chance sniggered. 'Ripley included.'

'Exactly,' Hoskins said. 'Perhaps he'll recognise the symptoms.'

They crossed the traffic lights, past a disused Baptist church, the self-confident gothic of a prosperous Victorian suburb.

'Jack Cam really going to buy you a drink, is he?'

'Might do,' Hoskins said.

'Bit cheeky. Reciting a list of cock-ups like that.'

'Yes,' said Hoskins. 'Still, they happened, didn't they?'

'All the same.' Chance braked sharply at the lollipop crossing outside the red brick primary school with its church windows. 'Bit cheeky.'

'I look forward to summer,' Hoskins said. 'Always have done. But this one, Jack! I cannot tell you how pissed off I am with the whole bloody thing.'

CHAPTER TWENTY-SIX

The sun of the summer evening had gone down behind the hills, ending the day in a flush of golden light that always reminded Hoskins of the seascape on Players cigarette packets of his boyhood. From the window of his flat, the hills were the furthest point of the view. With the light behind them, they were grey and sharp-edged, like the ribs of slag-heaps. Near at hand, the last of the warm day drew slant shadows down Longwall and across the city centre. The Prudential Assurance building, that had won a prize in 1950, rose in modernistic ivory-white, its rounded end suggesting the stern section of a Blue Riband Cunarder.

By their construction, the flats were insulated from the shouting and the slamming outside the two commercial pubs in St Vincent Street. Across the turf of Lamb's Acre, the embattled concrete of the new terrace and the rib-cage of the old stand, he caught the drifting of belated church bells. Even in Canton it was Sunday.

Lesley had not cried when he told her. So far as he could see, she had registered neither surprise nor resentment, certainly not betrayal nor misery. He lifted a saucepan-lid, sniffed and then went tactfully back to the bedroom. She was still lying on her side with her back to him, just as he had left her, still naked on the covers of the bed. The room seemed too warm for anything else. Her hands were folded under her head, as if she might be sleeping. The upper leg was straight and the lower one bent at the knee, the effect being to increase and distort the swell of her hips a little, as if in erotic suggestion. She was awake. No two ways about that. Hoskins sat down on the side of the bed.

'I'm sorry,' he said gently, 'but you had to know. Sooner or later you'd have heard something. Read something in the papers, perhaps. You know: "There is no truth to the rumour that. . . ." And so forth.'

'What sort of girl was she?'

He stroked the softness of her straight fair hair from the high crown to its trimmed line at her nape and jawbone.

'Not your class, that's certain. All right, I suppose. Unbalanced, though. A kind of quiet vacancy.'

'It's the one possibility I never thought about. That the whole thing might have to do with Robbo screwing someone else.'

Hoskins stared at the window, seeing the roofs and chimneys of the other flats.

'His interest in Mount Pleasant was genuine. It probably happened once with the girl. That's all.'

'I wonder what she had that I didn't.'

He smiled and kissed her neck. 'Nothing.'

Lesley turned on her back and looked up at him, touching his face.

'But you don't understand, do you?' she said. 'About Robbo and me? Not really.'

'Perhaps not.'

'We had an open relationship. We didn't possess one another. That was the agreement. If you've always lived in a possessive relationship, it's hard to understand. I'd had another man while we were together. It wasn't a guilty secret. And there was Eve.'

'Not a secret either?'

'We never had the chance to discuss it.'

'And Robbo?'

'I'm sure there were women. I don't know who. Except of course the girl in the car.'

They caressed one another in silence for a moment. Then Lesley said, 'It's a lot easier, you know. That sort of relationship. When something like that happens. If you possess a person and lose them, it can destroy you. Not Sam Hoskins, perhaps, but it does destroy people. It's not the kind of attachment I wanted. I'd been through all that before. I couldn't take it any longer.'

'That's fair enough,' Hoskins said, 'but I'm sorry I had to tell you about him and the girl.'

She pulled herself up and hugged her knees, sitting there like a thoughtful child.

'I wouldn't resent her,' she said, 'I really wouldn't. In fact, I feel terribly sorry for her. Will they put her on trial?'

Hoskins shook his head.

'I don't see how. They could try and get a couple of other psychiatrists to examine her and say she's fit to plead. But I don't think they will. The prosecution service isn't very keen on the idea. A vast waste of public money to no purpose. That's all they're bothered about. But in any case there'd be a conflict of medical evidence over the girl's state. Never does much good in court. And the rest of it is too circumstantial. First of all, you'd have to show Cooney was lying about her being at Hawks Hill when it happened.'

'How do you know he's lying?'

He stood up.

'Because I know Cooney. But you saw him on television with Eve Ricard: he'd put on a performance that a prosecuting counsel couldn't match. And the rest of it is circumstantial. You'd have to show why Sian Jones was so desperate that she killed Robbo. To do that, you'd practically need her confession. And that's something we haven't got and can't get. Even if we could, it's useless in court so long as she's out at Roseland.'

Lesley fished for her pants and sweater.

'I'm glad.'

'She'd have a good defence counsel. The best. I'd bet money that he'd hang the whole thing on the Mouse, or try to. Either Neville or his friends. Driving the stolen Caddie on the overcliff. Ramming a bike off the edge, either in an accident or out of devilment. A jury might go for that. The Mouse was on the Cakewalk that evening; I passed him in his own car, not the Cadillac. He couldn't have driven them both at the crucial time. But by the time their brief got through with it, no jury would believe I'd had time to recognise Neville flying past in a split second.'

'Then it's over,' she said, brushing her short hair into place perfunctorily. 'I'm glad.'

'They'll have to reconvene the inquest sooner or later, but there's no reason that you should be involved.'

She locked her arms round his neck.

'Let's go and eat,' she said.

It was a subdued occasion. They ate and talked quietly. For the first time in their affair, Hoskins felt an awkwardness between them. After Chance's jovial accusation, it had seemed better for Lesley to come to Lamb's Chambers. At least for the time being. When the meal was over, she admired his models of the Paris Hotel and the Odeon at Ocean Beach.

'It seems odd for a policeman,' she said at last.

'Even policemen take their boots off and become human.'

Before she could say anything else the phone rang. Hoskins picked it up.

'Mr Hoskins?' The voice was one he did not at first recognise. 'Chief Inspector Hoskins?'

Only then did he realise that, distorted a little by the vibration, it was the voice of Carmel Cooney.

'Speaking, Mr Cooney.'

'I was wondering, Mr Hoskins, if you could spare the time to come out and see me at Hawks Hill? It's a matter of some importance and concern to yourself. In your professional capacity, of course. Nothing to do with the business that you and I and Mr Cam was on about the other day. That wouldn't be etiquette, naturally.'

'It's rather late,' Hoskins said.

'Indeed it is, Mr Hoskins. And it's Sunday too. But I don't know that this should be left waiting. I've been looking through a video tape out here. And I think I got something you'd like to see. Something that relates to your little dust-up with Mr Lobo at the inquest.'

Hoskins looked up quickly and stared at Lesley as he spoke.

'A video?'

Cooney chuckled richly down the wire.

'You won't believe this, I daresay, Mr Hoskins. But it gives me no satisfaction, as a member of the Police Committee, to see my officers in trouble. And you are in a bit of trouble there, aren't you, Mr Hoskins? What I'm offering you is a good turn. A good turn in the matter of your career. And I promise you it don't affect your freedom of investigation in the other matter at all. Not a jot. This is all down to Neville the Mouse.'

'What video is this?'

Cooney chuckled again.

'Now, Mr Hoskins! Really! I'm not going into details on the public line. Not when there's an outfit in Cheltenham that can monitor four million calls at a time. You want to see it, you come over. It's hardly ten now. I'm impatient, Mr Hoskins, for you to have a look at this.'

Cooney's voice was rich enough to be heard almost anywhere in the Lamb's Chambers sitting room. Hoskins looked up at Lesley. She nodded.

'All right, Mr Cooney, I'll be up in about fifteen minutes. But I must be back here as soon as possible.'

'Would I keep you without reason, Mr Hoskins? I would not.'

Cooney chuckled again and hung up.

Hoskins stood, undecided for a moment, by the uncurtained window.

'Wait for me,' he said, hoping that she would take it as an instruction rather than a suggestion.

Lesley nodded. 'All right.'

'Stay the night. I'm not on until eight.'

She clasped her hands behind his neck and he allowed himself to touch the cool smoothness of her bare thighs below the level of her pants.

'I never intended to do anything else.'

He reached for his jacket. 'And in case anything funny happens, remember the gist of that conversation. Carmel Cooney wants to show me a video for my own good. Something to do with Neville the Mouse.'

Going down the communal stone stairs to the car, he was suddenly possessed by a cold thought. There had been a vindictive streak in the Mouse – capable of training a video camera on Angie, the red-haired biker's girl, during her last moments. How such a tape might have come into Cooney's possession, Hoskins could not tell. He prayed that it would prove to be nothing of the kind.

The blanched light of the ornamental lamps across the trees of the Mall shone on empty streets and occasional cars. Canton lay quiet in anticipation of Monday morning. Hoskins took the deserted route past Connaught Park and up Godwin Road again. It was twenty past ten when the grey steel gates purred open for him and he stopped the car in the porch light that illuminated Cooney's gravel drive.

There was no indication that they were watching for him. He rang the bell at the panelled double door in pastel grey and waited. It was opened for him by a girl whom he did not at first see clearly against the light and whom he did not then recognise at once. She was quite tall and tightly dressed in black trousers with a short jacket. The honey-blonde hair was strained back into a chignon from a face whose straight features appeared a little too prominent for beauty. There was a hardness in the face that did not surprise him and the crude ear-rings jingled as she moved. It was a second later that he knew her for the girl whom Cooney was supposed to have given to old Torrence in exchange for services rendered: Tracey. Hoskins recalled her at sixteen, the lithe willowy figure and graceful movements, the veil of hair floating as she walked. As clearly as Cooney himself, Tracey at twenty-five or so bore upon her the ineradicable symptoms of mortality.

The host appeared in grey suit and carpet slippers at the far end of the cool vestibule with its cornice lighting.

'Mr Hoskins! Good of you to come! We're in the saloon here. Come in and see if we can't find you something to break the ice!'

CHAPTER TWENTY-SEVEN

'Mr Hoskins!' Cooney ushered him into the long cool room, where the cornice lights illuminated neutral grey and silver. For a moment Hoskins thought Cooney was about to extend his hand and, defensively, he clasped his own behind his back. From the twin speakers, rich and pure, came the splendid leaping chords of a romantic piano. It was the only weakness that Hoskins shared with Cooney. He recognised the last jubilant variation of Schumann's *Etudes Symphoniques*.

'Have a seat, Mr Hoskins. Drink?'

Hoskins took the deep chair opposite Cooney.

'I won't drink, thanks. I must drive back soon.'

Cooney gave a short emphatic nod of his large head, as if he approved.

'First off, Mr Hoskins, this is nothing to do with my poor little girl. Your duty there is quite apart. Not that you could do much as things are – she's gone worse since they took her out to Roseland.'

'Sorry to hear it, Mr Cooney.'

Cooney leant forward, his knees fattening in the tight grey trousers as he shifted.

'Mind you, Mr Hoskins, they been wonderful to her out there.' He sat back and drew a magisterial breath. 'Wonderful, they been. I'm intending to donate a brain scanner, on condition it's used two days a week for patients from the National Health. Poor little kiddies from Barrier and Peninsula. Families that's as poor now as I was when I started. I don't forget, Mr Hoskins.'

'No,' Hoskins said. 'And about this other matter, Mr Cooney?'

Cooney raised his hand in acknowledgement.

'Quite right, Mr Hoskins. Well now, you and I haven't always seen quite eye to eye. But I still had a great respect for you. Always had. You been straight. Not like that little shit Roberts and his kind. Not like them two comics I hear about out Lantern Hill, knocking off confectionery on night patrol. And now, me being on the Police Committee, we got all the more cause to work together.'

'It's not customary, Mr Cooney, for a member of the committee to deal directly with a police officer.'

Cooney looked up at him in astonishment.

'Would I, Mr Hoskins? Would I do anything not customary? I respect you and wish you well. And, being on the committee, it gave me no pleasure seeing that snake Lobo try to slag you off at that inquest. But you're here, Mr Hoskins, as officer in charge of the case of Neville the Mouse. I'm offering you evidence as a member of the public. And if you can work it up Lobo's arse, so much the better.'

'Then let's have it, Mr Cooney.'

Cooney rang the bell. Tracey, the graceful figure in the tight black costume, entered with a video cassette. It was the immobility of the features as well as their boldness that aged and hardened her.

'Just load the tape in the machine, sweetie, and then see no one disturbs us,' Cooney said.

As Tracey knelt at the player on the lower shelf, he nodded at her for Hoskins' benefit.

'That's Noreen's girl, off the estates. You remember her? Father gone, of course. Married that daft old bugger Torrence. But these last few days, you no idea what she's been to me. With my little girl sick and so on.'

Tracey stood up and Cooney reached forward to ensure that he was able to pat her as she passed him on her way to the door.

'Now, Mr Hoskins,' he said, 'you know me as a careful man. My telephone calls are recorded and the security system down the Emporium is of the best. The punters don't see it and we don't mention it, but them cameras is turning all the time. Now, we don't keep the tapes. End of the day, we stick 'em back in and use 'em again. See? But when there's a try-on or a knock-off, we keep a copy. Savvy?'

'They do the same at Jones and Gower, Mr Cooney, and the chain stores.'

Cooney scowled.

'Public-school poofs with degrees,' he said scornfully. 'It's me the punters can thank for keeping the old Emporium going. Now, Mr Hoskins. Any day now, you are going to have to face an internal inquiry over the death of Neville the Mouse. And you're going to get a load of fucking fanny from Lobo and his crew about how the Mouse was just a high-spirited lad. Hounded to his death by vicious police officers. Right?'

'Probably, Mr Cooney.'

'What we got here,' Cooney said, 'is the answer. The security tape for the time Neville was in the Emporium that afternoon. He's on it, Mr Hoskins. And when the committee sees the Mouse carrying on at his nastiest, old Lobo is going to climb the wall.'

Hoskins controlled his excitement well.

'And what's your interest in all this, Mr Cooney?'

'Not to buy you, Mr Hoskins. You can't be bought. I want to see you get a fair deal. I want this city to have policemen that everyone knows where they stand with.'

'All right,' said Hoskins cautiously. 'Let's see the tape, then.'

Cooney pressed the button on the commander and the screen flickered with light.

'Two cameras,' he said proudly, 'able to see him from both angles, according to how the chap monitoring wants to play the game.'

'A view out the door, Mr Cooney? People on the pavement?'

'Course we have, Mr Hoskins. You know as well as I do, a thief can't be stopped until outside the premises. Nowadays, when it's some young buck, that probably means a fist-fight in the street. We have that on tape. Otherwise, we get a lot of old puddin' about our security staff assaulting the little bastards, when all the time it's the other way round.'

Hoskins watched the screen carefully. He was surprised at the quality of the recording.

'Nice bit of picture, Mr Cooney.'

'New Sony. Eight mil. None of the Mickey Mouse stuff they sell for home video.'

The camera had picked up the Mouse and Breaker Weekes, scuffling and laughing outside the window. There was an oblique view of the window, the girl with the sharp features and the mane of Pre-Raphaelite ringlets.

'Who's that girl, Mr Cooney?'

'Ah,' said Cooney, 'Liz or one of 'em. Just some young horsey that Benson hired to do the display.'

'Not the Mouse's? Not on the game evenings and weekends?'

Cooney sniggered.

'You got an old-fashioned mind, Mr Hoskins. If she was on the game at all, she wouldn't be doing the display for what old Benson shells out.'

She was stretching now and the Mouse, young face drawn into a savage leer, was making his unambiguous gesture behind her for the girl to see.

'Mind you, she was sticking it out for him a bit,' Cooney said. 'Giving him a taste of the old fat and cheeky. Makes you wonder if she fancied herself.'

Hoskins said nothing. He had noticed that as the Mouse and Breaker Weekes stood there, they spent some time staring at their own feet. It was odd. At least it was that.

'They were trying to put the wind up the girl,' he said vaguely, 'so's she'd run from the window and leave Neville to loot it.'

'Mean little prat, he was, Mr Hoskins. Who'd go to all that trouble over a load of cheap costume jewellery? It's only trippers' souvenirs. Wives of the young punters likes it. They don't know better. But it's hardly worth carrying away. He must have known that. Why bother thieving what he could hardly sell again?'

Hoskins stared at Cooney. The question was one he had not even stopped to consider. It began to acquire an ominous importance.

The girl was scrambling from the window now, almost running through the store. There was a glimpse of Neville behind the glass, stuffing his pockets, and Weekes crouching down outside as if tying up his shoelaces.

Hoskins frowned.

'Can you turn this thing back, Mr Cooney?'

'Whenever you say, Mr Hoskins. Look at this, though! Look at this!'

The camera had caught a glimpse of the fiasco on the pavement: Neville shrugging off his leather jacket, kicking Chance in the ribs. Then there was the chase through the store. The Mouse had drawn his lips back from his teeth in a breathless snarl. There was a mixture of hatred, indifference and resolve on the tense brown-skinned face. As he hurdled the perfume counter, it was clear that he had knocked down the girl behind it with a fist deliberately clenched.

'Doesn't look much like Mr Lobo's high-spirited boy now, does he, Mr Hoskins? More like a wicked little thug.'

Hoskins saw himself, a bulky greying figure lumbering in pursuit. Then they were gone, out of range, and there was nothing on the tape but the mute and stupid faces of the onlookers staring after them.

'That it, Mr Cooney?'

'Yes, Mr Hoskins. What you think of it, then?'

'Illuminating.'

'Illuminating!' Cooney's tone suggested that Hoskins would be the death of him with such humour.

'Turn back to the bit where the girl ran out of the window and the Mouse looted it.'

Cooney ran rapidly through the chase in reverse until the picture settled down again.

'Now,' Hoskins said, 'let's have it slow up to the point where Pope tries to grab the Mouse.'

As if the whole thing were being performed with difficulty under water, the images of the actors began to move. The girl with the reddish-brown mane of ringlets was on all fours, polishing the shiny white surface of the pedestals, the grey-blue denim tight as skin over the swell of her haunches. The Mouse, standing over her and grinning through the glass until he caught her attention, made his unambiguous gesture behind her. In a slow balletic movement, she rose and loped from view. The Mouse was lost to view and then reappeared in the window, casually stuffing his pockets. Breaker Weekes went slowly down to a squat, his back to the camera, his head bowed, hands busy somewhere near his feet. Then he turned slightly sideways, as if reaching down.

'Hold that!' Hoskins said sharply. Cooney froze the picture.

'You shall have a copy of the tape to take away, Mr Hoskins. Done on the other format for you.'

'There're gratings in the pavement outside some of those windows,' Hoskins said. 'He could be reaching in to one of them.'

'He wouldn't reach much, Mr Hoskins. Too far down. Any case, there's nothing down there. Only shit the public drops. Not used nowadays. Used to be where they shot coal, I think, in times gone by.'

'Let it run on slowly,' Hoskins said.

The looting continued and, this time, Hoskins could just make out the white van from which he and the others had emerged as the Mouse came out of the shop. Neville slipped free of Pope. Chance fell on top of Weekes. Then Neville paused and kicked.

'Hold it there again, Mr Cooney.'

Instead of running off, Neville turned towards Chance and Weekes. He kicked once, at Chance. Through the legs of the crowd it was possible to see Chance rolling clear to avoid the second kick. But now it was clear that the Mouse had not aimed the second kick at him. It was directed at, or upon, something lying on the pavement. Even in slow motion it was impossible to tell, from the video, what that might be. All the same, Hoskins felt a distinct excitement, tinged by hope. It was an experience that had come rarely in the past few months.

For Cooney's benefit, he sighed and made little of it.

'If you wouldn't mind letting me have a copy of the tape, Mr Cooney, I'll issue you the receipt first thing tomorrow. I'm not sure it tells us anything we didn't know. Still, it certainly shows how the Mouse could act when not on his best behaviour.'

'From what I hear of the little prick, Mr Hoskins, this was his best behaviour. He was rubbish. I'm just happy, for your sake, that any investigation should know it.'

'I'm working on a case, Mr Cooney. I don't accept evidence as if it were a personal favour.'

'Course you don't, Mr Hoskins. I know that. As a committee member, I don't offer favours to my officers. But if this does you some good, no one'll be more pleased than me.'

'Tomorrow, Mr Cooney. Tomorrow we'll see how much good it is.'

He got up, determined to leave. Cooney rang the bell again for Tracey.

'Find Mr Hoskins the copy of the tape, my pet. The one Mr Benson made.'

She went to get it.

'When she was sixteen or so,' said Cooney confidentially, 'she used to work in a jeans boutique. You never saw anything so beautiful, them long slim legs in tight pants and a bum like a twisted cherry. Some punter from the insurance office opposite used to follow her home at night after work. Right to the door. So close she reckoned he must have his tie caught in her necklace. One day he wasn't there. Gone right off. Not seen for a year or two.'

Hoskins acknowledged the story with a nod and took the tape from the girl.

'Right,' he said briskly. 'Thank you, Mr Cooney. I'll let you know what develops. You'll be hearing about the receipt.'

'What'd I want a poxy receipt for?' Cooney asked generously. 'I can afford a bit of tape, Mr Hoskins. Any time you're short, you only got to come round and ask.'

He stood in the porch and watched Hoskins drive away, the steel gates purring open and closed.

Lesley was stretched out on the bed in the darkened room. She was still awake.

'But it can't be to do with Robbo,' she said when he told her what had happened. 'Not the business at the Royal Peninsular Emporium.'

'I shouldn't think so. I don't know that it's to do with anything at all.'

They lay together for a moment. Then she took her hand from his face.

'You should have more women in the Division. Cooney wouldn't know how to deal with a woman investigating him.'

'He dealt with your friend Eve Ricard all right on the television show.'

'But you don't have many women working with you, do you?'

Hoskins shook his head.

'Lady crime-fighters are strictly for television series round here. Makes the viewers think equality's all the rage. That's what the producers want: your regulation female and regulation black member of the team. Truth is, we've almost stopped putting women into our part of CID. They have them for children and rape cases and so on. That's about all.'

'Why?'

He yawned.

'Too bloody dangerous. Any inquiry nowadays might involve a punch-up. Front-line stuff. You take a young buck, a yobbo from Barrier or Orient. He loves the feel of fisting some wanker's face. If it's a policeman, that's cloud seven. If it's a real bossy cow of a policewoman and he feels the nose break, face going all directions under the old knuckles, that's multiple orgasm.'

She was silent for a moment. 'You're cynical,' she said at last.

'I've seen it happen once or twice,' Hoskins said. 'Not to mention the steel-toecap kick to the stomach and the rest of it once she's down.'

'It's frightening,' Lesley said.

'It's bloody terrifying, if you stop and think about it. Which I'm not going to do until tomorrow morning.'

There was silence for a moment more.

'Try turning over this way and see how it goes,' Hoskins said gently. The frame of the bed creaked a little under the movement.

CHAPTER TWENTY-EIGHT

Chance steered the motor-pool Fiesta into the car park behind Jones and Gower, a rubbled wilderness where the Gaumont super-cinema with deep pullman seats had once stood.

'You want to watch it, Sam,' he said as he slammed the door. 'Cooney and his video is a bit like getting cosy with a porcupine.'

Hoskins hitched the waist of his trousers higher.

'Yes. Well, we'll see about that presently.'

Monday morning was a quiet time in Great Western Street and Atlantic Wharf, except for the hoarse-voiced sellers of sheets and towels from cardboard boxes along the access lanes at the rear of the Paris Hotel and the department stores. Quick-eyed and light-toed, they scanned the summer shoppers for the approach of a police helmet.

Benson and the girl were waiting in his office, beyond the accounts window of the Royal Peninsular Emporium. Hoskins began with the girl. She was shorter than she had appeared in the video and there was enough plumpness on her hips and buttocks to give her a waddling look in the tightness of the jeans.

'What exactly were these two young men doing? Did you see?'

'They were being nasty,' she said primly. 'At least, that one was. The one that died.'

'What were they doing as they stood there, before that?'

'I never saw anything else. Only that one of them was being nasty. I thought he might break the glass and grab me or something. He had a cruel look. As if he wanted to hurt someone.'

It was hopeless. There was nothing more to be got from her.

'Right,' said Hoskins patiently to Benson. 'Let's go downstairs and outside. See what we can find.'

The morning had grown warmer. Under the sunblinds shading the pavement, they studied the gratings that had been set at intervals before the long windows. Each was about three feet in length and eighteen inches wide, the slim iron bars spaced at intervals of an inch or two.

203

'These covers come up still, do they, Mr Benson?'

'They could, Mr Hoskins. They don't very often. There's no cause.'

'But a smart little bugger like Neville or Weekes could do it perhaps. Go the other end and give us a hand.'

'Need a lever, Mr Hoskins.'

Two chisel blades were fetched from the works office of the Emporium. Slowly, Hoskins and Benson lifted the grating up and clear. A couple of inches below the level of the pavement a ledge ran round the opening, wide enough to catch gum-wrappers and the smaller cigarette packets. The main drop went down about four feet to a dry bed.

'Not used for years, Mr Hoskins.'

'Cleaned out sometimes?'

'Not that often.'

Hoskins lowered himself more than waist-deep into the opening until his feet touched the hard bottom.

'Got to muck that lot out, have we?' There was no mistaking the disapproval in Chance's voice.

'Get a few of the clear plastic bags from the car, Jack,' Hoskins said.

He waited with Benson.

'Pity that girl never saw anything more, Mr Hoskins.'

'Matter of luck,' Hoskins said. 'Nothing a bit iffy about her, is there?'

Benson chuckled. 'She wouldn't be working here, if there was. And you don't tell me that Neville would have gone to a lot of bother to set her up in trade, just to snatch a few glass trinkets.'

'No,' said Hoskins thoughtfully. 'His little caper was a diversion. Make us all look the other way while his friend went for the grating.'

Benson looked down.

'The crap that's chucked in there, I'd have paid them to take away.'

Chance came back with the clear plastic envelopes.

'Hold 'em open,' Hoskins said. 'There's all sorts down here. Right little gold-mine.'

After several minutes of gum-wrappers and cigarette cartons, crisp packets and shop receipts, he stood upright and paused.

'Put this on its own, Jack. Someone's plastic ticket for the city library. They'll be glad to have that back. Hold it by the edge.'

Chance slipped it into one of the clear envelopes.

'And this,' Hoskins said. 'Someone's cheque-book, or what's left of it. No cheques in it. Only stubs.'

'That the lot?'

'Not much else that I can see.'

Benson helped him out and slid the grating back.

'Any good, Mr Hoskins?'

'We'll be in touch, Mr Benson. Need a little time to think first of all.'

Back in the car, Chance said, 'You think Weekes and the Mouse'd go to all that trouble over an empty cheque-book and a library card?'

'Nope,' Hoskins said. 'Any case, that cheque-book had been down there a while. Marked by rain, from the look of it.'

'And the Mouse was that crazy over reading that he had to have an extra library card?'

Hoskins held up the plastic envelope and looked at the card through it.

'Mr Morrier of Clearwater might be glad to have it back. Daresay he's not that bothered about a used cheque-book.'

There was no doubt of Hoskins' good humour as he went up the stairs of the headquarters building, past the carefully tended plants on the first-floor landing. It was some hours later, early in the afternoon, when he went into Ripley's office.

'No sign of Neville's prints on the cheque-book cover or the library card,' he said cheerfully, 'but Breaker Weekes once did three months' youth detention for housebreaking. We've got his prints. And they're on Morrier's library card. It must have been on that ledge just under the grating, where he could reach it.'

'Just grubbing about,' the Ripper said. 'Who wants a library card?'

'He did.' Hoskins smiled reassuringly. 'And having got it, he was grabbed by Chance. Dropped the card. And the Mouse goes to all the trouble of kicking it back down the hole. This time it misses the ledge and goes right down to the bottom. He'd got no objection to kicking Chance. But you can see from the video that he's after something else first. And it was important enough for him to turn back towards the men who were trying to grab him. He should have been off at the first sign. That's the first thing that's odd about the library card.'

Ripley sat down, impressed at last.

'Might be worth enquiring, Sam.'

'I'd say so, Max. There's another little gem that came my way over the network just now. CRO. Mr Morrier's on their files. Not for a while, but he's there. Not much, but he's got a criminal record as well as a library borrowing card.'

Ripley opened his mouth, but Hoskins had not quite finished.

'And there's the empty cheque-book, Max. The bank's been quite co-operative, hearing the circumstances. Not that we needed anything extremely confidential. That cheque-book was down there in the rain last week. Stained and blurred. But the last three cheques weren't drawn until the fine weather came again. In other words, someone tore those cheques out and threw the cover down the grating. Not the way I'd run my bank account, Max.'

Ripely frowned.

'Weekes saw it as he was standing there, thought it might have cheques inside? Fished out that and the library card?'

'Not that simple, Max. Hardly worth that much trouble for them. And, as for the library card, not worth anything at all.'

'You can't get anything more out of Cooney?'

'I don't think he's got anything more to give. I'll have a word with Morrier, though. He might be glad to have his card back.'

Ripley's face tightened with concern.

'I hope we're not off on another wild-goose-chase.'

Hoskins, half-way to the door, turned and looked back. He seemed surprised by Ripley's warning.

'I'm not interested in wild-goose-chases, Max. If I'm right, this is the big one after all.'

CHAPTER TWENTY-NINE

In the afternoon sun of Clearwater, Hoskins and Chance stood in the tiled porch of the Victorian semi-detached before the coloured glass of the inner door. Someone was evidently in. The bell trilled its second summons. Beyond the low wall of the little paved garden at the front, Clearwater Road ran away in the distance through a vast suburban uniformity. It dipped and soared again, between the procession of red brick houses with their little gardens and shrubs. The diminishing ribbon of tarmac was straight and empty as a race-track in the heat.

'Mr Morrier?' Hoskins made his hopeful enquiry of the cautious ginger-haired man who opened the door. But the man stood his ground and then turned over his shoulder.

'It's someone for you,' he said firmly.

Hoskins waited courteously until a dark-haired head replaced the ginger.

'Mr Morrier?' he said pleasantly, offering a glimpse of the warrant card. 'Chief Inspector Hoskins, city police. You've had a bit of bother, I think?'

The timidity in the dark-haired man's face tensed into anxiety.

'I'm not sure what you mean. What do you want with me?'

Hoskins smiled reassuringly.

'I understand you had a little mishap with your cheque-book, Mr Morrier. And I'll be able to give you back your library card. Can't do it this minute, but I've got it safe for you. Might we come in and have a word?'

Morrier stood back and led the way to the front sitting room. Hoskins was aware of the ginger-haired companion pottering inquisitively in the breakfast room or kitchen at the back of the house. The sitting room was a place of old padded furniture well cared-for, lace curtains and framed photographs of the honoured dead. It was a shrine in which the loyal son had grown up and which he tended now in his own middle age after his parents' death. With the aid of the other middle-aged figure, the ginger-haired acolyte.

They sat down.

'You've had a bit of trouble, Mr Morrier. That's all. I'd like to sort it out for you. If I can. If you'll let me.'

Morrier's face grew tighter still.

'Something of the sort was said to me once before, Mr Hoskins. Inspector Roberts. He wanted to help me. Help me into the dock.'

But Hoskins shook his head.

'Nothing like that, Mr Morrier. And, in any case, your little bother then wouldn't count for anything nowadays. It wouldn't come to the police, as the law stands now, let alone the courts. I'm not interested in that at all. But I am interested in you losing your plastic library card.'

The parlour clock that resembled a black and gold pantheon ticked the seconds away. Morrier looked up, curiosity replacing alarm.

'Why?'

Hoskins swept it all aside and started again.

'Mr Morrier. You lost your card in King Edward Square, didn't you? Monday afternoon of the May bank holiday. And your cheque-book and wallet, I daresay. You may have been lucky not to lose your life.'

Morrier sat in silence, staring at his hands in his lap.

'Mr Hoskins is right,' said Chance quietly. 'No one wants to harm you now. There's nothing against you.'

After a long pause, Morrier spoke again, talking to his hands in his lap.

'We discussed it, Harry and I. I couldn't go through all that again, as I did with Inspector Roberts. The money I lost was nothing. And there weren't more than two or three cheques in the book. Of course, they'd use them. But we'd stand the loss. I just couldn't bear . . .'

Hoskins prompted him gently. 'And the cheques were used?'

Morrier nodded. 'Almost four hundred pounds, all told.'

Chance looked up at Hoskins, quickly and uncomprehendingly. Hoskins frowned a warning at him.

'Four hundred?'

Morrier raised his head, the flushed face close to anger and tears.

'Yes! But better that than what they might have done to us.'

'Us?' Hoskins asked the question as if he understood and sympathised. 'Harry was there?'

'Across the square,' Morrier sobbed. 'But there was nothing he could do. Was there?'

Another pause followed this. Hoskins nodded to Chance.

'I'll just go out to the kitchen and have a word with Harry,' Chance said.

Alone with Morrier, Hoskins became more gentle and confiding yet.

'There's nothing to fear, Mr Morrier. Really there isn't.'

'What they'd say in court. They'd crucify us again.'

'They'll be offered a plea of guilty, Mr Morrier, and an easier road. If they know the game's up, they'll take it. There's two of you and other witnesses. And a man died trying to save you, Mr Morrier. A man with a wife and two children. A brave honourable man. That's the crime I'm talking about. Don't you owe him something?'

Morrier was mumbling to his hands again as the afternoon sun caught the lace and the padded flowers of the furniture.

'I know,' he said at last. 'I'm sorry. I should have had more courage, the courage to come forward. But I remembered the time with Inspector Roberts. I was robbed then, you know. The boy in the house robbed me. And I was the one called to account.'

'It's not the same,' Hoskins said. 'You've nothing to answer for now.'

Morrier drew a deep breath and looked up.

'I know,' he said. 'Tell me what you want me to do.'

Hoskins fished in his pockets.

'These two faces,' he said hopefully. 'Take your time. Then tell me if you recognise either.'

Morrier frowned.

'Not that one,' he said. 'But that one? Yes. Definitely, yes.'

Hoskins feared that he might appear to be trembling with excitement.

'Good,' he said. 'Thanks, Mr Morrier.'

'That's all?'

Hoskins stood up.

'We'll need a statement in due course. Have a word with your solicitor, if you like. Apart from that, it may be all over. It usually is. Contrary to what you see on telly, there aren't that many who plead not guilty.'

Chance was coming out of the back room.

'Any luck?' Hoskins asked.

'Twigged one.'

Morrier was behind them.

'I was sorry about that policeman. Really sorry. I shouldn't have waited. Of course, I shouldn't. You were quite right.'

'Never mind, Mr Morrier,' said Hoskins cheerfully. 'You've done the right thing now. I'll see about your library card as soon as I can.'

Outside in the car, he said to Chance, 'Made the old flesh creep a bit in there, wouldn't you say, Jack?'

'Yes,' said Chance thoughtfully, letting in the clutch, 'but then me personally, I'd rather have a glass of beer any day.'

'Gay!' Hoskins stared down the switchback of the long suburban avenue. 'I could imagine funeral parlours that might be gay compared with that little lot.'

Back at the headquarters, they rode the lift to the fifth floor.

'Right, my son,' Hoskins said in the corridor. 'I've got a couple of calls to make. So dust off the old truncheon and polish up the rhino whip. And then we'll go and have an evening out, down the Peninsula.'

He closed his door behind him and dialled a number.

'Any chance of Charlie Blades? Charlie? Sam Hoskins. Your exhibits. Reports on footwear in the Royal Emporium business. What've we got?' There was a pause. Hoskins reached for a pencil.

Blades returned to his end of the conversation.

'Just read it out, Charlie,' Hoskins said. 'What's the silica, then? Is it? Does it? Good show. And the manganese peroxide. No one said anything about it, Charlie, that's what I don't understand. Well, I suppose they didn't see the point of manganese peroxide. Not exactly topic of the day round the CID office. Nor the lime? Right, lime. That's the trouble, Charlie, too many ignorant young buggers here. Bloody schools don't teach 'em nothing now. Thanks anyway. The odds against this stuff being in the boots in the normal way must be pretty massive? Good. Smashing. Thanks, Charlie. That's definitely a nod and a smile down the drinker for you . . .'

Chance was waiting outside.

'We need permission from the Ripper, do we, Sam?'

'Not with what I've got,' said Hoskins merrily. 'Any case, he's not here today. Management conference at four o'clock on cost-centre funding. In other words, do away with central finance and make each department responsible for its own budget.'

'Fuck that,' Chance said as the lift doors closed. 'Not what I joined the Force for.'

Hoskins shrugged.

'No,' he said, 'I suppose not. Still, you can't expect us to be having fun all the time. Can you?'

CHAPTER THIRTY

'Watch my back,' Hoskins said to Chance. 'And watch your own while you're about it.'

As he eased himself out of the passenger seat of the Fiesta, he turned to DC Parrish behind him.

'Keep an eye on this limo, my son. Don't let some half-smart yobbo distract your attention while his fancy friend nicks it.'

'There's our first back-up stopped about fifty yards down the street, boss,' Parrish said reassuringly. 'And there's Mr Nicholls with a mini-bus of tin soldiers down Colenso Road.'

Hoskins grunted. They were parked just by the columns of the pier-head National Westminster, close to the dark and disjoined timbers of the old steamer landing. The jetty's railway signals for guiding the ferry-boats in now leant at a perilous angle. A long section of railing was just visible above the cocoa-coloured sludge into which it had fallen. The night-tide was flooding in along the dredged channel, lapping across the flanks of mud in the dusty pink light of sunset. A scattering of seabirds stood on the sleek expanse of dockland foreshore, impassive and unimpressed.

Hoskins led the way back to the Realito. After the heat of the city during the day, the calm evening air of the pier-head felt cool and fresh. A thump of music came from within the painted barley-sugar of the club's bulb-lit entrance arch.

'Monkey music for the teenies,' Hoskins said. 'Even the Realito's had a clean-up.'

The display cases were plastered with stickers for the acts: 'Young Revolution. . . . Smash Their Cars. . . . The Hangman Sings To-Nite. . . .'

'Nice healthy change,' Chance said. 'Biker's gaff, is it?'

'Off and on.' Hoskins tucked his warrant card into his palm. 'The Hangman had a spot on the TV rock show last week. Young-looking, angry, hair like a girl of sixteen. Full of stringing up the daddies and screwing the mummies, and bleeding everyone to death at thirty.'

'Charming,' said Chance.

Hoskins chuckled.

'Joke is, he's old Wadman that used to be an actor. Never made the grade. Arse-end of pantomime horses and pierrot shows or kids' stuff on the sands. You know, "Uncle Willie: Punch and Judy, Conjuring, Pederasty." Never see forty again. Take the wig off him and he's anybody's uncle – or auntie. And, as he says, this murdering the bourgeoisie is strictly for middle-class kids. They're the only ones hung up enough to get a thrill out of dad being bled on the pig-sticker while the natives gang-bang mum. He reckons they've got more spending money anyway. Last couple of years he's collared a house, two cars and a job-lot of under-age girls. Up Challoner Road, near Cooney. His popular culture is definitely not for the poor.'

'Bloody comics!' Chance said.

They walked into the din, the flashing and the rotation of coloured lights. The Realito was less than half full, despite the energy of the groups. No one paid much attention to the two intruders. For the benefit of the pedestrians, the lead singer was snarling into his microphone, urging someone to begin pissing in the petrol and cutting up the tyres, shattering the windscreens and reconquering the roads for peace.

Through the door at the side of the stage, they came to the old vestry, now used as a communal dressing-room. Louise was there in a short leather skirt and black stockings, a black jacket and make-up more heavily applied than usual. Beyond her stood Breaker Weekes with two girls and a boy.

'Right,' said Hoskins, indicating Weekes and Louise, 'I want a word with him and her. The rest of you, clear out into the other room.'

The other three went out. Weekes made no attempt to escape. Instead he came forward, a sallow youth of eighteen with tight dark curls. He assumed a leer that Hoskins guessed was copied in homage to the Mouse.

'You come here after me, did you?'

'A word or two,' Hoskins said.

'Spoken with a fat lip if necessary,' Chance suggested.

Hoskins frowned and the leer brightened more fully on the Breaker's mean young face.

'Touch me, Hoskins, and I'll bloody 'ave you!' He smirked jubilantly. 'Touch me and I'll have you for assault as well as harassment. Lobo knows the rules. Once you lay a finger on me, that's legally assault.'

'I'll be touching you all right, Breaker,' Hoskins said, quietly reassuring. 'You can count on that. No two ways.'

Chance closed the door and stood with his back against it.

'Touch me and I'll have you!' Weekes was still warning him now but high-pitched with it. 'Touch me and I will! And this time I've got a witness.'

Hoskins took a step forward and Weekes took a step away. Then the boy stopped, dumbfounded. He had recited Lobo's incantation, the witch-doctor's spell, and it proved powerless. With surprising speed, Hoskins moved and grabbed him. Weekes turned, only to find his arm twisted up behind his back.

'There now, Breaker,' Hoskins said affectionately, 'I'm touching you. All right?'

'That's technical assault! Mr Lobo said so!'

There was a hint of self-pity, even tears of humiliation in the voice. Beyond the door, the music thumped and snarled.

'And it's technical arrest, Breaker. I hope he told you that too.

Once I'm touching you, that's technical arrest. All right? Got that, have you? Now, I'm arresting you, in the presence of Sergeant Chance and this young lady. You'll be taken to police headquarters, to the bridewell. And the duty inspector will formally charge you with the murder of Sergeant John Stoodley. And when you've gone through the statutory time for questioning, you'll be permitted to see Mr Lobo or any other solicitor of your choice. Provided you can find one that wants to see you.'

The Breaker stared, immobile and uncomprehending as a landed fish.

'I got nothing to say,' he muttered at last.

Hoskins nodded.

'That's fair enough. We don't need you to say anything. You've been picked out by some very impressive witnesses. Your prints are all over the contents of one gentleman's wallet. Running off down Great Western Street, from Jones and Gower, leaving John Stoodley to bleed to death in agony, you tore the cheques out and threw the book down the grating of the Emporium. Right? And you dropped a plastic card down there. Okay? After the trouble began, you went back for it. Didn't want it found on that ledge, I daresay. Or perhaps you were thick enough to imagine it might be one of his credit cards.'

'You got nothing!'

Weekes almost spat with contemptuous bravado.

'And then there's the broken glass,' Hoskins continued affably. 'Tiny fragments of it, embedded in the soles of your boots. We had a look at those when you were rounded up for thieving the Cadillac. And when we come to search your things and do the full range of tests, there'll be all sorts of bits and pieces.'

Weekes tried to pull against the arm-lock, then gasped and blinked back involuntary tears at the pain of it.

'And you'd better get used to discomfort, Breaker,' Hoskins said gently. 'Murdering a policeman is life. Still, I suppose you reckoned on that. And I daresay you can imagine how some of the prison staff are likely to feel about you. One sneeze out of tune and you'll be banged up day and night with just your pottie and mattress for company.'

'I want to see Lobo! I never did it!'

'And then there's the hard cases in there. I can't see you as pretty myself. But tastes change in there. You'll find out a bit of what it's like to be on the game, my son. See how the other half lives.'

'I never did it! I want Lobo.'

'What's going to make it worse,' Hoskins continued conversationally, 'is that you'll be the only one sent down. If you choose to take the punishment for the others that thumped Stoodley, fair enough. But so long as you cover up for them, you could kiss goodbye to parole. In that case, as they say, life means life.'

'I never did it.' There was a subdued catch of despair in the voice now. 'I was with her!'

'Both hands together behind the back,' Hoskins said politely. 'That's better. Don't try pulling away, you'll only hurt yourself.'

The metallic click of the cuffs was like the rifle-cocking of a firing-squad.

'Take him out to the back-up car, if you please, Mr Chance.'

Hoskins watched them go out of the rear door and caught a glimpse of the uniformed man posted there. He turned to Louise.

'Now, young lady. You and I have had this sort of conversation before, over a stolen Cadillac. As things are now, you could be charged as accessory to murder. But then, perhaps you want that. You and Breaker going down together like Bonnie and Clyde.'

She shook her head, slowly and dumbly, the colour rising in her face.

'He was with me.'

'What time?'

'All the time!'

It was a fine flaring of defiance, but it died almost at once.

'You're not even a good liar,' Hoskins said sympathetically. 'You were with the Mouse that Monday. Out the Beach. On the Cakewalk. Remember?'

'That was later. I was with Breaker when it happened.'

'That's clever,' Hoskins said admiringly. 'But you don't know exactly when it happened, do you?'

She stood, hanging her head, unresponsive.

'Do you?' he suggested gently. 'If you do, perhaps you'd like to tell me. Always remembering, of course, that you could do a long stretch for perjury as well.'

'I'm not saying any more.'

He sighed.

'How long do you suppose you'd last as his alibi, once a prosecuting lawyer started tearing into you? And how long do you suppose you'd get as accessory, or for perjury? There's witnesses that saw him when Stoodley was killed.'

She stood there, head bowed, mute and miserable.

'Don't be a fool,' Hoskins said softly. 'We've got his fingerprints on the evidence. An alibi won't work, even if he deserved one.'

Still she would not look at him.

'Another thing,' he said. 'You'll need heavier make-up and thicker stockings, if you want to keep those bruises out of sight.'

'No.' Louise was suddenly desperate to convince him. 'You don't understand.'

'Breaker and the Mouse always liked a female punch-bag,' Hoskins went on casually, 'but that one on the cheekbone was careless. The Mouse was careful never to let it show as clear as that on his girls. Make-up doesn't cover it. There's one showing through your stocking as well. And when you're medically examined, as you will be later on tonight, we'll have the whole sad story.'

'We were fooling around . . . that was all . . .'

She bowed her face into her hands and stood there, crying quietly. Hoskins knew that the issue was finely balanced.

'It won't be fooling around next time,' he said, as if explaining a simple proposition to a child. 'He was just getting you used to a bit of rough handling in play. That way, you're less likely to complain about the real thing. But you belong to the Breaker. Even if he hasn't made you earn your bread yet, it's just a question of time. And then there's customers you can't face. The ugly ones or the things you won't do. So the money's short and there's a row. You'll be knocked about until one day it's more serious. Broken nose or arm. And perhaps much worse than that.'

'I can't . . .' But it was a whimper of indecision.

'I don't want evidence in court. Only the truth between us now.'

In the shabby vestry, there was a moment of complete stillness. 'I don't know . . .'

But the wail of doubt was a pebble that began the avalanche.

'Take your time,' Hoskins said. 'He's going down anyway. But he'll go down for a lot longer if he drags the trial out with a load of twaddle. That's how the judges play it.'

'Breaker . . . Breaker told the Mouse. They'd caught this queer, he said, and taken his wallet and some cheques. Near King Edward Square. He never said anyone was killed. Only a fight and a window broken. I never knew it was that policeman killed, I swear it.'

Hoskins led her to a chair and let her sit down.

'Who were they? The others? If Breaker has to take it alone, it'll be a lot worse for him.'

'Jerry down Monmouth Terrace,' she said, as if suddenly angry at those who had escaped, 'and Boxer and Arnie. And Wildey and a boy called Joe, from the Kalif. And Didier and Fox. And I don't know the rest.'

'That's all right,' Hoskins said. 'You've done all you need.'

She looked up at him, the mascara streaked on her young face. The bruise on the cheekbone was tighter and shiny.

'And me?' she whispered. 'What about me?'

Hoskins smiled at her reassuringly.

'We'll need a few particulars. You can have a wash and brush-up at the headquarters building. Then we'll get someone to take you home and stay with you, if necessary.'

'Home?'

'Barrier, isn't it? Or else wherever your parents are.'

'I gave up the room in Barrier. And I can't go back to his place,' she said miserably. 'I'd have to go back to them. To Hawks Hill. Godwin Road.'

Hoskins stared for a moment. Then he recovered his equilibrium.

'Right,' he said briskly, 'we'll sort something out.'

He went out to the car and handed Chance a sheet of paper.

'Seven more names as well as Weekes. I want 'em identified, where necessary, and picked up. Half of them I know already.'

'Bloody hell, Sam!' Chance spoke with unconcealed admiration.

'This lot? Tonight?'

'Straight off,' Hoskins said. 'The girl's coming to make a statement. Then I'm going to have her taken home to her parents. To the posh end of Hawks Hill.'

'You're joking,' Chance said.

'Not my evening for jokes. Just put out the call for those seven names. I want them pulled in simultaneously and held separately. This has gone too far to risk a cock-up. Get Morrier and his missus with the ginger hair. I'll want some identifying done.'

'And Weekes?'

'Take him back and stick him in the cooler. And get a policewoman for the girl. I'll finish off here and follow you back in the other car.'

It was almost an hour later, the last of the summer dusk had deepened into night, when Hoskins emerged from the lift into the corridor of the fifth floor. There were voices everywhere, raised in argument, assertion and enquiry. Everyone was talking and no one was listening. Strangers stood about in attitudes of indignation. Unrecognised, he reached his room and closed out the din.

The phone on his desk was ringing.

'Sam? Gerald Foster, *Western World*. What's going on up there? There's stories buzzing around the news desk. CID swoops and mass arrests. And specifically a call from two outraged parents about thugs in CID hammering on the door and snatching young kids from their very arms. You fisting the yobs again?'

'Seems quiet enough here to me, Gerald. I've just this minute got in. I'll ask around and let you know.'

He put the phone down. It rang again at once.

'Sam? Tom Nicholls. I'm down the bridewell. Look, we need some help down here. No one warned us about this lot coming in.'

'No one warned me either, Tom. I'll see what I can do.'

There was a knock at the door. Chance came in and closed it against the swelling babble of voices outside.

'It's like bloody world-cup night out there, Sam. What comes next?'

Hoskins unlocked his desk. 'Depends on the state of play.'

'Oh, we got 'em all,' Chance said. 'Four mean-looking young

thugs of eighteen or twenty, all short hair and tattoo marks. Two sixteen-year-olds. And two distinctly juvenile: fourteen and thirteen. You've got three parents, by the way, all shouting the odds. One of them's trying to phone his MP. At least, he says he is.'

'We'd better have Ripley here.'

Chance sniggered.

'He's been phoned. He'd already had his Ovaltine and tucked himself up in bed with Mrs Ripper. All hair-nets, moustache-curlers and two sets of choppers smiling in the same glass. Anyway, we got him out of his pit. He's on his way. And Weekes volunteered a statement.'

'Did he now?'

Chance handed over the sheet of paper.

'Nowhere near King Edward Square that day. But one of the windows in his gaff was smashed and he must have trod some glass into his shoe. He picked that card out of the Emporium grating from curiosity. Hence his dabs. He's a much misunder-stood lad, is the Breaker. We've got him in the upstairs interview room.'

'Good.'

'But there's not enough rooms, Sam. We've got nine of 'em here, if you include the girl. Not to mention the parents. And I reckon you'll have Lobo and his team on the doorstep any minute.'

Hoskins grunted. 'And what about the girl anyway?'

'Been sick twice. That's about all. I put Hannah Cody in charge of her.'

'Right.'

The phone rang again.

'Sam? Gerald Foster again. I'm getting something about a Mr Levins and his MP. Police brutality towards his thirteen-year-old son.'

'I'll look into it, Gerald.'

'Wish you would, Sam.'

Hoskins put the phone down again.

'One of those buggers is on to the *Western World* again, Jack. No more phone calls to be made from this building by members of the public. Right? Anyone who wants to phone can go and find a call-box in the Mall. With any luck, they'll all be out of order.'

He picked up the statement again and led the way to the door.

'Hang on,' said Chance. 'We also got Mr Morrier and the very lovely Ginger-Nuts here. They identified Weekes. Morrier also picked out three of the others. His friend picked out two from the same three. Those two are talking up the business of being innocent bystanders. But they don't deny they were there.'

Hoskins shook his head as if to clear it.

'It's what you might call a break, Jack. This morning, John Stoodley could have been done to death by almost anyone in the city. Now we've got eight suspects under arrest, three solid witnesses, cast-iron forensic evidence and a couple of confessions coming up.'

'Right,' said Chance enthusiastically. 'What's next, then?'

Hoskins pulled a face. 'Let's go and see Breaker Weekes.'

The bleak distempered box of the interview room with its square opaque window of meshed security glass was lit by unshaded fluorescent strips. There was a bare wooden table with an unemptied ashtray and a wooden chair either side. A uniformed constable sat on another chair by the door. Weekes, staring grimly at his cigarette packet, refused to look up as the two men came in.

Hoskins flourished the statement.

'You're a liability to your profession, my son.' He sat down opposite Weekes, head lowered, as if trying to look into the boy's face. 'A bloody amateur.'

'I got nothing more to say. That's the lot.'

Hoskins sat back.

'You've said more than enough, my young friend. This cobblers about fishing the card out from the grating through curiosity. Don't you know it had been rained on down there, apart from anything else? And don't you know that they can tell the fingerprints that were marked by rain and those that were made later? And that there's both sorts of yours?'

'Bollocks,' Weekes said. 'Any case, I wiped the poxy thing on my trousers when I picked it up.'

'Why'd you do that, then, if there were no prints on it to begin with?'

Like a boxer rebounding from the canvas, the Breaker came back. 'It was dirty, that's all. I wiped it clean. Now stuff that!'

Hoskins shook his head.

'You were on the security system video. There's a complete tape of you. You never wiped anything. Any case, if you did, there'd be fluff from your trousers on the card. Sticks to plastic like glue. And there won't be a sign of it.'

Weekes was visibly crestfallen. 'Nothing to say.'

Chance picked up the other chair from which the uniformed policeman had risen. He set it down at the far end of the table and slid into it.

'You're in the shit, my lad,' he said philosophically to the young prisoner. 'Right in it.'

Weekes tightened his mouth.

'Then there's the boots,' Hoskins said. 'The tiny bits of glass embedded in the plastic soles.'

'I told you!' said Weekes desperately. 'It's down to the broken window in my gaff. All right? In the bloody statement, isn't it?'

Hoskins nodded.

'Living in a Crystal Palace, are we?' he asked.

'What's that supposed to mean?'

'What it means, Breaker, is manganese peroxide.'

'Fuck that.'

But Weekes was now in a world he could not begin to understand. He was uneasy and then visibly frightened by his incomprehension of what was happening, what was being done to him.

'And then,' said Hoskins, 'there's extract of lime. Refined to a standard specification. You could even tell who manufactured the glass, according to the quantities.'

'Don't waste my time,' Weekes said wretchedly.

Hoskins leant forward.

'I'm not wasting your time, Breaker. I'm doing you a kindness. Before you get any further in. Window glass doesn't have that extract of lime nor that manganese peroxide. That's used for plate-glass. Display windows. The formula in this case is a manufacturer's in Walsall. They only got one contract in this city: Jones and Gower.'

Weekes was beaten. He hung his head, unable to speak.

'See?' said Chance simply. 'I told you you was in the shit.'

'Murder of Sergeant Stoodley,' said Hoskins simply, 'and attempted murder of two police officers in Martello Square. That's us. Still on file. Assault of Sergeant Chance outside the Emporium while resisting arrest. Robbery with violence in the case of Mr Morrier. Car theft, along with the Mouse. And there was a girl in the storm drain that might have your marks on. Not to mention Louise. I can't begin to imagine when you're going to see the light of day again. You'll be medically examined, of course. If they reckon you're a psychopath, then you're banged up for good and all.'

'He looks a bit like a psychopath to me,' Chance said.

'Acts like one,' Hoskins added sadly.

The Breaker lowered his face on to his folded arms. Hoskins and Chance watched the dark curls of the head. The shoulders heaved once, There was a muffled but unmistakable sobbing.

'What you need, Breaker,' Chance observed, 'is a friend or two.'

CHAPTER THIRTY-ONE

'You're a lovely boy, Samuel Hoskins!' screeched Chance in a subdued parade-ground falsetto. 'What are y-e-e-w?'

'I'm a lovely boy,' said Hoskins obediently, 'and I still don't understand it.'

Chance grinned down at the Mall from the office window. The long avenues were deserted in the heat of the late July afternoon. The civil servants and their families had departed for Ibiza or St Ives. Their vaulted corridors were quiet. Groups of children from the nearby houses rode bikes along the paths between the Edwardian civic buildings and the Stalinist towers of the 1960s, all laminated stone-dust and precast concrete ornaments. These more recent blocks represented not architectural style but prosecutions for municipal fraud, sentences served and files long since closed.

'My God!' said Chance. 'I have never known this place so chuffed. You did it, Sam! You really did it!'

Hoskins chucked a folder aside.

'I didn't get Cooney, or Sian Jones, or anyone else for the Robbo Smith business. I didn't get near whoever murdered that biker's girl.'

'But you got the bastards that killed John Stoodley. After everyone thought it was a real write-off. You've no idea the lift that's given the sergeants' room. Bloody conquering hero, that's you, Sam. And eight of Weekes' lot pleading guilty. Game, set, and match.'

Hoskins stood up. 'Mostly luck, Jack.'

But Chance's large red face beamed with ill-concealed affection and pride.

'No!' he said dismissively. 'You don't get a result like that just from being lucky. The reckoning next door is that it's down to nifty footwork. And your footwork, Sam, is shit-hot.'

Hoskins turned to pick up another folder, disguising his pleasure at Chance's enthusiasm.

'That's nice,' he said blandly. 'When I kick the bucket and get the municipal eighteen-inch plot in the ash-can section of Boot Hill, I'd like an inscription on the regulation two-by-two marble look-alike. "Here lies Samuel Hoskins, late of this parish. His footwork was shit-hot." I reckon that just about says it all.'

Chance grinned.

'Come down the Harp and I'll buy you a drink.'

Hoskins shook his head.

'A word with Ripley. I'm booked in now.'

'I'll go down there and see you later.'

Hoskins opened the door and let Chance out.

'Okay,' he said, 'you're on. But if I'm not there in an hour, you can assume I'm stuck.'

Presently, the folder still in his hand, he went across the corridor and tapped at Ripley's nameplate. The Ripper was rising from his desk, folding his glasses into their case. Uncharacteristically, he greeted Hoskins with a smile.

'That was nice, Sam. That was really nice. I've had the commissioner on the phone. He says, and I agree with him totally, that he's never known morale in this building higher than it is now. The entire Division's cock-a-hoop over the Weekes business. We've shown the yobs that they can't hit us and run. We've shown the lads that we look after our own. The public's right behind us now, backing the winning side. And neither Ms Ricard nor Mr Lobo can open their mouths in public without fouling their own nest.'

Hoskins sat down in obedience to Ripley's gesture.

'I'm just glad it worked out, Max. For John Stoodley's sake, most of all.'

Ripley shook his head, marvelling at it all.

'Eight of the little swine in the dock, Sam! That'll show people whether this town's being policed or not. And Stoodley killed going to the rescue of a civilian. That's worth more than any amount of riot shields or plastic bullets. I can't tell you the sheer goodwill I've felt towards us on all sides the past couple of days. And it's down to you, Sam, first and foremost. I'm not going to let anyone forget that.'

'I wouldn't like Jack Chance and the others overlooked,' Hoskins said.

'They won't be, Sam. But you're not going to duck the credit on this. You've taken enough stick in the Neville business.'

The Ripper beamed indulgently at him. Hoskins sensed an indefinable unease.

'I'm glad everyone's pleased,' he said feebly.

The Ripper perched on the edge of his desk, informal and expansive.

'Oh, they are, Sam. That's why I thought this would be the best time to discuss you – your immediate future – with higher authority. To be perfectly honest, they started discussing it with me. Your stock stands very high just now. There's got to be a formal inquiry into the death of Neville, but we can deal with that. No one's going to believe Weekes' version any longer. Not since his arrest. And you've got Cooney's video. That substantiates your previous evidence absolutely. If we take this one carefully, they can't touch you. They'd like to, of course. Lobo and his friends. But I don't see that they can.'

'Is there something I don't know, Max?' Hoskins asked.

Ripley's tone had a single blemish of insincerity, like one wrong note in the great span of an orchestral chord.

'No, Sam.' The superintendent shook his head. 'Absolutely not. But there is still your answer to Lobo at the inquest, about insensitive enforcement of policies on race. That's going to die the death, don't worry. But it might take its time.'

'Meaning?'

The Ripper sighed.

'The commissioner thinks, and I agree with him, that a low profile might be in order for the next month or so. You've got a hell of a future here, Sam. It'd be a tragedy to put a foot wrong now.'

'What sort of low profile exactly?'

'We had a request for a senior officer from CID on secondment, until the first week of September. Ocean Beach Division . . .'

'Ocean Beach!'

'Ocean Beach made the request. The commissioner thinks, and so do I, that it's the perfect answer. The city's quiet, as a rule, this time of year. What's six weeks, Sam?'

'I don't want to go to Ocean Beach, Max! I've got a job to do here.'

Ripley's voice hardened.

'The commissioner put it to me as a suggestion, Sam. If necessary, he'll make it an order. I wanted to say something to you, just as a matter of courtesy.'

'What am I supposed to do in Ocean Beach?'

Ripley studied the polished gloss of his neat toecaps as he swung his feet gently.

'There's a problem there, Sam. It could get well out of hand. This time of year, the sands are crowded. The beach goes way past the built-up area at either end. Some of it's a bit remote. There's been complaints about attempts at indecency, where families have been sitting. Families with kiddies.'

'Indecency? What sort of indecency?'

'Exposure,' Ripley said, self-consciously.

'Flashers?' The anguish in Hoskins' voice was unconcealed.

'More topless bathing, Sam. But if people want their kids protected, they've got a right. If we disregard topless, what about bottomless too? And if we let that go, what if the men demand the same right? And, if that happens, where does it end? That's what Martin says out at the Beach. Could you have a man with an erection walking along in the middle of family parties? Where does it end, if you don't draw a line now?'

'What you mean,' Hoskins said in his dismay, 'is that I'm being put on the old "Pervert Patrol"! Me and a couple of Ken Martin's bucks in bathing trunks, pretending to play volley-ball up and down the sands for six weeks! Fuck that, Max!'

Ripley slid off the desk and stood up.

'If all that happens is volley-ball, Sam, you'll have done your job. And done it well. After that, the sky's the limit. A lot of people are prepared to bat for you. You're riding high. Don't blow it by making a scene over this. Keep clear until the inquiry's over and come back to glory in September.'

'Six weeks in swimming trunks, pretending to be a punter!'

'Don't be a stupid bastard, Sam!' Ripley's colour was up a little and his face was dangerously mobile. 'You could have been out on your neck after that smart answer to Lobo at the inquest. A lot of people have taken a lot of trouble for you. But the balance is still pretty fine. Don't balls the whole thing up!'

'Someone should prosecute the commissioner for wasting police time. *My* time!'

'Sam!' It was a pathetic painful cry. 'If someone had been there at Bank Holiday, we might have closed the file on Robbo Smith by now. It's not a waste of time if your presence saves a child from being molested, hurt or even killed. All right?'

Hoskins turned his face from Ripley and glared at the window.

'That's marvellous,' he said bitterly. 'Six weeks of that, or else collect my cards and get a job shunting the motors in Cooney's car park.'

The Ripper walked round his desk. He picked up a sheet of paper and frowned at it, ostentatiously shifting his attention away from Hoskins.

'Sorry, Sam, but that's how it is. We'll discuss the details in the morning.'

Released earlier than he had expected, Hoskins walked through the warm air of early evening, away from the Mall and into the avenue of gabled Victorian villas that ran from its nearer end. Half-way down Rossiter Road was the Harp, a mock-Tudor pub of bar snacks and middle-class pretensions. Chance was there with two of the other sergeants in the buzz of the carpeted saloon. He came across alone.

'Look at your face, Sam! Can't have been as bad as that, surely?' Without waiting for a reply, Chance signalled to the barmaid.

'I've been seconded to Ocean Beach, Jack. Six weeks. On the sands. Holiday gear. In charge of the "Pervert Patrol".'

To his discomfiture, Chance emitted a half-suppressed squittering laugh.

'You haven't, Sam! The old swimming trunks and volley-ball routine? Watching for the flashers?'

Hoskins sensed what was to come.

'Don't bother asking the funny one, Jack, about how we manage with whistles and truncheons. You'll find out.'

'Hang on, Sam! Fair's fair.'

'There's no such thing as fair in this business, my son. I've known that a long time. First thing tomorrow, I've got to see the Ripper again. I'm asking for you as back-up the next six weeks. It's been a pig of a summer so far. Someone else can have a little share of it from now on.'

He took the beer from the counter, drank off the first couple of inches and began to feel better. Dudden came up and was talking to Chance.

'There's this one about Eve Ricard and Lobo cast away on a desert island,' Dudden was saying, grinning in anticipation. 'And no one else there but this fantastically sexy native girl with no clothes on. Anyway . . .'

Hoskins relaxed in the warm smoke-tinted air of the saloon. The carpet was soft under his feet and the polished mahogany supported his elbow. The voices around him were familiar and affable. The six o'clock sunlight of Canton through the leaded windows grew thick and fiery. Taking another inch of the beer into his mouth, he listened indulgently to Dudden's story.

227

CHAPTER THIRTY-TWO

It was November before the case against the murderers of Stoodley was heard and the sentences passed. The inquest on Robbo Smith, adjourned from time to time, was concluded in mid-December. On its last day, a Siberian freak of weather brought a foot of overnight snow, a fortnight before Christmas. From the window of his office, Hoskins looked down across the gardens and buildings of the Mall. Above the even spread of white, the domes and bronze chariots of the civic skyline, the long avenues, pillars and flights of steps brought a suggestion of Prague or Budapest to the civic centre of Canton. Against the expanse of frosted brilliance, the black bronze casts of Victorian industrialists struck noble attitudes on the plinths of the public gardens. The dead city fathers had a monolithic air in the reflected wintry brightness. Their new background turned them from entrepreneurs into heroes of the Soviet Union.

Hoskins glanced at his watch. The bronchial whine of a single car, wheels spinning ineffectually on hardened snow, rose from the avenue below. As if in a tradition of municipal ineptitude, the snow had taken the city authorities by surprise. Almost nothing had been done to clear it. The buses had stopped. Only the metro-rail link still connected the city with Lantern Hill. Lesley had kept clear of the inquest. Hoskins was to bring her news of the verdict.

He pulled on his coat and went out into the corridor, the tiling puddled from melting snow on the shoes of the new watch that had come on duty. Walking down the Mall was slow going, the snow soft but still deep. King Edward Square was quiet, a scene of stranded custard-yellow buses deserted in their bays. For the first time, going that way on foot, he was confronted by the 'Closing-Down Sale' of Jones and Gower, the city's original department store. Henceforward, Carmel Cooney's Royal Peninsular Emporium would reign unchallenged as the purveyor of life's 'little extras' to the people of Canton.

He made for the Longwall entrance of the store, in order to cut a corner and walk under cover. The display windows on that side, where Stoodley was killed, had been hung with a curtaining of red tinsel strips to conceal their emptiness. There was to be no new store and no redevelopment here. Another fragment of the city died and was forgotten. With his lifelong memories, a cut-price purchase in the last week of Jones and Gower seemed to Hoskins a bit like robbing a tomb.

As he walked through the shell of the family store, there were still areas on the ground floor and corners of the upper floor laid out for bargain-hunters, as if business might go on for ever. But round these carpeted islands, the interior dimensions of Edwardian prosperity had been stripped bare. Only the square pillars were still faced with brown hessian. The bleak spaces were huge and empty as an aircraft hangar. The carpeting had gone and the rubber-tiled floor was chipped. Boxes and rolled mats, a step-ladder and a pile of dismantled fittings were all that indicated where the shop was still being cleared.

Hoskins walked through the ill-lit spaces of the upper floor, fascinated as if by a ship on its way to the breakers. At a whim of managerial irony, the public address system was still relaying an endless tape of Christmas music, jollying along a seasonal trade the store would never see. Hoskins took his leave to the dirge-paced accompaniment of 'We Three Kings of Orient Are'. At the Great Western Street entrance, the display windows were already hidden behind sheets of new plywood to protect them against the midnight stoning that closure and failure attracted.

The metro-rail platform and a shelter with a wooden seat were all that remained of the Victorian station at Lantern Hill, built in the style of a Swiss lake resort. Across the road, Carmel Cooney's Cloud Seven Arcade was doing bad business in the freezing weather. So far as Hoskins could see, it was empty except for a young woman at the change kiosk and a swarthy middle-aged minder. Everywhere was quiet that day in the winter chill. He trudged to Arran Street and knocked at the door. Lesley was booted and long-skirted again.

'You look like a snowman,' she said.

Hoskins nodded and followed her into the kitchen. She stood waiting, chastened a little in expectation.

'It's all right,' he said quietly. 'They brought in an open verdict. They couldn't do anything else as it was. The main thing is, it's over.'

She took a step towards him, holding her arms up, waiting to be hugged.

'That's all I wanted now,' she said indistinctly into his chest. 'For it to be over. Now there's nothing to stop us. Is there?'

'Being a bit careful wouldn't come amiss,' Hoskins said. 'They won't do any more about the case. There's no point. But they won't close the file either.'

She shook her head, brushed her fringe into place with the edge of her hand and helped him off with his coat.

'Have you had lunch?'

'Yes,' said Hoskins, lying.

'You know what I'd like to do?'

'I've got a fair idea.'

It was, he supposed, the relief of tension, the inquest being over. It was the end of the ordeal, so far as it concerned her. Whatever the cause, for a self-possessed young woman of her kind she was almost skittish that afternoon. Presently she stood, as before, bare-legged in her boots.

'The boots,' he said thoughtfully. 'I wonder what it is about boots?'

Lesley sat down and began tugging at them in a businesslike manner.

'I think it's called fetishism, dating back to boyhood and the ladies in the magazines,' she said.

'I suppose so.'

'Women don't need that sort of thing. A harem in photographs.'

'I suppose not.'

'Lord and master of all he surveyed,' she said, throwing down the second boot. 'The boy Hoskins. Absolute sexual power. A harem could run rings round you. In reality, you'd be scared stiff.'

She was standing up now, hooking down the waist of the pants, the fringe falling forward a little.

'Would I?'

'I should think so.' She stretched out on the bed.

'I doubt it.'

Lesley rolled over on her side towards him.

'All right,' she said, 'I'm yours. For this afternoon. I'll do anything you want me to. You wouldn't know where to begin. Would you? The boy Hoskins would run for his life.'

'Anything?'

'Yes,' she said, a little uneasily, as if the game might have gone wrong.

'Absolutely anything?'

'Within reason.'

He undid his belt.

'Oh, this is within reason all right, so far as I'm concerned.'

She watched him lay down the belt and move to the buttons.

'What is it?'

'Just stop yakking,' he said gently. 'At least that's it for a start. We ought to play this game more often.'

But they were still talking, lying together, when the chirrup of the telephone disturbed them. Lesley went barefoot and naked to answer it, moving demurely as a little girl. Hoskins heard her voice, quiet and puzzled. She came back.

'It's for you.'

'How the hell can it be for me? No one knows . . .'

But as he got up, he thought that someone did know, after all. It was Chance's voice on the other end.

'Sam? Look, I'm sorry about this. Honestly. I thought I ought to get to you before anyone else.'

'What about?'

'That girl,' Chance said. 'The one Harold Moyle was on about. You know, the fancier after school and so on. Went missing from home two days ago. The Lantern Hill gendarmerie found her body this morning. Something to do with a pensioner clearing snow from his path.'

Despair swelled like nausea in Hoskins.

'Hell's teeth,' he said wearily. 'That's all we need.'

'Harold Moyle's been trying to get hold of you. He's been making a few waves as well. Warned us months ago that this would happen, he says.'

'Leave him to me, Jack. I'll be back in action in half an hour.'

'There might be a connection with the biker's girl, Sam. The two things look a bit similar. There could be a nutter on the loose.'

'If there wasn't a nutter, it wouldn't have happened,' Hoskins said glumly. 'I'll be in as soon as I can, Jack. I'll have to take the metro-rail again.'

He walked into the bedroom and sat down beside Lesley as she stretched out, patient and waiting.

'That girl at Harold Moyle's school,' he said dully. 'The one he was on about. Some man following her. We never found anything, never saw anything. With Robbo and John Stoodley and the biker's girl, I couldn't spend the summer watching Shackleton Comprehensive. When we put men out there, no one saw anything. Anyway, someone's done it after all. They uncovered her body this morning.'

'That's dreadful,' she said, sitting up and putting out her arms to him. 'Poor girl.'

'It's bad,' he said. 'Bad news.'

'You couldn't have done any more, Sam.'

'Six weeks playing volley-ball on the sands didn't help. But in the end, it's my fault. Someone must have been watching her, planning the whole thing. And I missed it. We all missed it, somewhere. Next time you suggest that a companion can do anything he or she likes with you, remember that there's one or two who fancy murder.'

She shivered, naked in the winter room.

'A thing like that, it makes the blood run cold,' she said.

Hoskins took her hand and shook his head.

'No,' he said vaguely, 'that's the funny thing about blood. When it's cold, you're already dead and it doesn't run. It only runs while the heart's still beating. I've seen a fair bit of it in the course of the job. Whatever they may tell you, if it runs at all, the blood runs hot.'

>>> If you've enjoyed this book and would like to discover more great vintage crime and thriller titles, as well as the most exciting crime and thriller authors writing today, visit: >>>

The Murder Room
Where Criminal Minds Meet

themurderroom.com